EVERY TIME WE TOUCH

LUCY MITCHELL

B

Boldwood

First published in Great Britain in 2026 by Boldwood Books Ltd.

Cover Design by Head Design Ltd

Cover Images: Shutterstock

A CIP catalogue record for this book is available from the British Library.

Paperback ISBN 978-1-80703-183-1

Large Print ISBN 978-1-80703-184-8

Hardback ISBN 978-1-80703-181-7

Trade Paperback ISBN 978-1-80703-182-4

Ebook ISBN 978-1-80703-185-5

Kindle ISBN 978-1-80703-186-2

Audio CD ISBN 978-1-80703-176-3

MP3 CD ISBN 978-1-80703-177-0

Digital audio download ISBN 978-1-80703-178-7

This book is printed on certified sustainable paper. Boldwood Books is dedicated to putting sustainability at the heart of our business. For more information please visit https://www.boldwoodbooks.com/about-us/sustainability/

Boldwood Books Ltd, 23 Bowerdean Street, London, SW6 3TN

www.boldwoodbooks.com

For Mum

1

'Could you order this book for me, please?' the man asks. 'It's titled *Curses and How to Break Them*, by the author J.K. Fielding.'

I flinch, accidentally knocking the box of glittery pens off the till counter and onto the floor. There's no time to pick them up. A man and a woman are standing in front of me. He is in his mid-twenties with pale blue eyes and styled blond hair. The woman is about his age, with wavy brown hair and is gazing adoringly at him. She turns to me and gushes with pride, 'Marcus is doing some research on curses.'

Raising an eyebrow at Marcus, I ask, 'Academic interest or personal issue?'

I already know the answer to this. He's not battling a troubling curse dressed in a designer short-sleeved polo shirt, sunglasses perched on his head and flashing me that charming, lopsided smile.

He chuckles. 'Academic. I've heard this book on curses is…'

My brain loses control of my mouth, and words I would never dream of saying to a customer fly off my tongue. 'Save your money. It's not that good. This author, J.K. Fielding, doesn't know what he's talking about.'

Marcus blinks, caught off guard. He wasn't expecting me to have read J.K. Fielding's lengthy book and to have formed an opinion on the author's thoughts about curses.

The young woman rushes to Marcus's aid like she's his own personal bodyguard. Casting me a frosty look, she says, 'I think Marcus will be the judge of the book, thanks.'

Her clipped tone spikes my agitation. Marcus rewards her with a kiss.

I tap the book's details into the computer and request a copy. 'It will take three to five working days. Do you want to collect, or shall I get it delivered?'

'I will collect,' he says, reaching for one of the bookmarks that are on sale at the till counter.

His girlfriend pulls a disapproving look. 'They look trashy, Marcus.'

He waves his phone near the card machine while words jostle on my tongue. I want to tell her that the bookmarks are not trashy, and, if she must know, I spent hours painstakingly searching for a local supplier who could make bookmarks with the name 'Once Upon a Spine' on the front.

As they walk away, I bend down to pick up the glittery pens and hear Marcus's girlfriend. 'So rude. What would that woman on the till know about curses anyway?'

Her words echo inside my head. What would I know about curses?

I let out a heavy sigh and place the box of pens back on the counter. The romance book display table always catches my eye. Today, those pastel covers promise laughter in a field of flowers with a love interest, cuddling up to a sun-kissed crush on a beach towel, or kissing a handsome stranger in the rain. My heart lets out a series of aches, which I quickly stifle. A woman approaches the counter, wearing a bold blue, sleeveless summer dress and clutching one of the romance books that everyone on TikTok is raving about, titled *Espresso Yourself*.

'I love a good romance.' She chuckles before handing me the book so I can scan the barcode. Her fingers come dangerously close to mine. Fear takes over and I let the book fall onto the counter. She doesn't mind and starts to explain her rationale for choosing the book. 'My boyfriend works in a coffee shop and looks a bit like the male character on the front cover.'

My eyes flick to the man on the cover, who's casually leaning against a café counter, his confident smile, tousled hair, and dark, piercing eyes promising excitement once the café closes. I glance at the woman and notice the freshly in-love glow on her face as she takes out her phone. A twinge of envy stirs within me as I catch sight of the photo on her lock screen; she and her barista boyfriend are kissing in front of a gleaming silver coffee machine.

Her payment goes through. I slide her book into the paper bag and am distracted by a man walking past the counter, running a hand through his mass of dark curls. He makes me think of Sam. I stop myself and push his face to the back of my mind, but it's too late. My focus has gone. As I hand over the book bag to the woman, our fingers brush. I hold my breath and silently hope their love story lasts a lifetime, ending with them both, old and crinkly, holding hands and reminiscing about how they fell in love over a vanilla latte with an extra shot of love many years ago.

A flash of white light crosses behind my eyes, and when it passes, I see her sitting opposite the man on her lock screen.

They must be in his coffee shop. He's talking about timing, needing space, and how she deserves better. She sits very still, her hand resting on the mug as if it might keep her steady. Her eyes are watery, and her bottom lip has that sad quiver.

The woman hurries away with her book, and I reach under the counter for my bag of sugary boiled sweets. I pop one in my mouth, savour the sweetness, and wait for the weird, muffled sensation that always follows one of my visions to pass. When the sounds from the bookshop return – a small child crying about his mother's choice of book for him, two people talking about a book's plot twist, and the doorbell jangling – I think about the woman with the barista boyfriend who will soon let her down gently in his coffee shop. The soft pink and blue covers of the romance books catch my eye again. They might promise idyllic meet-cutes and kisses in the rain, but they fail to mention that love, like milk, has an expiry date.

Miranda, my boss and owner of this bookshop, Once Upon a Spine, pulls me out of my thoughts. She hands me a mug of steaming tea and whispers, 'Cute male book customer alert. He's in the crime section browsing that new serial killer best-seller. The one where he takes his victims on dates to the cinema and murders them in the back row. He matches the description of the sexy serial killer.'

I look up and spot an older man with black hair, a rugged face and arms the size of tree trunks. 'Miranda,' I sigh. 'You have Frank, and last week you celebrated your fifteenth anniversary.'

Miranda giggles. 'If that cute man over there wants to take me to the cinema, I wouldn't say no. We could skip the murder part, and he could just devour me...'

Fortunately, a customer comes up to the counter and rescues me from one of Miranda's fantasies. He's embracing the

May heatwave in a blindingly pink Hawaiian shirt splashed with palm trees.

Spring and summer are my sworn enemies. The warmer it gets, the fewer layers people wear, and the more complicated my life becomes. I often daydream about living in a cold country where everyone spends the year wrapped up in thick clothing, and long sleeves are non-negotiable.

With a big smile, my customer reveals he's buying a cycling book for his wife. 'I am proud of her,' he beams, running a hand through his greying hair. 'She's rediscovered her love for bikes at fifty-nine.' I smile and process his card payment. 'I bought her a new bike last Christmas. Extra wife-points for me.' He chuckles. 'It's like the bike she had as a girl, lavender-coloured with a basket, white wheels, and a bell. It's been great seeing her cycling around town.'

My senses are on high alert; I don't want to have any physical contact with this man. He clearly loves his wife, and I don't want to see how things end for them both and that lovely bike. My hands become jittery, and I fumble with the bag and the book. 'Careful,' he says, catching the bag. I get careless and assume the danger has passed, but he turns sharply to wave at his wife through the shop window, and his bare forearm brushes my hand. Damn – short-sleeved Hawaiian shirts!

A flash of white light fills my vision. I gasp and grip the counter. As the light clears, I see two police officers in my mind. They're standing in a living room, exchanging concerned looks, while my customer sits on the sofa with his head in his hands. My heart thumps as they tell him about the fatal road accident involving his wife, and I glance at the framed photo on the wall where she's sitting on her lavender bike and laughing at the camera.

I blink and gulp as the vision fades.

The man is smiling and speaking to me, but I cannot hear him. It feels as though I'm underwater. His tear-stained face from my vision will stay with me for ages. He nods and walks towards the door. Reaching for another boiled sweet, I shove it in my mouth and survey the bookshop as the sight of it always calms my agitated state.

Nestled on a cobbled side street off the main road, Miranda's bookshop, feels like stepping into a good friend's living room, complete with quirky bookcases, sagging armchairs, and colourful rugs. It smells of old paper, fresh coffee, and vanilla-scented air spray. Wooden shelves line every wall, tightly packed with books of every hue. There are several display tables, curated entirely by Miranda's whims, such as 'Books that will make you feel like a hot mess' and 'Hot people doing bad things'. A string of fairy lights zigzags across the ceiling all year round, and the till is cluttered with pastel notebooks, glittery pens, and bookish stickers.

My eyes wander around the shop. They spot a customer flicking through a non-fiction book on dogs, an elderly man reaching for a cookery book, and a woman ordering her three teenage children to look for the romance book she's pointing to on her phone screen. The sound of the bookshop rushes back to me. I smile as one of her children moans at being in a bookshop with his mother and siblings looking for a romance book. His mother snaps and reminds him of the hours she has spent watching him play football. She reminds him of how much this book means a lot to her.

Two women approach the till, each carrying books. I go to great lengths to avoid physical contact and pretend I have a cold, so I don't pass on any germs. They ignore me, and I listen to their conversation about Psychic Medium Cynthia, who, according to one of the women, never disappoints. 'Cynthia can contact anyone on the other side,' explains the woman. 'She has a team of helpful spirit guides who track down deceased loved ones or unearth family secrets that were taken to the grave. That woman knew what my shady Uncle Malcolm was hiding before he died.'

Her friend blinks in surprise. 'You've never told me about shady Uncle Malcolm. Do we need to go for a glass of wine and have a chat about him?'

As they walk away talking about shady Uncle Malcolm and what he was doing before he had a fatal heart attack, an idea forms in my mind. Cynthia could contact Mum and Dad. They would surely give me the answers I've spent years searching for. The thought of speaking to Mum and Dad again after all this time makes me feel a little odd, and my mind tries to replay the memory of sitting in the back of the car, but I block it out.

Miranda gives me a break from the till, and I take the opportunity to hide away in my favourite place, the science fiction and fantasy section. It is both a magical and chaotic corner of the bookshop. Miranda has hung an old replica sword to the wall and added a note in old handwriting that reads, *Please do not duel unless you're arguing over a book.* The walls are lined with tall bookcases, crammed with epic fantasies, spell books, and sleek dystopian thrillers. I always think the air in this section of the shop feels a little cooler, which, combined with Miranda's twinkly lights, gives it an out-of-this-world vibe.

While I am there, I do some internet sleuthing about Psychic Medium Cynthia. After I've requested an appointment for tomorrow, Miranda calls me back to the till so she can make an important business call in the back room. What she really means is that she wants to chat with her online fashion stylist on Zoom about her latest clothing purchase.

I head for the till and serve two customers. As the last one walks away with their vegan cookery book, the doorbell jingles. I glance up and freeze.

Sam.

He's standing inside the door, looking just as he did a year ago. Still distractingly attractive with his olive skin, dark curly hair, and muscular arms that could effortlessly carry me out of a burning building if I needed rescuing.

2

'Nelly,' he says with a surprised warmth, stepping closer to the till like we're old friends and not cautionary tales.

As I force out a smile, I grip a pencil so hard that it snaps.

He runs a hand through his hair. 'I was passing by. Thought I'd pop in.'

'Lovely,' I mumble, avoiding his gaze.

When Miranda broke her leg last year, she hired Sam to help me. At that time, he was between bookshop jobs. Sam and I got along immediately, and I fell hopelessly in love with him from afar.

Sam made me want to believe in love. When we laughed and joked while stacking bookshelves, or when he held my gaze a little longer than necessary, he made all my worries disappear. He used to write me funny handwritten notes and leave them in romance books for me to find. Considering what I know about love, spending time in the bookshop's romance section is challenging. Sam's notes gave me a new source of happiness, and being among romance books stopped being such a struggle.

To my surprise, Sam admitted he felt the same way about

me. He did it through one of his notes. It read, *I can't stop thinking about you, Nelly xx*. I remember my heart pounding wildly. He was watching me when I looked up. I blushed, and he smiled.

The rest of my shift was spent imagining what he looked like... naked. My emotions were running wild, yet there was an undercurrent of anxiety. I was worried about what I would see when we touched, and I was also agonising over something else that has been making me feel uneasy for years. I don't like to admit it aloud. Not because it feels shameful, but because it feels out of step with how life is meant to unfold. I am thirty-three and still a virgin. I blame my teenage years. From what I observed from the girls at secondary school, having sex seemed only to speed up one's inevitable heartbreak. When I touched the girls' arms at school, I saw how their love would end. Shortly after losing their virginity to their boyfriends, two of them would discover that their beloved boyfriends were two-timing them, and in Elaine Smith's case, she would find out that her boyfriend mocked her body parts in his biology class. This made me put an imaginary lock on my knickers and steer clear of sex and love.

Sam was going to be different, I told myself. After a lot of ruminating, I concluded that being a virgin would work to my advantage with Sam. What helped was remembering what Miranda, my boss and regular over-sharer, once told me her partner, Frank, likes to whisper in bed: 'Can we pretend you are a virgin?'

From Miranda's experience, being a virgin would give me added appeal. It could make Sam love me more. Later that evening, as we closed the bookshop, Sam reached out and grabbed my hand. I squeaked as I wasn't ready for the monumental touch.

That was the crucial moment.

Until then, I had never envisioned a positive form of love. Everyone for whom I've had strong feelings – fancied or loved from a distance – had eventually hurt me in some way.

I held my breath and prayed to see a happy future for us. The familiar flash of bright light behind my eyes made me gasp, and when it faded, I realised how our love story would come to an end. I saw him and his ex-girlfriend caught in a passionate embrace in the back room of the bookshop. I recognised her face; she was a regular. Although Sam assured me they were over, I had a nagging doubt that they still liked each other. I looked devastated, in my vision, standing in the doorway and watching them kiss. Our love story would end with him cheating on me.

Looking back, I should have suppressed my emotions and told him I wanted to remain friends, but I got carried away. I told myself that Sam and I were different. He was going to be the exception. In a moment of madness, I convinced myself that breaking a curse was just a matter of maintaining a positive mental attitude. So, I vowed not to flinch when I heard him mention her name, or question why she spent every lunch hour wandering aimlessly around the bookshop. I ignored the painful reminders from the past and my curse's unfailing accuracy. Sam was the start of a new chapter in my life.

For three perfect weeks, we had passionate embraces in the back room before we opened, and we slow-danced after he'd put the closed sign on the door.

On that grey Thursday, the sight of him leading his ex-girlfriend by the hand into the back office caused an earthquake inside me. Just like my vision predicted, I left the till unattended, sprinted into the back room, and burst in on them kissing. After Sam, I vowed never to fall in love again. I promised myself no more crushes, daydreams, or hoping.

'You look well,' he says, bringing me back into the present.

I ignore his compliment. 'How are you?'

He raises his hand. 'Married. She didn't want a big fancy wedding, so we booked a registry office and became Mr and Mrs Clark. We've just returned from our honeymoon.'

My stomach plummets towards the floor. He married his ex-girlfriend. I force out a fake smile. 'Well, congrats.'

'You know I still feel guilty about how we ended.'

I can't listen to this. 'Let me know if you need any help, Sam,' I say frostily. 'The romance section is over there.' I fake a quick check under the counter, so he won't see my watery eyes.

Marcus's girlfriend's comment from earlier today echoes in my mind as I wipe a tear from my cheek. I know more about curses than she and Marcus will ever know.

In my pocket, my phone buzzes. I have an appointment with Psychic Medium Cynthia tomorrow.

3

'Can you help me contact my late parents, as I want to ask them what they know about my curse,' I say, and instantly regret it.

I'm sure Psychic Medium Cynthia was not expecting to hear that today. She's been staring at me for a while; I can't recall the last time she blinked. My question is unusual and must represent a dramatic shift from her usual requests, such as finding out how loved ones in the afterlife are doing or when that life-changing lottery win will happen.

She even looks the part with her silk headscarf, constellations of tiny silver stars on each cheek, large gold hoop earrings, and long silver nails. Her garage has been transformed into a magical gateway to the other side, with candles, crystals, posters of enchanted forests, sticks of burning incense, and a round table creaking with tarot cards and glittery clutter.

A trickle of saliva runs down the side of her mouth. I don't know whether to worry or offer her a tissue.

'Are you okay?' I ask, waving my hand in front of her eyes.

Her face flickers back to life. She smiles and dabs at her mouth with a tissue. 'Can you repeat your question?'

'I need you to get in contact with my mum and dad. They died when I was nine years old. I am cursed, and I want to ask them some questions.' With a trembling hand, I take out a little notebook, flick to the first page and start to read. 'Question One. Did they know I was cursed? Question Two. Do they know of any family relation who—'

She waves her hand, and I stop. Her beady dark eyes are narrowing. 'A curse? Can you give me more details?'

'It's romantic and tragic...' Words hover on the tip of my tongue, but I can't quite release them. She leans in closer, and I wonder why I'm sitting in a stranger's garage, filled with cheap stars and overpowering incense, about to reveal my deepest secret.

'This sounds interesting. Tell me about this romantic curse.' She reaches for a glittery lip balm beside her and smears it onto her plump lips.

Last night, I lay awake for hours in bed, imagining how Cynthia would react when I told her about my curse. My brain always starts with the worst-case scenario, so I visualised her giving me a terrified look while I talked about it. This would undoubtedly be followed by her calling the police, and me spending the rest of my life imprisoned in a science lab with wires connected to my head and being studied by scientists. Once my heart had stopped trying to burst out of my chest and I had calmed my breathing, I thought about a different scenario in which Cynthia helped me by casting an ancient spell. The lights overhead would flicker, and we would hear a thunderclap in the sky. The spell would succeed and free me from my suffering. I fell asleep imagining my new life.

I take a deep breath before crossing my fingers in my lap. 'When I touch people, I see a vision inside my head.'

Cynthia frowns. 'A vision?'

I nod. 'It shows how their love story will end.'

'What do you mean? Can you see if they are going to get dumped?'

'Yes,' I sigh. 'I see the ghosting, the awkward let-downs in coffee shops and the accidents – which always happen to the nice ones on their way to work.'

She fiddles with one of her hoop earrings. 'Do they come true? Your visions?'

'Always for the things I see about others. However, with my own life, I have the option to change my fate. If I decide not to pursue love with a person who, in the future, will hurt me, the vision doesn't come true.'

'But if you choose to ignore what your curse is showing you—'

Raising my hand, I interrupt her. 'It comes true.'

'What about if the person isn't in love with anyone?' Cynthia is stroking her chin. I can see she's giving my curse some serious thought.

'I see how they spend their time alone.' I think about the older man in the football shirt, who had sat next to me on the bus. He'd been wearing shorts, and his bare knee had touched my hand when the bus came to a juddering halt. His vision showed him sitting alone in a tiny studio flat, watching the world go by outside his window. His face was etched with sadness as he watched the loved-up couples walk hand in hand past his house. On his lap was a framed football-themed wedding photo, and on the coffee table in front of him was a book titled *How to Mend a Broken Heart Post Divorce*.

Cynthia arches an eyebrow. 'Are they enjoying being single in your visions?'

I shrug. 'Some fully embrace not having anyone special in

their life, whereas some struggle with loneliness and a broken heart.'

She applies a new layer of lip balm. 'My best mate is married but is also having an affair with her driving instructor. She's failed her test six times, but that's another story. If you touched her hand, what would you see – the saucy driving instructor or her poor husband?'

'In that situation, it would depend on who has captured her heart.'

Cynthia nods. 'You would see how things end with the driving instructor and his lessons, which are conducted from his back seat.' She sighs. 'And you want to get rid of this wonderful gift?'

I nod and correct her. 'It's a curse. Not a gift.'

'Does this curse work on demand?'

'Yes.'

She lights a silver candle beside us. 'Do you have to touch a specific part of someone for it to work?'

'It must be skin-to-skin contact. I can't see anything through clothes.'

Her eyebrows rise. 'Interesting. Do your visions ever change?'

This feels more like an interrogation than a psychic reading. 'What do you mean?'

'Do you see different visions every time you touch someone?'

I shake my head. 'I see the same vision unless something has changed, like if someone has died or a new person has entered their life.'

She extends her heavily spray-tanned arm towards me and smiles. 'Touch me. I have some suspicions about my boyfriend, so let's see how good your curse is.'

After a deep breath, I touch her fingers. There is a flash of bright light before my eyes. It clears, and I see a burly man with a bald head sitting in a lorry cab kissing a woman with long black hair who wears a skintight pink dress.

It makes me gasp.

Cynthia smooths down her headscarf. 'Don't hold back. I'm ready.'

She doesn't flinch as I tell her. When I finish describing his lorry cab in detail – including his black-and-white fluffy dice, his lorry-shaped mug, his silver roadster kettle, and his black T-shirt emblazoned with the words 'I just dropped a load' – and his shiny head and how tight the woman's dress was, Cynthia leans closer. 'That's not a curse – that's a money-making gift. You have a talent,' she gushes as the world around me feels muffled. I watch her mouth move, but I can't hear anything. Reaching into my back pocket, I take out my emergency packet of boiled sweets and suck on one until I can hear Cynthia again.

'The woman you described is my boyfriend's boss's wife. She's been sniffing around my man for ages. I knew she would make a move.' She smears on another layer of lip balm. 'You have confirmed what I suspected, and the details you provided were spot on. I mean, how would you even know what his favourite T-shirt says across the front? I will deal with him when he gets home. That is an amazing gift.'

'I don't always get a sense of timing with my visions,' I explain. 'He might not be cheating on you right now, but he will in the future.'

She rolls her eyes. 'His cab smells of her cheap perfume. He claims it's his new air freshener from Sainsbury's. I am not stupid. Anyway, enough about him. I could do with an extra pair of hands.' She lets out a heavy sigh. 'My mother has decided to go away for a while. I have three kids to pick up from school, a cheating boyfriend, and a thriving psychic business she was helping with, and she selfishly books a three-month cruise around the world.' I watch Cynthia place her head in her hands. She lifts it a few seconds later. 'If you worked here, I could sort out my kids and my relationship. Your gift of romance prophecy would have my customers queuing out the door. Come and join me.'

Shaking my head, I clasp my hands together. 'It's not a gift. It's a curse. Please help me find my parents in the afterlife. They must know more about my curse, possibly even how to lift it.'

She casts me a bewildered expression. 'This is a wonderful gift you've been given. It's not a curse. I think you should consider my business offer.'

My skin prickles. Her eyes have sharpened. They are bright, with the unmistakable glint of someone doing mental maths and seeing some eye-watering business numbers in their mind. She views my curse as a money-making gift. Sitting up straighter, I take a deep breath and try to sound calm. 'I need your help, not a business offer.'

It comes out more like a low growl.

Cynthia is oblivious to my annoyance. She shakes her head. 'You have been blessed with a fantastic gift. I don't understand how it is ruining your life. You get free dating spoiler alerts in your head.'

This woman has no idea what I endure with my curse. My cheeks are heating up, and I am on the verge of tears. 'Can you help me or not? It is ruining my life.'

Cynthia tries to reach out and touch my hand, but I yank it away as I don't want to see her trucker boyfriend kissing that woman again.

'Go away and think about my offer,' she says.

Has she not listened to anything I have said?

'Think about the money we could both earn from your gift.'

'You don't understand.' My voice wobbles. Irritation bubbles inside me. 'Every time I meet someone, I see how love ends.' The face of the man from the bookshop who bought his wife a cycling book comes rushing back to me, triggering a series of aches in my chest.

She lets out an excited shriek. 'We could be rich. I can see the advert now.' I watch as a dreamy, faraway expression takes hold of her face. 'Meet Mystic...' She falters. 'Sorry, what's your name again?'

'Nelly.'

To my horror, she screws up her face. 'Nelly? We would have to give you a magical name.' She draws an imaginary poster square in the air with her fingers. 'The poster would read: "Meet Mystic Nelwynna, who will predict how your love will end."' She lets out a contented sigh.

I am wasting my time here, and I am not being called Nelwynna as it would sound like I sing to woodland creatures in my spare time.

My face feels hot and my heart is thudding.

Before she can say another word, I leave and hurry out of her garage in tears.

4

I wake up frightened after a cold drop of water lands squarely on my forehead. The brown stain on my ceiling, which I reported to Gary, my landlord, a few months ago, is now leaking. I told him it had started after a bad storm and that I thought it was a roof issue. He dismissed what I said with a shrug and a grin. 'Old buildings get stains, Penelope,' he'd said. 'It's all part of their character.'

He didn't hear me mutter under my breath, 'Character, my arse, Gary.'

After showering and dressing, I go downstairs to his basement flat to report the leak and gloat. A small, petty part of me enjoys being right, but that joy only lasts a few seconds.

Gary comes to the door in a grubby dressing gown and old slippers that look like they've been half-chewed by a pack of wild dogs. His wiry black hair appears slicked back with grease. He casts me a creepy smile, revealing a row of his yellow-stained teeth, and says, 'Calm down, Penelope.'

The familiar prickle of agitation I get when I speak with Gary makes me clench my fists. I have told him countless times that I am called Nelly. My parents named me Penelope. Becoming Nelly after the car crash made my life easier. Gary, however, continues to ignore my wishes regarding my name.

'I'll look at your ceiling later.' He hands me an envelope, as if it were a birthday card. 'You've saved me a trip,' he said. 'It's a rent increase. Sorry.'

Gary is never sorry.

My name, Penelope Blake, is scrawled across the front in his distinctive, messy handwriting, which always gives me serial killer vibes.

I rip open the envelope in front of him. My heart is pounding. The rent is already extortionate on my bookshop wage. Once the numbers stop dancing, my mind begins to process the increase. The extra amount I will need to find makes my stomach drop.

'I know it's an increase, but times are hard.'

Tears rush to my eyes. I blink furiously to stop them from rolling down my cheeks.

'Tell you what,' says Gary. 'If you have a friend who wants to share, I am happy for you to split the pain.' Something flickers across his face. 'There were two of you when you moved in. You and... Eva.'

The way he softly pronounces my ex-flatmate's name is tinged with creepiness and turns my stomach.

Gary had a soft spot for Eva. When Eva and I were flatmates, the rent never increased. Any issue, no matter how small, was resolved seconds after Eva complained. Gary couldn't do enough for her, and the flat practically glowed.

Waves of guilt still crash over me when I think about how my friendship with Eva ended. She was one of my few friends, and I ruined it. I want to blame my curse, but honestly, it was me.

'Would Eva come back?' Gary's beady, dark eyes have grown wide. 'I miss seeing her smiling face.'

I don't want to discuss Eva with Gary, and I don't want a new flatmate either.

Feeling gloomy, I return to my flat and rest Gary's letter against Mum's vase on my hallway table. The slender white vase always lifts my spirits. I stare at it for a few moments, and a smile spreads across my face. It's one of the few keepsakes that remind me of my parents. Dad used to come home with flowers, and Mum would laugh about not having a lovely enough vase for them – especially when they were tulips, her favourites. One evening, he brought home both a colourful bunch and this slender white vase. We had a lot of fun arranging them.

I will deal with the rent increase later. Grabbing my bag, I spot a flash of silvery, grey fur out of the corner of my eye. My heart sinks, and I get ready to stop Lenny, my cat, from escaping. He's been doing this a lot lately. I've told him repeatedly that he's an indoor cat, but he thinks he knows best. If only he could understand that I don't have many people in my life, mainly because of my curse, and that if he ever escaped, my heart would break.

I am quicker than him, and I win the battle. Holding him in my arms, I bury my face in his fur as he emits engine-like purrs. 'Mummy needs you, Lenny Spartapuss.'

Later at work, while wrapping up book purchases and trying to get the temperamental card machine to work, I think about how I can manage financially with the upcoming rent increase.

The sensible option would be to find somewhere cheaper, but I love my flat too much. It's part of a Georgian terrace house, which has been converted into flats. Gary's rich elderly aunt left him the house in her will. He told me he struggled to maintain the property, so he started renting out the flats to cover costs.

The building is constructed of honey-coloured limestone and is three storeys high.

My flat is on the top floor, sitting beneath the roofline where the walls slant inward and the ceilings press down. It was once the servants' quarters and has been carved out of a maze of small rooms connected by a narrow hallway. In the living room, there's a small sash window overlooking a cobbled street lined with shops and cafés. The ceilings are low and sloping, the floorboards are uneven, and there are two bedrooms tucked under the eaves. Although it is costly, has a leaky bedroom ceiling and a creepy landlord, I am still fond of my little flat. I love how it crouches beneath the roof and makes me feel safe.

It gives me sweeping views from the windows, and at night, my flat comes alive with sounds of birds nesting in the roof, creaking pipes, and footsteps across wooden floors below. I love its hidden history and often drift to sleep thinking about the servants who once slept under this roof and the lives they must have led.

If I moved out, I don't think I could afford anything in the town centre. I live and work in a picturesque, historic town that boasts a highly sought-after high street lined with characterful buildings, boutique shops, and stylish cafés. Leading off the high street are charming cobbled streets, always busy with tourists and shoppers. Rent prices are rising rapidly, and even though Gary has just increased the rent, I know it's still a bargain compared to other places. I would be forced to rent a shabby studio flat on the outskirts of town. I wouldn't be able to walk to work, and I would miss my flat terribly. Additionally, I have Lenny and finding landlords who don't mind pets can be challenging. I can't move out.

The bookshop wage is abysmal, and Miranda, my boss, is a nightmare. Every day feels like a private diary entry, as she over-shares her relationship issues, the clothes she's wearing, and the male customers she fantasises about. Her one saving grace is that she owns Once Upon a Spine. Books are my lifebuoys; they keep me afloat when my curse tries to pull me under.

My stomach growls. Perhaps the only way to handle my rent increase is to reduce my food expenses. I'm already down to beans on toast most nights, and lying awake in the small hours with hunger pains is becoming a regular occurrence. If I cut down further, I'll be reduced to a pile of bones and still cursed.

5

I look up after handing a customer their purchase – a poetry book – only to see Miranda smiling at me and gesturing to her dress. I let out a silent groan.

Earlier, before we opened the shop, I was too busy worrying about Gary's rent increase and forgot to notice Miranda's latest outfit. Last year, Miranda hired an online fashion stylist who has completely overhauled her wardrobe. The stylist, a twenty-five-year-old fashion student who, Miranda claims, wears pyjamas, works from her bed and charges an eye-watering amount, was recommended by her best friend, Anna. According to her, the stylist is costly but will perform miracles. In Anna's case, her wardrobe overhaul led to a steamy relationship with an airline pilot who, she claimed, looked like George Clooney and gave her discounted long-haul flights.

Miranda now expects me to give her daily feedback on her outfits. The fact that she asks me for fashion feedback is still a surprise, given I only wear black long-sleeved T-shirts and grey jeans. Today she's in a pink floral tea dress with short sleeves and a heart-shaped neckline. Her curly brown hair is piled high in a messy up-do.

'You look good, Miranda,' I tell her.

'My fashion stylist says the theme for the week is cute pink dresses,' she says, with a heavy sigh. 'Before you ask, Frank didn't notice.'

During Miranda's first Zoom consultation with her stylist, she was asked about her fashion ambitions. Miranda explained that her main aim was to capture her partner, Frank's, attention. After fifteen years together, she feels invisible to him and believes a new wardrobe might alter their relationship. This serves as another poignant reminder of the complexities of love. Once you have found your beloved, there's no guarantee that the intense feelings that brought you together won't fade away and compel you to spend thousands on reinventing yourself in the hope that those exhilarating sensations might someday return.

Miranda has not yet achieved her goal.

Nearly a year has passed, and Frank has not made a single comment about her outfits. Some weeks, he doesn't even look up from his granola when she comes downstairs looking as though she's stepped out of a glossy fashion magazine. It's been painful to watch as Miranda has spent a considerable amount of money, had a new wardrobe fitted in her bedroom to accommodate her clothes, and her online fashion stylist has enjoyed several luxury holidays, which Miranda claimed were for research purposes.

'He might mention it tonight,' I say, trying to lift Miranda's spirits.

She walks over to the till. 'I don't think he'll say anything positive later after visiting his mother, Nelly. She's still busy crocheting that doll, which Frank keeps saying looks like a voodoo doll and has an uncanny resemblance to me.'

I serve a customer who buys a book on carpentry. Once the woman has gone, Miranda leans over the desk. 'Do you know someone who needs extra cash and wouldn't mind a hot guy wandering around their home in boxer shorts?'

Miranda never fails to shock me. I blink a few times in surprise. 'What?'

'I know a guy who needs to rent a room.' She gets distracted and beams at two older ladies hovering by the door.

'Where are the crime books?' one lady asks.

'I like my crime novels to be grisly and dark,' pipes up the other. 'Just like my divorce.'

Miranda smiles and points them towards the crime section. She turns back to me, already halfway into one of her fantasies. 'If I were in my thirties again and not living with Frank, I would offer this hot guy a room and the keys to my heart. Or my bedroom.' With a dreamy, faraway look, she murmurs, 'Given who this hot guy is, I would offer all three.'

My fifty-five-year-old boss has a vivid imagination and tends to share it with others. I have learned that it's best to shut her down quickly before the situation escalates.

'Sorry, I don't know anyone, Miranda.'

She stares at me. 'You have a spare room, Nelly.'

'I do, but I'm not looking for a flatmate.'

Miranda's dark, beady eyes study my face. 'In the back room earlier, you told me about your "crippling rent increase" and how you were living on beans on toast and black coffee.'

Why did I tell Miranda about Gary's letter? My face is getting warm. 'I did.'

'Well, this is the perfect solution. You get help with your rent and a bare, muscular chest to gaze at while you eat your cornflakes.'

'I don't want to gaze at a—'

She interrupts me. 'Nelly, you're an attractive, single, young woman. I worry about you not dating. You also live like a hermit.'

'I'm not interested in dating.'

'When I was your age, I was wild. I had a string of fellas after me and a permanent dent in my mattress.'

She winks, and I die a little inside.

If there's one thing I hate more, it's listening to one of Miranda's pep talks. When will she accept that I'm not like her?

'If you're worried about this chap being a weirdo or a potential serial killer with a doll collection, don't be,' Miranda says, tapping me on the arm.

There's a flash of white light. When it clears, I see the same vision I've had for years: Frank pushing a pram and calling himself 'Daddy'. I've never told her about my curse or what I see for her and Frank. Their future makes me uneasy. She's always claimed that children were never on their radar. The future, apparently, disagrees. I shove the vision into the darkest depths of my mind and pop a boiled sweet into my mouth.

Miranda is looking over at the romance section. She's pointing and speaking but I can't hear her.

The sound of the bookshop comes rushing back to my ears. Miranda is mid-sentence. '...he's the son of Frank's boss and...' She enjoys dramatic pauses. 'His books are in this shop.'

'Who are you talking about? Books? What do you mean?'

She draws an imaginary heart shape in the air with her fingers. 'The guy who needs a room – he's a romance author.'

'Really?'

She nods. 'Oliver James.'

Ugh – that name rings a bell. I glance at the new romance book display table Miranda set up last week. It's currently dominated by Oliver James's latest pastel-pink novel, *Love Me Forever*. The cover features a lovestruck couple gazing into each other's eyes. His name is emblazoned across the top in swirly gold letters. I can't walk past the table without rolling my eyes or physically flinching.

Romance authors like Oliver James spend their lives writing books that convince readers that love conquers all and that soulmates can be found in idyllic settings, such as florists or bakeries. They make me want to believe in love, but my curse always reminds me of the lies, the ghosting, the serial cheaters, the tragic accidents that take the good ones while they are cycling around town or those who can't seem to forget their ex-partners.

Miranda tidies up the array of glittery pens, notebooks, and bookmarks by the till. 'I only found out this the other day,' she explains. 'You'd think Frank would have told me sooner that his boss has a son who's a bestselling romance author. Frank knows the bookshop has been struggling financially. Having direct access to the author everyone's talking about right now would be a game-changer for me.' She sighs. 'Sometimes I wonder what goes on inside his head.'

'Oliver James is moving here?'

Miranda nods. 'He's selling his flat in London and wants to rent a room for six months.'

'Why would someone like Oliver James come here?' I murmur.

She shakes her head. 'I have no idea. You'd think Oliver would go live with his father, who, I might add, lives in Cornwall in a large, flashy house, and each week, a new bikini-clad woman sits in his hot tub. I've seen his Instagram photos. I bet

Oliver's late mother is rolling in her grave, watching her husband behave like a wealthy playboy. Oliver should head for Cornwall and join his father.'

This is a helpful reminder to me. Heartbreak still finds you in the afterlife.

'Maybe Oliver doesn't want to live with his father.'

Miranda ignores me and pulls out her phone. 'I know I'm technically old enough to be Oliver's aunt, but if he were interested in a fun, fifty-something woman with a lively personality, a pair of flexible hips, and a personal fashion stylist, I wouldn't say no.'

'Miranda, you have Frank!' I exclaim.

She rolls her eyes. 'I don't think Frank knows I exist.'

I watch her take out her phone, scroll, then hold the screen in front of me. I find myself staring at a photo of Oliver James. He looks like he's from a romance novel. My heart skips a beat. He is annoyingly handsome, with perfectly tousled hair and dark eyes that evoke thoughts of a rich, dark coffee.

'Do you like what you see?'

I blink at him and then at Miranda.

Her eyes twinkle. 'Imagine bumping into him after he's just had a shower.'

'Miranda, I don't want a flatmate.'

'Oh, Nelly, come on,' she groans. 'This would also be a good career move for you.'

My eyebrows are almost touching my hairline. 'A career move?'

'Think of all the promotion we could do. You could sweet-talk him into doing some book signings or an event or two.'

My irritation levels have spiked. She only wants me to offer Oliver James a room because she thinks it will boost her business. I don't think she ever intended to ask anyone else.

Before I tell Miranda where she can shove her idea on flat-sharing with Oliver James, a customer asks why the bookshop's free Wi-Fi isn't working. I leave Miranda by the till and assist them with their Wi-Fi issue.

The next few hours are filled with my attempts to ignore my hunger pangs and the image of Oliver James, which refuses to leave my mind.

I repeatedly tell myself that I don't want a flatmate and certainly don't want a male flatmate who writes romance novels. Money is tight, but I'm not desperate.

6

Miranda leaves early. 'Think about what I said earlier,' she says with a wink. 'Frank tells me Oliver is house-trained and owns a Le Creuset set. If that's not husband material, I don't know what is.'

'No thanks, Miranda,' I snap and start a vigorous shelf stack.

Later, as I lock up the bookshop, my phone rings. It's Aunt Polly.

When my parents died in a car crash, Aunt Polly became my legal guardian. She is everything to me. I often think about how dramatic a change it must have been for her when her brother died, and she became the guardian of a nine-year-old girl. At the time, she had no plans for children of her own, and we barely knew each other, as she and my father had not been close. We bonded immediately over a massive slice of cake, her copy of *The Secret Garden*, which she let me borrow, and her promise to paint my new bedroom in her house any colour I wanted. She was the first person I confided in about my curse.

After moving away, Aunt Polly now lives by the coast, an hour away by train, and we keep in touch during the week with calls and FaceTime. When we meet, it's coffee, cake and long walks on the beach.

'Nelly, I have some news.' I detect something unfamiliar in her voice. Her cheerfulness and sing-song tone have been replaced by one tinged with sadness.

I sense something is wrong. 'Are you okay?' My heart is thumping against my ribcage.

'I have breast cancer, Nelly.'

My chest tightens. I struggle to breathe. 'Cancer?' I croak.

'Yes.'

My body starts to tremble. 'You haven't told me about this.'

'I didn't want to worry you.'

'Okay – is it treatable?' My legs feel weak. I sit on one of the plastic chairs in the children's section.

Aunt Polly continues. 'Nelly, the doctor tells me I have a good chance of beating it as it hasn't spread to my lymph nodes. I need to have a course of chemo and possibly a mastectomy.'

Hot, stinging tears rush to my eyes. 'We'll get you through this. I'm coming over. I'll get on a train now.'

'Not now. Come on your day off on Sunday.'

'I'll be there.' My voice is wavering. Hilary's face flashes up inside my mind, which is followed by a sad ache in my chest. My aunt and Hilary were best friends. They were so close that my aunt often referred to Hilary as her 'fourth emergency service'. Ten years ago, they fell out and have not spoken since. My aunt refuses to tell me why she won't talk about Hilary. She says some things are better left alone. It's moments like these that I wish Hilary was still in our lives.

'Let's talk when you're here, Nelly. There's something I want to ask you.'

'What is it?'

'I'll tell you when I see you.'

A cloud of gloom passes over me. What does she want to tell me? 'I can't wait, Aunt Polly, tell me now.'

She lets out a sigh. 'Nelly, I wanted to ask whether you would come with me to have my chemo. They want to start it on Wednesday, and I know that's your day off from the bookshop. I was worried it would be a lot of—'

I interrupt her. 'You don't have to ask. I'll be there.'

Aunt Polly gave up her time, energy, sleep, and possibly her sanity for me. The least I can do is be there for her when she's unwell and needs to have treatment.

'The course is weekly. It would be every Wednesday. But... what about the cost of the train fares?'

'I'll sort it, Aunt Polly,' I croak. 'You don't have to worry; I'll be by your side.'

My aunt's sobs come in bursts. Hearing her cry and knowing I am not there to comfort her makes my heart break. 'I'm sorry, Nelly.' She sniffs. 'I'm just scared.'

'It's okay to be scared,' I say as tears roll down my cheeks. 'We're going to get through this together. I am going to be holding your hand, bringing you book gifts, and I might even treat you to one of our new bookmarks.'

'Oh, Nelly, you don't have to go to any trouble, but I wouldn't say no to one of those.' She blows her nose, which makes me hold the receiver away and smile. My aunt has always favoured an extra-loud nose blow. 'Let's talk on Sunday,' she says, her voice sounding a little stronger. 'Would you like to join me at the café when you arrive? My treat.'

'Only if we can eat far too much cake.'

I can hear a weak laugh. 'See you on Sunday.' She hangs up, and I wipe my watery eyes.

Gary's envelope is waiting for me when I get home. It sits where I left it on the hall table, leaning against Mum's vase. I should have shoved it in a drawer or, even better, set it on fire. Snatching the envelope, I tear it into pieces. After tossing the remains in the bin and apologising to Mum's vase for leaning Gary's letter against it, I wander into my bedroom. A note on my bed greets me. It reads, *Fixed it*. Gary claims he has repaired the hole in the ceiling. This is surprising. I glance up at the ceiling and groan. The stain has been covered with sheets of white paper stapled in place. He hasn't solved the problem at all.

Aunt Polly's news weighs heavily on my shoulders. I sit on the bed and let my tears fall into my lap. She means the world to me. Over the years, when my curse has shown me nothing but heartbreak and darkened my world, my aunt has answered it with cake at her favourite café, long talks about books, and slow walks along the beach. These small, steady things have given me the light to find my way again.

Sensing that I need some emotional support, Lenny weaves his body through my legs while emitting a loud purr.

'Where would I be without you, Lenny?' I whisper, giving his chin a good stroke. 'You are Mummy's best boy.'

We sit in our favourite spot in the living room. I've placed my chair by the small sash window, creating an ideal spot for unwinding after a bad day and perfect for people-watching. Beside my chair is a stack of my favourite go-to reads for when my days feel heavy and I turn to reading about other lonely but resilient souls. On top is *Jane Eyre*, and beneath it is *Anne of Green Gables*.

Below the window lies a cobbled street lined with cafés, restaurants, and shops. The evenings stay light for hours because it's May. My chair used to belong to my mother. It's a classic wingback in a rich ruby colour. I am possessive over it, and even when Eva lived with me, I never let her sit in it. This is my happy place. It's where I sit night after night watching the world beneath my window while listening to my vinyl records (mainly Coldplay), enjoying music, safe in the knowledge that there's no risk of anyone touching me.

Tonight, people-watching, Chris Martin's voice and Coldplay's latest album do little to ease my stress. The worries about Aunt Polly and my financial situation are gnawing at me. I decide to make myself a comforting plate of beans on toast.

After my tea, I do some research on what Aunt Polly is about to endure with her treatment. I read several articles and watch a few YouTube video diaries from breast cancer patients. They all mention that the fatigue due to the chemo is debilitating. I need to change my original plan to visit her once a week. I am Aunt Polly's only family, and she's going to need support. I'll accompany her to chemotherapy on a Wednesday, but I'll also see her on Sundays, which is my other day off. I can do her laundry, clean the bungalow, and run errands. I checked the train prices earlier, and travelling twice a week will be costly. With my rent increase, my weekly budget is becoming alarmingly tight.

Cynthia's face comes to mind. I know she made me cross with her business offer, but maybe I should now consider telling people how their love stories will end for money? I feel the same prickle of irritation that I did when I was sitting in her magical garage. Witnessing disastrous endings to relationships, marriages, affairs, and situationships is tough enough, but taking people's money makes me feel uncomfortable.

But I also don't want a flatmate, especially one who writes about first kisses, soulmates, and meet-cutes in cake shops.

However, I need to do something. I don't want Aunt Polly to undergo chemotherapy on her own.

An idea unfolds in my mind. I could advertise for a flatmate. There must be better flatmates than Oliver James out there.

7

The cries of seagulls and a cloudless blue sky greet me as I step off the train. Journeys on packed trains can be challenging and emotionally draining, especially in the warmer months. And today, this train was packed with beach day-trippers and stopped at every little station. Despite pressing myself against the window and trying to avoid physical contact with my fellow passengers, they ignored all the signs I was giving. My curse was busy showing me an endless reel of melancholic visions about love. The little packet of boiled sweets I bought at the station was a lifesaver as they helped me feel better when the world went quiet.

The train reached the station before my aunt's stop, and I didn't think my journey could get any worse. 'Is that seat taken?' I looked up to see a young lad, clutching a skateboard. He had blond surfer hair, baggy faded jeans and a boyish smile. A door opened inside my mind, and my memories of Luke rushed out. I couldn't get the words 'yes, it is taken' out of my mouth fast enough.

By the time I reached Tide-Leigh, a lively seaside town on

England's southwest coast, my head was aching with sadness and salt air. The road to Aunt Polly's house was chaos; tourists hurrying towards the beach, screaming children, inflatable rings and cars blaring loud music. As I weaved through it, I thought of the flat share advert I had posted last night. My criteria are simple:

No scary doll collection.

Must like cats.

Must agree to strict no-physical contact rules.

Above all, must not write books about love.

'Hello, Nelly, you took your time,' says Aunt Polly with a wry smile.

'It's hell out there.' I chuckle. 'I'll need extra cake after that journey.'

Entering Aunt Polly's bungalow feels like stepping back in time. The walls are decorated with framed photos of me growing up and images from before her falling-out with Hilary. When Hilary wasn't arguing with her three daughters, her ex-husband, or playing a supportive role, she was Aunt Polly's social sidekick. Aunt Polly and Hilary knew how to enjoy themselves, organising babysitting for Hilary's daughters, then going on drunken trips to Blackpool, where they got tipsy, sprayed their hair pink, and took silly photos. They would also go to Spain for wild weekends, raving with whistles and glow sticks, or head to London to drink cocktails and shop. Seeing Hilary's photos, I still hear her high-pitched laugh and the sound of her high stilettos on Aunt Polly's tiled kitchen floor.

'Let's go to the café,' says Aunt Polly, grabbing her cardigan and bag from the hook. 'Those cream cakes have got me through a difficult week.'

After she locks up her house, I take her hand. A flash in my mind shows Aunt Polly's hand holding someone else's, recognisable by a delicate silver chain on their wrist. Hanging from the bracelet is a tiny padlock. I've seen this vision since my aunt moved to Tide-Leigh ten years ago, and it has never changed. I believe it's a sign that my aunt's ex-girlfriend, Sandra, still holds the key to her heart and will one day return. This always makes me feel uncomfortable.

My father and his sister weren't close. I remember asking my mum at a family wedding who the woman with black hair was and why she was holding hands with the woman with long golden hair like Rapunzel. Mum explained that the black-haired lady was Aunt Polly and Sandra was her girlfriend. They broke up six months after the crash. I had confided in Aunt Polly about my curse and told her every time I touched her hand, I saw Sandra kissing the woman across the street. It turned out Sandra was having an affair with the woman who lived opposite my aunt. I will never forget the nights I sat in my bedroom listening to my aunt cry in the next room after Sandra left.

When Aunt Polly asks me what I see when we touch, I always lie and say I see her enjoying a wonderful single life in Tide-Leigh. I don't mention Sandra's bracelet with the tiny padlock. However, my curse is never wrong, and at some point, I do need to accept that she and my aunt will reunite one day. This is a future I'm not yet ready to face.

A cooling sea breeze greets us as we walk up her street. I squeeze her hand. 'We are going to get through this together.'

She casts me a weak smile. 'Thank you, Nelly. It's been a bit daunting. Come on. There are two cream cakes and a pot of tea waiting for us.'

Aunt Polly's café, The Sailing Boat, is on Tide-Leigh Bay's pedestrian street. Facing it are pastel-coloured shops and a promenade of golden sand leading to the sea. The royal-blue exterior features a hand-painted boat with white sails. Inside, the nautical theme continues with a ship's wheel on the counter and plastic menus with tiny boats. Once we're seated in our favourite spot by the window and have given the waitress our order, I look at Aunt Polly.

'Why didn't you tell me sooner?'

'Everything happened so fast after my regular mammogram. Before I knew it, I was having a biopsy and then sitting in front of a consultant being told I had cancer. I had to have a lumpectomy, and then I was told I needed to have chemo.'

Shock at what she's gone through by herself takes hold of me. 'You went through all that without calling me?'

She tries to calm down her mass of black hair. 'You know me, Nelly. I don't like being unwell. I tried to shrug it off and told myself I would handle it on my own. A few days ago, the thought of having treatment scared me. I realised I needed help.'

'I'll come to the hospital with you on a Wednesday, and we will fight this. I'm also going to come over every Sunday to help with housework.'

I notice her jade-coloured eyes are watery, and she's trembling. 'I'm scared, Nelly.'

'I know, but we're going to get through this. In the meantime, you need to eat more cream cakes,' I say, gesturing towards the cakes on display by the till. We both chuckle, and she wipes her eyes.

'I've added you to my car insurance so you can drive me back from the hospital. Don't worry, Nigella will behave herself.'

Aunt Polly's car, Nigella – named after TV chef Nigella Lawson – is in immaculate condition for its age. My aunt pampers Nigella and treats her like a family member. Nigella's bodywork is rust-free, she has low mileage, and she receives daily compliments from my aunt. The trouble is that Nigella has been spoiled, and now the car has a mind of its own. It rarely starts on the first try, its seatbelts tighten unexpectedly, and it randomly switches off the radio or spits out CDs it dislikes. It stalls at inconvenient moments, seemingly to deliberately annoy its driver. My aunt has had mechanics look at Nigella and to my frustration, none of them can find any faults.

I groan. 'Can't we get a taxi?'

Aunt Polly shakes her head. 'Nigella knows this is a big thing for me. She will be as good as gold.'

'She's a car, not a small child.'

The café door swings open, and a fashionable couple walks in. Both have sun-kissed golden tans and broad smiles. They wear matching sweaters over their shoulders, as if they've just stepped off their yacht. Aunt Polly looks up and waves at the woman. She whispers, 'That's my friend, Karen, with Jack, her new younger bloke. We all think he's dodgy. See what your curse thinks.'

Karen and her new man head for our table. 'Polly,' she cries and throws her arms around my aunt. 'How lovely to see you.'

'Hey, Polly,' says Jack, who runs a tanned hand through his dark hair.

Aunt Polly points to me. 'This is Nelly.'

I stand up, and Karen grins. She outstretches her hand. 'I finally get to meet you.'

Our hands touch, and a white flash reveals the truth. When the light clears, I see Karen watching through a window in a rundown house. Inside, Jack sits on a grubby sofa with three children climbing on him, while a tired woman tells them to leave their father alone because dinner is ready. Everything goes quiet around me. I suck on one of my boiled sweets and pray my dentist has other things on his mind besides my teeth at my next visit. When the café's sounds greet my ears, Karen and Jack are leaving, as Jack has some business calls to make.

'What did you see?' Aunt Polly asks.

'He's a liar. Jack has three kids, a wife and lives in a shabby house.'

Aunt Polly gasps. 'I knew it. Poor Karen. Her first husband was a cheat, and now she's hooked up with a conman. Falling in love should come with a health warning.'

Our tea and cakes arrive. We both devour them in seconds.

'I went to see a psychic medium,' I say as I pour milk into my tea. 'To reconnect with Mum and Dad.'

Aunt Polly looks puzzled. 'Oh. Can I ask why?'

'I'm sure they must know about my curse. Maybe one of them knows who passed it down and how to lift it.'

I have lived with my curse all my life. When I was little, I assumed everyone experienced a flash of white light and a picture in their head. Every time I touched one of my parents, I saw them asleep in a car and covered in what I thought were sparkly jewels. This didn't trouble me when I was little. I saw lots of things in my head, but I never quite understood what they meant. As a child, I had a skin condition on my hands, and Mum made me wear little white gloves all year round. She used to say that the germs in the air were making my hands sore.

The car crash when I was nine changed everything.

My aunt sighs, dabbing her mouth with a napkin. 'Can you stop calling it a curse? It's an extraordinary gift.'

'Experiencing visions constantly is draining. Most are upsetting or tragic. I can't be the only one in the family to go through this. Was anyone else cursed?'

Aunt Polly shakes her head. 'I've told you, there's never been anyone like you with such a gift.'

I put my face in my hands. 'My curse has made me avoid love.'

'Your curse says a lot about love,' sighs Aunt Polly. 'I'm glad we turned our backs on romance. What did the psychic say?'

I roll my eyes. 'She said I have an extraordinary gift and offered me a job with her.'

Aunt Polly nods. 'If Miranda closes, you know where to find your next career.'

'I can't do that.'

My aunt casts me a bewildered look. 'If I were you, I would be making money out of it. I see all those celebrity psychic mediums on TV, and I always think, Nelly could do a better job.'

'I can't do that,' I mumble. I silently vow to carry on looking for a way to live curse-free.

'I have something to show you,' she says and takes a red leather photo album from her bag and places it on the table. 'Look what I've found.'

'Where did you get that?'

I watch her open the album. 'In a box in my cupboard upstairs. I don't think I got round to unpacking it when I moved here.'

The first pages show photos of Mum and Dad's wedding day, including one with them gazing into each other's eyes and another with guests. Seeing my parents in photos feels strange, as if they are from another world.

Dad used to say Mum and I were like two peas from the same pod with our red hair, blue eyes and scattering of freckles. We both loved to swim. Mum said water was her friend – strange to me then, but I was young. She said she felt free, like a bird.

I was good at swimming and joined the local club at the sports centre. For some reason, the chlorine didn't irritate the skin condition on my hands. However, once I came out of the pool, Mum whipped my gloves on. Aunt Polly liberated my hands. This is something I will always be grateful for, as other children always laughed at my gloves.

After the car crash, the mere thought of swimming made me think of Mum, and I would get upset. So, I gave it up and vowed never to swim again.

I gulp back a wave of emotion.

'Is this too much for you, Nelly?'

I shake my head. Aunt Polly turns the page to find a photo from my tenth birthday party. It was a turning point for me in so many ways. I didn't win the dance competition Aunt Polly had organised, and that sent me into a mood. I made the mistake of telling Helen and Olivia from school that I see things in my head when I touch people. Helen told me that I was weird, Olivia giggled, and I spiralled.

Aunt Polly smiles and turns a page in the album. There's a photo of me at fifteen with a golden-haired boy, Luke, hugging his skateboard, and I have books under my arm. I think of the boy on the train and how similar he looked. Aunt Polly starts to turn the page, but I stop her.

I remember Luke's soft lips and his dad's aftershave, which he put on before seeing me. Luke's family moved from California for his father's job. I fell in love with him at first sight, captivated by his obsession with skateboarding. He practised non-stop, and I was consumed by teenage love, spying on him from my bedroom.

We became friends, but I kept my distance, wary of my curse. We eventually touched, and the vision was so excruciatingly painful that it made me sick. Luke would die in a skateboarding accident on the way to meet me.

I hated my curse and back then, I was confident that I could change its fate. I convinced Luke to leave his skateboard at home whenever we had a date, and I felt free and happy for three weeks. But I knew my curse was watching and mocking me. One day, I had stomach pains; the nurse suspected appendicitis, and Aunt Polly took me to the hospital. Luke, hearing I was there, was on his way to see me but decided to jump a flight of steps on his skateboard, crashed, and hit his head.

After his funeral, I wouldn't come out of my bedroom for weeks.

Outsmarting my curse has never worked.

'Are you okay?' Aunt Polly asks me.

I blink away the tears in my eyes.

'Let's leave the past alone,' she says, reaching over to rub my shoulder.

We both sip our tea. Aunt Polly tells me about her chemo and what she will endure. Her voice crackles. I can sense she's feeling emotional and overwhelmed by the journey ahead of her.

A woman enters the café who reminds me of Hilary. She's tall with brown bobbed hair; not a strand is out of place.

'Do you ever think about getting back in touch with Hilary?' I ask.

Aunt Polly shakes her head. 'Let's not talk about Hilary.'

'I was thinking she might be a good—'

'Nelly,' says Aunt Polly, her voice edged with firmness. 'I said let's not talk about her.'

8

Tonight, I am interviewing three potential flatmates. I haven't told Miranda, as she will question me about why I'm not interviewing Oliver James. Hopefully, by the end of the day, I will have found the perfect candidate, which will allow me to tell Miranda that Oliver James can walk around someone else's flat in just his underpants, thinking about his next idea for a book.

Eva is on my mind. Like me, she's a passionate reader, and we met through a book club Miranda used to run. She worked in the clothes shop on the high street and would always make us all laugh by saying things like 'The real issue in this book is that nobody owns a decent coat,' and 'If the protagonist had worn a pretty dress with pockets, she would have better handled that emotional climax.' When we shared a flat, she would review books on social media in her free time. She was known for her dramatic live book reviews and once loved a book so much that she burst into tears while talking about it, which I found impressive. She was warm and funny, and we got on immediately.

The first time I accidentally brushed against Eva's arm, I had a vision. It was of a man with spiky red hair in bed with a blonde woman. It startled me, but as she was single, I ignored it and joked about avoiding untrustworthy red-haired men. She laughed and agreed.

For the first six months, everything was good. Then, one day, I came home to find him – the man from my vision – sitting in my kitchen with his arms around her.

'This is Karl,' she gushed. He grinned and gave me a wave.

I smiled, but inside, panic bloomed. I wanted to say something and warn her. All I could think about was what I'd seen and how Eva would get her heart broken by a two-timing, red-haired love rat. I kept quiet until Eva's estranged sister returned home from New Zealand; to my horror, she was the blonde woman in my vision.

One drunken night, I made the mistake of telling Eva about my curse and what I'd seen regarding the end of her love story. Eva didn't believe me and assumed I was trying to break up her relationship and turn her against her sister. Shortly afterwards, she moved out, left the clothes shop and stopped reviewing books. My big mouth and my curse ruined that friendship.

I take some deep breaths. There will not be another Eva. All I need to do is keep my distance and my mouth shut.

My first flatmate candidate is knocking at the door. I take a deep breath and grab Lenny, which will make handshakes as tricky as possible. I'm going to do my best to avoid physical contact. This is an ambitious plan, given that I live in a flat, once built for servants, with small rooms and a narrow hallway, but I must try. Also, holding Lenny means he won't dash out of the door. Last week, he discovered that the sweeping staircase outside my flat's door eventually leads to the ground-floor hallway. He also found that the large door at the end of the hallway leads to something exciting outside. If the guy who lives in the first-floor flat hadn't blocked Lenny with his mountain bike, he would have made a bid for freedom. I can't let that happen.

Francesca is a glamorous woman in her late twenties, dressed in a designer pink tracksuit and sipping an iced coffee.

'Hi,' she coos.

I cast her an awkward smile. Taking a big step back, I let her in.

With a flick of her poker-straight black hair, she glides past me. I watch as she struts up my hallway like it is a catwalk at a fashion show. Her hips sashay from side to side. As she enters the living room, I direct her to the sofa. She ignores me and flops onto my favourite chair by the window, as if she owns it. My agitation levels rise.

'That's my chair,' I say, with a firm edge to my voice. 'You can have the sofa.'

She sighs, gets up from my chair, and perches on the arm of the sofa. Can she be any more irritating?

I settle myself in my chair and take out my notebook. 'Why are you looking for a flat?' I ask.

'Darren and I broke up,' she says, inspecting her leopard-print nails. 'I wanted an open relationship.'

'Oh.'

She casts me a wry smile. 'Why stick to one man when you can have several? I love dating and I am meeting so many new people.'

I let out a silent groan. I will struggle to cope with the constant flow of strangers in this flat if Francesca moves in.

She runs her hand through her long black hair. 'I'm on social media a lot, so I do Insta Lives and TikToks. My followers are all night owls like me. I am hoping to go on TV soon.'

'Oh – what sort of TV?'

'It's a new show called *Naked Island*.'

I gasp. 'Naked what?'

With a flick of her hair, she giggles. 'It's where a group of hot people live on this luxurious island, but the twist is… no clothes are allowed. It's filmed day and night. Oh, and if I'm successful, I won't be wearing clothes in the daytime.' She smiles. 'I will need to practise.'

'Interesting,' I say, crossing out her name. The last thing I need when I walk through my flat door after a hard day at the bookshop is a naked Francesca wandering about.

After a few questions, I bring the interview to a close. 'I'll be in touch about the flat.'

Once Francesca has gone, I make myself a cup of coffee and confide in Lenny. 'She needs to live by herself. I don't think we would have made good flatmates.'

Steve is the next person on my list. He's in his mid-thirties, wears a shiny grey suit, and is an amateur magician in his spare time. When I read his flat-sharing profile, I thought he sounded interesting, and he could show me a few magic tricks.

As soon as we are seated, he pulls out a pack of playing cards. 'Pick a card, Nelly. Any card.'

His card trick is unconvincing and fails because he guesses my card incorrectly. An awkward silence follows. I remind myself that his one saving grace is that he redirected himself to the sofa when I warned him about my chair.

I start to interview him. 'You're a magician in your spare time. What do you do for a living?'

'Accountant,' he says. 'I wish I could cast some magic over some of my clients' figures.'

'What do you do in the evenings?'

He scratches his bald head. 'Practise magic tricks.'

I think about the disappointing card trick in the hallway. Maybe he needs to practise cards more.

'Do you do magic shows?'

He nods. 'Yes, I have a weekly show.' I watch as he pulls out a gold coin. 'Watch this coin disappear.'

His trick doesn't work, and I guess which hand he has the coin in. We both find interesting things to look at on my wooden floor to avoid eye contact.

'My assistant has left, and I have a vacancy if you're interested,' he says after a lengthy silence. 'You would help me behind the scenes and allow me to saw you in half.'

'No thanks, Steve.' The words shoot out of my mouth. Considering his dreadful tricks, I wouldn't want him coming anywhere near me with a saw.

I ask him whether he likes cats. 'I do,' he says, giving Lenny a stroke. 'I need to make you aware that I work with a live dove. She lives at my mother's house; however, there are occasions when I get home from a show, and I'm too tired to trek over there, so I stick the dove in the bathroom overnight. Does your cat like birds?'

'He watches them out of the window. He's an indoor cat so I don't know whether he would know how to hunt.'

I cross out his name. The last thing I need when I'm desperate for a wee in the small hours is for a mad dove to be flapping around my head while Lenny makes unsuccessful attempts to catch it, knocking over everything in the process.

Steve shrugs and brings out his cards for the second time. 'Pick a card.'

After another disastrous card trick, where he attempts to slide my card into his suit sleeve but fails, causing it to fall to the floor, he then asks if I want a coin trick, which I decline. He subsequently tells me our flat share wouldn't work and leaves.

My final candidate is called Paula. She's in her mid-thirties, single and a DIY enthusiast.

'I love doing up old buildings,' she gushes as I show her around the flat. 'This place is perfect. Would the landlord mind if I stripped all the kitchen cupboards and repainted them?'

'You could ask him.'

She grins. 'I am getting excited already. This place has so much potential.'

We sit down for the interview, and like the others, she goes to sit on my chair first. 'That's my chair,' I say, feeling agitated.

She smiles and runs her hand over the wooden arms. 'I will do wonders with this tatty old chair.'

Her words are like stinging drips of hot fat on my skin. 'It's not a tatty old chair.'

She ignores me and carries on gazing at it. 'When I have finished with this chair, it will look amazing.'

'You'll not be touching my chair.'

Paula sits down on it and screws up her face. 'Oh, God, it's saggy.'

Anger ripples through me. I've had enough of this. 'Get out.'

'What?' She looks horrified.

'Please leave. The interview is over.'

When she's gone, I sit in my chair, and Lenny jumps onto my lap. I stroke him and try to ignore my financial worries. Picking up my phone, I open Facebook and click on Cynthia's page. Perhaps I should consider working for her? I know the thought makes me uncomfortable, but this is a worrying situation. I could work after the bookshop has closed. She's currently hosting a Facebook Live event for her followers, so I log in to it. She's at her magic table, selecting tarot cards. 'Pat from Huddersfield,' she says, looking directly at the camera. 'Someone is returning from your past.'

Behind her, two young children are arguing. She tries to explain to Pat from Huddersfield, who I assume is on Facebook

Live, why the person is returning from the past, but is interrupted by a child's scream.

'Sorry about this,' she says and turns around. 'Lance – stop hitting your brother, and Vincent – stop kicking or I'll put you in a field and feed you carrots.'

A teenage girl wanders into the magical garage holding a phone. 'Mum, I'm trying to buy Drake tickets on your credit card, but it keeps getting declined.'

'Cassandra!' screams Cynthia, 'I never said you could use my credit card, and right now I am on a bloody Facebook Live.'

'Mum, I need Drake tickets,' snaps Cassandra. 'Your card has been declined seven times. I thought you were minted.'

I close Facebook. I can't work for Cynthia. My curse, combined with that level of chaos, would make me lose my sanity.

After a deep breath, I open Instagram and check out Oliver's profile. The only thing I know about him is that he's a romance author and his father is Frank's boss.

Scrolling through his Instagram grid, I notice it's filled with pictures of bookcases, stacks of notebooks, jars of pencils, a cat curled up on various chairs, and selfies of him writing alone at café tables. It feels so… nice, which is a little unsettling.

There are no photos of any girlfriends, which contrasts with Sam's Instagram grid, where his ex-girlfriend appeared in nearly every other picture. I asked Sam about this, and he said it would have been a hassle to delete all her photos, as they had been together for six years. Looking back now, I should have seen this giant red flag and listened to my curse.

Oliver might like to keep his personal life off social media, which is probably the case. Perhaps Sam isn't a good comparison?

I go onto Google and look at a couple of his recent author

interviews. His debut book topped the book charts, and his subsequent books have gone viral on TikTok. I look at Amazon – all his books have thousands of positive reviews.

After returning to Instagram, I stare at his profile picture. 'You are my last resort, Oliver James.'

9

'I've had a rethink.' After taking in a deep breath, I squeeze my hands together. 'About my flat.'

Miranda is busy telling me where she bought her leopard-print dress and its eye-watering price tag. It takes her brain a few seconds to process what I have just said. She stops talking, and her face lights up.

'I do need a flatmate and...' I'm struggling to push the words out.

'You're going to flat share with Oliver,' Miranda squeals, pulling me into an unwanted hug. I try to resist her, but she's stronger than I am. We end up in a strange tussle that ends with us banging foreheads and my vision of Frank pushing a pram. The sound of the bookshop disappears, and I shove a boiled sweet into my mouth. Miranda is speaking while doing a strange celebratory dance.

When my ears start to work again, I rub my sore forehead. 'I'll need to meet Oliver before I confirm anything.'

Miranda smiles sweetly. 'Of course. I'll call Frank. He can tell Oliver the good news.'

I watch as the pound signs in her eyes make her half-walk and half-run across the bookshop towards the till. My heart is thudding, and I feel sick. What am I doing?

If Francesca the reality TV star, Steve the magician, or Paula the DIY enthusiast had been normal, I wouldn't be in this position. I begin to tidy the shelves behind the display table in the science fiction and fantasy section. Aunt Polly's face flashes in my mind. This is all for her. Oliver's money will pay for my weekly visits. I will be able to hold her hand while she undergoes chemo. He will move out once his flat in London sells. This is not a long-term arrangement. It will just get me through this difficult time.

'Can I collect my boyfriend's book?' a familiar voice says, making me whirl around. Marcus's girlfriend is standing in front of me, clutching his receipt.

I nod and walk over to the till counter. She follows and lets out a heavy sigh. 'He sent me as he's terribly busy with his academic paper.'

'Here it is,' I say, taking out J.K. Fielding's book, which is heavy and lands on the counter with a hefty thwack.

'That's a tome!' she exclaims. 'Gosh – I didn't realise J.K. Fielding had done so much research.'

'He got carried away,' I say, casting her a sugary smile. 'If you ask me, your boyfriend should conduct his own research.'

She stares at me. 'Marcus is working on his PhD. I think he will be the judge of whether J.K. Fielding's work meets academic standards.' Her eyes travel up and down my body before resting on my face. 'I hardly think he needs your input on a published scholar.'

I make sure our hands brush as I hand her the bag with Marcus's book. The flash of white light clears, and I see her walking along a library and turning a corner to find Marcus passionately kissing a woman with short blonde hair in the ancient history section.

Her phone starts to vibrate. 'Hello, my love,' she coos, turning away from me. 'What are you up to? Oh... you're going to work in the library. See you later then.'

As she walks away, I let out a sigh and hope that today is not the day she discovers that her beloved Marcus is doing more than working on his PhD in that library.

'Nelly – where are you?' Miranda has spoken to Frank. Her voice is annoyingly shrill. 'Oliver can meet you tonight. If you're free?'

'Doesn't he have to travel up from London?'

She shakes her head. 'He's staying with us. Arrived yesterday.'

'What? He's staying with you?'

'Frank couldn't allow his boss's son to stay in the Travelodge. Anyway, I knew you wouldn't be able to say no. As I said to Frank, give Nelly a few days.'

I clench my fists by my side, and an angry red filter slips in front of my eyes. Why does it feel like she has masterminded this entire situation?

She twirls a strand of her brown hair around her finger. 'That angry look you're giving me doesn't suit you.'

I remind myself she is my boss, and I need this job. 'What is he like?'

'Oliver is a bit rough around the edges. Not quite like his profile picture, but you could tidy him up.' Grabbing my hand, she reluctantly leads me away from the till to the romance section. I silently groan at the Frank pushing a pram vision as she surveys our shelves filled with sugary, pink-coloured books, the display table, and the two dusty pink armchairs, where readers eager to dive into a book feel as if they're at home. The world becomes muffled. I can't hear what she's saying, which is a blessing.

Miranda is still talking when the sound returns to my ears. 'Forget my idea of dressing him in tight jeans and a white string vest. I would put Oliver in a tweed suit. I would also escort him to the nearest barber.'

'He might not want to tidy himself up.'

She ignores my comment. 'Oliver has got that brooding, tortured artist thing going on. Frank says he's struggling with writer's block.'

'As long as Oliver stays in his room, we will be fine.'

Miranda gives me a bewildered look. 'Nelly, the world needs Oliver's romance books. You must do all you can to support and guide him through this dark, creative time.'

'I would be his flatmate, not his therapist.'

She's not listening to me. 'When he does his book signing event...' She pauses, pointing both index fingers at me. 'We haven't discussed this yet, but you can work on him about that... I think we will place his signing table here, so he has the pretty shelves as a backdrop. What do you think?'

Being in this section of the bookshop for too long makes me uncomfortable. After clawing at my itchy neck, I check my watch. To my relief, I see that it's time for us to open. 'I need to open the doors.'

She doesn't hear me as she's lost in her thoughts about Oliver's book signing event.

A male customer excitedly enters, eager to grab the latest trending book from a well-known crime author, along with a stressed mother and her noisy little boy heading to the children's section. As she walks by, she grimaces and says, 'This is the only place that will keep him quiet for more than five minutes.'

I keep myself busy by sorting out the online book orders and try not to think about Oliver James becoming my flatmate.

'Is the free Wi-Fi working?' A young boy approaches the counter with his iPad. I call Miranda, who hurries into the back room to fiddle with the control box. I smile at the boy. 'It will be working again soon.'

'Excuse me, do you work here?' I look up from my online order list to see the woman with the little boy, smiling at me. His little hands try to grab the boxes of pens and glittery notebooks.

'Yes. How can I help?'

She beams and lets go of her son's hand. He races off, shrieking with delight. 'Do you have this author's debut book in stock? It was published a few years ago, but I can't find it.' To my horror, she waves Oliver James's latest book at me.

A groan escapes my lips, causing the woman's smile to evaporate.

'Sorry, I didn't mean to groan at you,' I say quickly, before my behaviour leads to a complaint. I must think on my feet since she doesn't want to hear that I don't seem to be able to escape this author.

'He's the author everyone wants to read right now. I bet you're deluged with requests like mine.' She has provided me with a way out.

'Yes, that's right.'

She gives me the details, and I check the laptop.

'It should be in stock.' I put on a fake smile, and we walk to the romance section, passing Miranda, who is back from fiddling with the Wi-Fi and is now busy taking photos of the display table piled high with Oliver's latest romance. 'Don't worry, I'll sort out the social media and watch the till, Nelly,'

Miranda sighs, with a dramatic hand to her brow. 'I think I am doing too much.'

My irritation spikes. 'Do you want to find this customer's book? I can stay on the till and sort out Instagram.'

Miranda casts me a sugary smile. 'Go ahead and look for the book. Once you're finished, I might need a little nap.'

I mutter under my breath about the amount of time she needs recharging in the back office when she does very little in the shop. While I search the shelves for Oliver's debut, the woman scrolls on her phone.

Behind me, I can hear the laughter of her boy and the sound of little feet thundering across the bookshop.

CRASH. Miranda's scream follows the sound. I turn around to see that the display table has toppled over, scattering books all over the floor. To my surprise, the small boy squeals with laughter and races back to his mother, who is still engrossed in her phone and oblivious to the chaos he has caused.

'My mother has just texted me to say she will have my son for the rest of the day,' the woman says, holding her phone. 'I need to get him to her house quickly before she changes her mind.' She grabs her son's hand and scans the mess. 'Thanks for helping me search for the book. I'll see if I can order it online.'

She hurries away, telling her son he will have a great day with Nanna and leaving me with a floor full of Oliver James's new novel.

Miranda comes over, dabbing her brow with a ball of tissues. 'I'll be in the back room if you need me. My nerves are in tatters after that incident. Can you put the display table back together, watch the till, restack the new fiction shelves, and can you also sort out Instagram?'

With a heavy sigh, I lift the table back up and begin to pick up the books as Miranda sashays away, complaining of exhaustion.

I am busy tidying up the mess when I hear Miranda's dulcet tones behind me. 'Oh, this is going to make a lovely shot,' she says, making me jolt. I thought she had gone.

I turn around to find her holding up her phone and pointing the camera at me. I'm sweaty, pissed off, and clutching piles of books in both hands. This won't be a good shot.

'Oliver will love to see his new flatmate posing with his new novel.'

'I am not posing,' I say through gritted teeth.

She gives me a wink. 'Photo is winging its way to Oliver. I need to rest.'

'Miranda,' I groan. It's too late. She flashes her phone, and I can see the photo has gone to Oliver.

Oh well, Oliver James and I can both look rough around the edges. That's one thing we will have in common.

There is a steady flow of customers for the rest of the day. I try my best to avoid physical contact, but they seem to gravitate towards me with their bare limbs. I found myself rewarding two customers with free bookmarks who accidentally bumped into me while wearing long-sleeved shirts and kept the end of their love stories to themselves.

I don't see Miranda until there are ten minutes left before closing.

She saunters over to stand by me at the till. 'He'll be at your flat for six.'

I let out a groan as tiredness washes over me. Every part of me is aching. The last thing I want to do is rush home. 'That gives me half an hour to get home, shower, sort out my hair and tidy up.'

She pats me on the shoulder. 'Let him see the natural you, Nelly.'

'I don't want him to see the natural me.'

Her eyes are shining. 'Frank used to love the natural me. Why don't you go early, and I'll close? Yes, I know I am a great boss.' She giggles, and I hurry away.

On my way up to my flat, I see Gary walking down the stairs. His black wiry hair is slicked back with gel, and he smells of Lynx aftershave. He grins at me. 'I'm off out on a date, Penelope.'

I feel the usual prickle of irritation. 'It's Nelly, Gary. Not Penelope.'

He shakes his head. 'I haven't got time for small talk, Penelope. My date is waiting for me.'

I recall how Gary accidentally knocked my arm the day Eva and I moved in. At the time, he was living with his third wife. My vision showed his wife catching him in bed with their cleaner. A few weeks later, Gary informed Eva that he was single yet again because, in his words, his wife couldn't handle the fact that other women couldn't keep their hands off him.

With a happy whistle, he carries on down the stairs.

Oliver James's face flashes up inside my mind. 'Gary,' I call out. He stops and looks up at me.

'I might have a new flatmate. Will you need to do any checks or anything?'

He shrugs. 'I trust your judgement, Penelope. Let me know their name and I will get the contract changed.'

'It's NELLY,' I shout.

'Penelope, I am going to be late. If you want to talk to me, my flat door is always open.'

The creepy look he gives sends me racing up the last few steps to my flat.

Once I've greeted Lenny, I take a quick shower, pile my hair up into a messy bun and change into a fresh pair of black jeans and a white T-shirt.

I'm poised to coat my lashes in mascara when there's a knock at my door.

My stomach dives for the floor. It's him. Oliver James is here.

Scooping up my cat, I whisper, 'Stay loyal to me, Lenny. We need to stick together.'

10

The man standing in the hallway does not look like the polished Oliver James I saw in his author photo. His wavy brown hair is a little longer, and a thick stubble coats his chin. His T-shirt is crumpled, and his jeans look well-worn.

And yet, annoyingly, he's still handsome.

Those dark eyes, the colour of strong coffee, make the word trouble flash up in capital letters inside my mind, and his boyish smile throws me off guard.

'You must be Nelly,' he says. His voice is smooth and polished, reminiscent of a male narrator on my audiobook app.

Oh, God, I can feel a tiny flicker of something inside my chest. *Stamp that out right away, Nelly!* This man tricks his readers into believing love is a good thing. Heartbreak would be inevitable with a man as handsome as Oliver. Someone as handsome as Oliver probably has a girlfriend – or even several – on his arm.

I hold Lenny tighter. 'Nice to meet you.'

He smiles at Lenny in my arms. 'Who is this little guy?'

'Lenny.' To my annoyance, Lenny starts to purr and stretches out a silver paw.

Oliver chuckles and gently shakes it. 'Nice to meet you, little guy.'

'Lenny,' I correct him. Lenny will be horrified to be called that. Oliver chuckles, and I look down to see Lenny lovingly rubbing his head against Oliver's hand.

Lenny, you are a traitor, and I will have words with you later. Now I need to let Oliver into the flat without touching him. This will be interesting, as my hallway is relatively small.

I step into my flat, set Lenny down, pull the door as far as it will go, and press myself against the wall so that our arms cannot touch. 'Come in. This is the hallway. It connects... things.'

Oliver casts me an odd look and steps inside. 'Hallways tend to do that.'

Ignoring his witty comment, I point him in the direction of the living room.

'Wow – this is cosy,' he gushes, looking around my living room with my chair in front of the small sash window, the tiniest sofa in the world behind it, the old fireplace, and the many shelves of books along the sloping wall. 'This would once have been the servants' quarters of this great house. I like it.'

A smile breaks out across my face. Apart from me, he's the first person to have acknowledged that about my flat.

He points to my chair by the window. 'That's a great spot to sit.' I watch him walk over and gaze out of the window. 'Can we have a rota on who gets to sit there?'

I can feel my smile fading. 'No.' My answer is firm and clear.

This makes him smile and turn back to me. 'Are you into accepting bribes?'

I shake my head. 'No. That's my seat.'

'I can give you a signed copy of my latest book?'

Forcing out a polite, tight-lipped smile, I say, 'I'm not a fan of romance novels so your bribes won't work with me.'

'You haven't read my books?' He seems shocked.

I shake my head. 'The covers are pink – that's all I know.'

His dazzling smile reappears. 'Well, that's a relief,' he sighs. 'I find fangirls hard to live with.'

He's not getting a smile out of me for that playful comment.

Leading him to the kitchen, I ensure there's a safe buffer zone between us. I am slightly ahead, opening random cupboards like an anxious estate agent. 'This is the kitchen. Fridge. Sink. Oven.'

He gives me a nod of approval. I hope he's considered my minimalist approach to work surfaces and my neatly organised cupboards.

I point him towards the bathroom door whilst standing far back. 'Open the door.'

'After you,' he says with a grin.

Shaking my head, I gesture for him to go first. He pokes his head inside. 'Tidy – I like it,' he says.

While he's surveying the bathroom, I open the door to Eva's old room. 'Here you are. I know it doesn't look big, but it has a double bed, a desk and a wardrobe.'

'Maybe this beautiful room will help me to start writing again,' he says, striding in, running his fingers over the desk, and gazing out of the window. 'Is that our garden down below?'

'It's a private communal garden shared by all the houses in the crescent.'

He nods. 'Do you use it much?'

I shake my head and refrain from telling him that I actively avoid human contact when I'm not working. 'Miranda said you had writer's block.'

He carries on looking out of the window. 'Yeah, it's been a while.'

I hurry away, as I don't want to get into a deep conversation about his creativity or lack thereof.

He enters the living room.

'Take a seat,' I say, gesturing for him to sit on my sofa. I turn around my comfy chair so I'm facing Oliver.

Miranda and Frank may think this is a done deal, but I need to assess this chap myself. Last night, I wrote a list of questions in my little notebook, which I've retrieved from my handbag. It is now on my lap with a bookshop-branded pen.

He eyes the sofa with suspicion. 'I don't think I've ever seen a sofa this size.'

The two-seater sofa is tiny and uncomfortable. 'It came with the flat. It was designed for a family of mice.'

He smiles and sits down, filling almost the entire sofa with his tall, athletic frame. Lenny walks in and leaps onto the arm of the sofa next to Oliver, as if they are old friends.

'Okay, I have some questions,' I say after glaring at my cat.

'Fire away,' Oliver says. 'Did you get this grilling from her, little guy?'

I ignore his attempt at friendly banter. 'I can see you don't mind my cat. Do you have any pets?'

His smile fades. 'I love cats. I had one, but she died of old age a few months ago. She was called Figgy Pudding, and she was my best friend.'

He gets a big tick as I like people who refer to their pet as their best friend.

'Is your cat just called Lenny, or does he have a full name?'

This gets him another tick, as true cat lovers give their feline friends first, middle, and last names. 'His full name is Leonard Frederick Wilson Spartapuss.'

Oliver nods. 'Impressive. My cat was Figgy Pudding Bojangles.'

I find myself giving him an extra tick for giving Figgy an amazing surname.

'Does Lenny go outside?' Oliver asks. 'Figgy went outside, and despite only having three legs, she was a phenomenal hunter.'

'Three legs?'

He nods. 'I got her from a cat rescue place ten years ago, as no one wanted her.'

I'm staring at him while my hand is frantically giving him loads of ticks for this act of kindness.

'So Lenny? Does he go outside?'

'Lenny is an indoor cat, although lately he's been trying to escape.'

Oliver nods and says with an air of confidence, 'He won't get past me, so don't worry.'

'What's your daily routine?'

He sits up straight. 'I get up at a reasonable hour.'

That's another tick from me.

'I spend the rest of my day staring at a blank laptop screen,' he continues, 'doomscrolling on social media and watching YouTube videos about how to write books.'

Glancing up from my notepad, I cast him a quizzical look. 'You have written many books. Why do you watch YouTube videos on how to write? Surely, once you've written one, you know how to do it again.'

He shakes his head. 'My brain blocks out the trauma of writing my previous books, so when I sit down to write something new, it's like I am starting as a new writer.'

'Have you had writer's block before?'

'Nope.'

'What do you like to do on an evening?'

'Well, as I've just moved back to this part of the world, I've been catching up with my mate, Jamie, a lot. He's just bought a flat in town, which he's renovating. We also like a game of pool.'

Hearing about his friend and their love of playing pool earns him another tick in my book. This could be an advantage for me. We wouldn't have to interact much, as I work during the day, and he would go out in the evening.

'You've lived here before?'

He nods. 'I grew up in Bristol. My mates and I used to come here for a night out. I moved to London after university, and then Dad moved to Cornwall.'

He smiles at Lenny and scratches him under the chin.

'Why have you moved back here?' I ask.

He pauses and the light dims in his face. 'The London life wasn't for me any more.'

There's more to that answer, but he doesn't elaborate. I make a mental note and move on to the next question. 'How neat or messy are you?'

He runs a hand through his wavy hair. 'I'm mostly a tidy guy.'

'Mostly?'

I observe a mischievous glint in his eyes. 'Nobody's perfect.' He grins, which makes my heartbeat accelerate. I find myself scribbling down the words, *Watch his dangerous smile, Nelly*.

I look down at the next question. 'What would you say are your annoying habits?'

He crosses his legs. 'I've been told I talk in my sleep.'

'Well, if you don't talk too loudly, I'll be happy. Any other bad habits?'

'I used to annoy people when I read my draft novels out

loud, but as I'm not writing...' His eyes survey my living room. They linger on the painting above the fireplace. 'That's intense.'

I turn to look up at Frida Kahlo's painting, *The Wounded Deer*. To me, there is something comforting about witnessing someone else endure my levels of romantic bad luck and be pierced by arrows. I appreciate how, despite all her heartbreak, she still stares ahead like I do.

'It's comforting,' I murmur.

When I turn back, he's casting me an odd expression. I ignore him, continuing with my interview questions. 'What would you say are your good habits?'

'Hugs,' he says, with an air of confidence. 'I have been told I give the best hugs.'

Every part of me flinches. 'You can keep those to yourself.'

An awkward silence descends upon the room. I flick my eyes to my notes.

He speaks first. 'You're not a fan of hugs then?'

'No,' I say, keeping my focus on my notes. Another peculiar silence follows.

I stare at the next question. This is an awkward one. 'Are you single or...'

He interrupts me. 'I'm single, and before you ask – no, I am not dating. What about you?'

'Single.'

'Are you dating?'

'No,' I scoff and then regret it, as the less he knows about me, the better.

'Terrible – isn't it?' he says lightly. 'All of it. Dating. Romance. Love. I think we have all been lied to.'

'Hang on – you're a bestselling romance author. You write about love.'

He shrugs and looks at my Frida Kahlo painting. 'Doesn't mean I believe in it.'

His answer makes me suspicious. Romance authors like Oliver James are experts in delusion. They spend their lives writing books that fool readers into thinking love conquers all. While he's stroking Lenny, I scribble the following.

He writes romance, but he doesn't believe in love – yet he makes a living selling it. Is this emotional manipulation? Is Oliver James a modern Mr Rochester but with better hair and a publishing contract?

I circle my Rochester observation several times.

'Are you writing good things about me?' he asks.

Heat rushes to my cheeks. I ignore his question and fire off several random questions. He raises his eyebrows at my question about whether he puts milk or hot water in first when making a cup of tea.

'Tell me about yourself, Nelly,' he asks.

What can I tell him about myself?

A simple question that should be easy to answer. Except it's not. I flick my attention to my notebook and realise I'm holding my pen like it's a weapon. Stabbing the page I'm on, I say, 'There's not much to tell.'

'Come on. There's always something. Do you like working in the bookshop?'

'It's good.' Words about avoiding the romance section jostle around on my tongue.

He's waiting for me to say more.

'What do you do for fun?'

I blink. 'Fun?'

'Yes, like hobbies or interests.'

His eyes search my face. I don't want to say that my social life is non-existent; that I don't do spontaneous coffee dates, drinks after work, or sports; that Miranda, my toxic boss, is my only friend – and the thought of that makes me want to cry. My curse has turned me into a burden to others.

'I like going to visit my aunt who lives by the sea,' is what I settle on. Could I sound any more like a servant girl from the 1800s?

He gives me a polite nod. 'Are there any flat rules?'

I grip my notebook with both hands and get ready to tell Oliver the most essential rule. 'No touching. This includes hugs, handshakes, shoulder taps, high fives, accidental brushes, toe taps, knee knocks, and reassuring back rubs.'

Oliver is stroking his chin, like he's considering each one. 'I understand the rule, but I think you are missing out on my comforting back rubs.'

'This chair is mine,' I say slowly and clearly, like I am talking to a small child. 'No debate, negotiation, or literary inspiration.'

He lets out a sigh. 'That's a tough one.'

I point to Lenny, who is gazing adoringly at him. 'Lenny chooses who he loves. Do not try to win him over.'

Oliver strokes his soft back. 'No secret cuddles for you, little guy.'

I watch my cat behave like Oliver's biggest fan. Lenny needs to get his priorities right.

I recall what Miranda said about Oliver wandering around my flat in just a pair of boxer shorts. I need to stamp this sort of behaviour out from the start. 'No nakedness in the flat or cooking breakfast in just your underwear.'

He blinks and stares at me. 'I would never—'

'Clothes must be worn at all times.'

I watch him flick his floppy fringe, and I notice a mischievous glint in his eyes. 'I agree with you about not cooking breakfast in my underwear, but does that mean I can cook lunch and tea in my boxers?'

'That is not funny, Oliver.'

Leaning back slightly, he studies me with a crooked smile. 'So, did I pass the interview?'

Glancing down at my notes gives me a shock. My page is a sea of ticks. That's unsettling.

'You didn't completely fail,' I say, trying to sound indifferent.

'I'll take that as a yes.'

'I didn't say yes,' I mutter, but it's too late. Lenny lets out a purr of approval and climbs on Oliver's lap.

'Lenny says yes,' Oliver says with a wry smile.

'Fine,' I say, rising to my feet. 'But if you sit in my chair you're out.'

He grins. 'Message received.'

As I walk towards the kitchen, I hear him mutter to Lenny, 'Is she always this fun?'

11

'Oliver is thrilled about moving in,' gushes Miranda, before handing me a coffee. 'This morning, he wouldn't stop talking about your flat and that gorgeous chair by the window. He reckons sitting there and watching the world go by will cure his writer's block.'

My shoulders and neck feel as though someone has inserted rods of iron into them. Yesterday, I made it abundantly clear that the chair by the window was mine. I set the hot cup of coffee down for safety. 'That's my chair,' I say through gritted teeth. 'He has the sofa.'

Miranda's eyes widen dramatically, and her mouth forms a perfect O shape. 'He's a writer, Nelly. The view out the window will inspire his books. For goodness' sake, show the poor man some kindness. He's in a dark, creative time.'

'I made it clear last night that the chair is mine.'

She gestures towards the romance display table. 'Oliver is an international best-selling author who has been struggling for some time to write. You need to do all you can to help him create those wonderful romance books of his.'

'Oliver has a desk in his bedroom. If he's desperate to write, he can do it in there.'

With a flutter of her false eyelashes, she offers me a saccharine smile and tilts her head in a patronising way. 'If I were in my thirties, single and sharing a flat with Oliver, I would do whatever he wanted.' Her eyes brighten and she giggles like a lovesick teenager.

I can't listen to this. Grabbing my coffee, I go and calm down in the science fiction and fantasy section. It takes a good hour of shelf tidying to bury my agitation over Oliver James wanting to use my chair.

As I tidy up the display table, I sense someone staring at me. Looking up, I see a young man with black curly hair and blue eyes, wearing designer glasses with thick, square frames. A feeling of familiarity washes over me. I recognise him from somewhere. A friendly smile breaks out across his face. 'Penelope Blake,' he gushes. 'It's you. Wow – I didn't expect to find you here.'

I blink several times. He knows my old name. My brain frantically tries to remember who he is.

'We were at the old swimming club together. Our mothers used to sit next to each other when they watched us train,' he beams. 'Don't you remember me – Henry Stevens?'

I can feel my eyes widening with surprise. My mind has become awash with memories of Henry, the skinny little lad who was my friend at the swimming club and gave me his sweets after training. We used to laugh and fool around when the coaches weren't looking. I remember Henry left before my world turned upside down. 'Henry? Is that you?'

'Yes, it's me. Do you remember eating all my sweets?'

I giggle. 'My dentist and I both blame you for my boiled sweet addiction.'

He laughs. 'We would sit in the sports centre café before training, and you used to hide my bag. I would then get in trouble for being late.'

'You gave me unnecessary feedback on my crawl stroke.'

He grins. 'My mum said you were a bad influence.'

We both chuckle. 'How are you doing?' I ask. 'You moved away – right?'

'Mum and I moved away after my father...' He pauses and strokes the spine of the book he's holding. I read the title: *The Water Holds Me*, by Margo Lane. My eyes flick to Henry's smile, which has almost gone. I tactfully change the subject. 'Do you still swim, Henry?'

He laughs. 'No. After we moved away, swimming wasn't the same.' I can hear a phone bleeping. 'I had no one to mess around with,' he beams, while reaching for his phone in his back pocket. Henry sends whoever is calling him to voicemail. He lifts his gaze to mine. 'I must dash as I have a train to catch. Listen, I'm back here in a few weeks with work. Do you fancy going for a coffee sometime? We can reminisce about old times.'

Words jostle on my tongue. I can't seem to push them out of my mouth.

'It's okay, no pressure about the coffee. Hey – do you still have that weird touchy thing?'

My heart grinds to a halt. 'What?'

He nods. 'You told me once about how you touch...'

I can't remember confiding in Henry. My nervous laugh makes him stop talking. 'I don't know what you're talking about, Henry. You must be mistaking me for someone else.'

The urge to get away from him is strong. How dare he call my curse a weird touchy thing! 'Look, I'm busy...'

His face has dimmed. 'Oh, I'm sorry. It was nice seeing you, Penelope. I'd better go as I can't miss my train. Can you keep this book for me? I will collect when I return.' He hands me Margo's book. 'It's for my mum.'

'Nelly,' I mumble. 'My name is now Nelly.' After casting him an awkward smile, I flick my eyes to the display table. 'I will put this book aside. I'd better do some work.'

'Bye, Nelly.' He walks away and stops. 'Say hello to your mum for me.'

My heart stops beating. I spin around to see him standing at the entrance of the section.

'I know our mothers argued,' he says, 'but it was years ago, and my mum says she wishes she'd listened to her...'

Memories of Mum rush into my mind. Henry left the swimming club a few months before the car crash. He doesn't know what happened to my parents. Tears prick my eyes. If I explain, I will get upset. 'Goodbye, Henry,' I say and turn my back on him.

I close my eyes and take some deep breaths. Henry needs to stay in the past. It was a good decision of mine to not accept his coffee offer.

Miranda wanders over. 'Oliver is excited about moving in tomorrow. Will you be on hand with tea, coffee, and perhaps a light lunch for him?'

I bite my lip and shake my head. 'Oliver will be moving in by himself. I am out for the day.'

Tomorrow is Aunt Polly's first chemo session. I told Oliver he could move in alone and get accustomed to the flat. He agreed and asked if he could prepare a meal for both of us when I get home. 'A moving-in celebratory meal,' he said, his eyes twinkling. I tried to put him off by saying I wouldn't be in the mood for celebrations when I get home, but he was annoyingly persistent. He doesn't know about Aunt Polly, and I don't plan on telling him. There are many things that I don't want Oliver to know, and this is one of them.

Miranda gasps. 'You're not going to help him settle in?'

'Oliver is a grown man, Miranda,' I snap. 'I am sure he can move a few boxes from his car and carry them up to my flat. If you're so concerned about Oliver's welfare, why don't you let him live with you?'

She lets out a heavy sigh. 'Frank's mother is moving in with us for a while. She hasn't been the same since her hip operation.'

'How do you feel about that?'

With a shake of her head, she sighs. 'His mother is a difficult and bitter woman. Nothing positive has come out of her mouth for decades.'

'I'm sure she'll be grateful that you're looking after her.'

Miranda scoffs. 'Pigs might fly.'

We are distracted by a customer: an elderly man with tufty white hair and twinkling pale-blue eyes. Miranda leaves me to deal with him while she sorts out paperwork in the back room.

'Can I help you?' I beam at the old man.

'Hello,' he says in a gravelly voice. 'I am trying to track down a book.'

He hands me a crumpled piece of paper. In scrawly handwriting, it says, *Barbara Plum's Family Cookbook.*

'I've never heard of Barbara Plum. Let me have a look.' I gesture for him to follow me to the till. Once there, I type the title into the laptop.

'It was the only cookbook she ever used.'

'She?'

'My wife, Joan,' he replies and takes a breath. 'Joan died a few years ago. I miss her terribly.'

His words make me look up.

'I've been trying to cook the meals Joan made. Her shepherd's pie was delicious, and we raised our children, grandchildren, and great-grandchildren on her chicken casserole. Everything Joan cooked was from Barbara Plum's cookbook.' He chuckles. 'It used to be dog-eared, covered in pencil notes and gravy stains. After she passed away, when I moved house, it went missing.'

He blinks and takes out a white handkerchief with a cluster of pink embroidered flowers on one corner and the stitched initials J.C.E. 'This was her favourite handkerchief,' he explains. 'I always carry it with me.' He dabs his watery eyes. 'If I can get hold of Barbara's book, I can make her chicken casserole and…' He pauses and stares down at the handkerchief. 'For a few moments, I can believe that it was Joan who made it and she's just popped out to the shops.'

My throat tightens. I remind myself that this is what love does to perfectly sane people. It makes them do strange things, such as chasing chicken casserole recipes and pretending it will bring back their loved ones.

He sniffs. 'My family are scattered over the world nowadays. If I wanted to see them, I would have to fly. There's no one near me any more, so I think about Joan and Barbara's cookbook a lot.'

I return to the laptop, still carrying Henry's book. The old man follows. Once at the counter, I slide the book on the shelf underneath the till. I tap in 'Barbara Plum's cookery book' into the database.

'I am afraid it has been out of print for years.'

The old man's smile wobbles. 'Well, I tried. It's just an old cookbook.' He blinks and holds my gaze.

'I'm sorry.'

'Can I give you my details in case you come across Barbara's book?'

I nod, and he gives me his name, phone number and address.

As he hobbles towards the door, Miranda appears at the till counter. 'Was that Mr Ellis?'

'Yes, why?'

She stares wistfully at the elderly man leaving the shop. 'Was he in here asking for Barbara Plum's cookery book?'

'Has he asked you about it too?'

She nods. 'He usually comes in on a Wednesday when you have your day off. That book is out of print, but I don't think he understands that we're unlikely to obtain a copy. He will give you his details and be here next week. Poor old Mr Ellis.'

His words 'it's just an old cookbook' still echo in my mind as I walk home that evening. Crossing the road, I consider trying to find it for him. I know of second-hand book shops that are great at acquiring out-of-print books. But would that cookbook only worsen his suffering?

I tell myself that, just like love, books come to an end, too.

12

Exhaustion washes over me. As I walk home from the station, my legs feel like lead. It has been quite a day.

Aunt Polly drove us both to the hospital in Nigella, who, I might add, was like the world's most angelic car. There was no stalling, no seatbelt strangulation, and we even listened to a classical music CD to calm Aunt Polly down.

Watching her go through her first cycle of chemo was stressful, emotional, and thankfully event-free. The nurses were excellent, and we felt special and supported.

After the chemo, I drove us back, and Nigella reverted to her old mischievous ways. She stalled as I was trying to negotiate a busy roundabout, nearly cut off my blood supply with the seatbelt, and spat out Aunt Polly's Classic FM CD.

'Ignore her,' Aunt Polly said, tapping the dashboard. 'She's worked up about my chemo.'

I looked away and muttered to myself about Nigella needing to be on the scrapheap.

On the way home, I asked Aunt Polly about hair loss. She gave me one of her optimistic smiles and said she would embrace a new, shorter look, including wigs and hair scarves. I looked out of the window and hoped she would maintain her optimistic outlook about her hair.

Aunt Polly didn't fancy tea and biscuits, so she sat on the sofa while we watched an interview with a woman who had swum the Channel. I tried to concentrate, but Henry's face kept intruding on my thoughts. My mind replayed our encounter in the bookshop, and I felt a little twang of guilt for my abruptness and turning my back on him. He triggered me with his talk about Mum and my curse. Back when we swam together, we were good friends. I remember how he made the Saturday morning training sessions bearable. The book he wanted me to put aside for him comes to mind. I will make sure Miranda doesn't put it back on the shelf.

I glanced over at Aunt Polly. I'm glad the first session is over, and I hope the side effects aren't too severe. There was one low point. I asked again about Hilary and whether we should re-establish contact with her. In my defence, I grew up with Hilary being our fourth emergency service. When I see my aunt suffering, I want to call Hilary.

She had a knack for making my aunt smile even in the darkest moments. I remember when Aunt Polly lost her job at the factory office and came home in tears. It was me who called Hilary. Six minutes later, we heard the familiar screech of tyres, the slam of a car door, and heels clattering up the path. Hilary burst into Aunt Polly's, clutching a bottle of red wine in a bandaged hand and an overnight bag slung over her shoulder. 'Polly,' she cried from the hallway, 'I am here for the night. Let's get pissed. Sod your job. I never liked your pervy boss. Oh, and before you ask...' She put the wine down and held her bandaged hand aloft. 'Lilly slammed the car door and didn't realise I'd not taken my hand away.' Lilly is one of her daughters.

'You still came over?' gasped Aunt Polly.

Hilary grinned. 'Polly, my arm would have to be hanging off for me not to come over.'

'Let's not talk about Hilary, Nelly,' muttered Aunt Polly, and shook her head with disapproval, as if I had said the wrong thing.

When I said goodbye, she became tearful at the door. I hugged her and told her I would visit on Sunday. Hilary was still on my mind, and as Aunt Polly wished me a safe journey back, I looked at the photos of the two of them still on the wall. If I wasn't allowed to talk about Hilary, why did my aunt have an entire wall covered with photos of her?

I'm a few streets away from my flat. My nerves are jangling at the prospect of entering and seeing Oliver. He's a stranger, and I only have Miranda and Frank's word to rely on. For all I know, he could have spent the day rummaging through my underwear drawer. Panic blooms inside me. If he's sitting in my chair or if there are any signs he has been in it, I will be so cross.

I also need to avoid all physical contact with him for as long as possible. He claims he's single, so there's a good chance I will see him spending his days sitting at a desk staring at a blank sheet of paper and trying to work through his writer's block.

In his interview, he claimed he was single, but for all I know, he could secretly have his eye on someone. If I touched him, I could see how that ends. Considering how good-looking he is, I might see anything – from a vision of a furious woman spilling a drink on him in a pub, shouting about his wandering hands and broken promises, to something tragic that happens to Oliver after he leaves a book signing. I would then have to watch him tuck into what would be his last meal and silently groan at the thought of having to find another flatmate.

An elderly man is sitting on the bench near the corner of my street. His crop of white hair reminds me of Mr Ellis and his quest to track down *Barbara Plum's Family Cookbook*. I think about the way he held my gaze. 'It was just a cookbook,' I say to myself. The look on Mr Ellis's face comes to the forefront of my mind. There was something about it, and it wasn't about the chicken casserole. I pause and wait for my brain to unscramble my thoughts. 'He was holding on to something.'

An uncomfortable feeling takes hold of me. I dismiss it.

As I approach the corner of my street, I hear a man shouting, 'LENNY.'

My heart comes to a shuddering halt. Oh, God, Oliver has let my cat escape.

Panic takes hold of me as I break into a sprint. Tears prick my eyes as I pump my arms and beg my legs to go faster, even though I haven't done any cardio for years.

I can't lose Lenny.

Looking up, I see Oliver with his hands in his hair, standing outside my flat.

The entrance to my flat is at the back of the house, which is away from the hustle and bustle of the cobbled street. It's quiet and backs onto a private communal garden, which is scattered with mature trees and shrub beds, has a centre patch of grass and is hemmed in by a black ornate railing fence. The garden is kept locked to stop unwanted visitors.

Oliver catches sight of me, and a look of terror takes hold of his face. I'm not sure whether that's because he's lost my cat or it's the sight of me half running, half staggering with a red face, breathless and close to tears.

'Nelly, I am so sorry—'

I don't let him finish. 'You promised me you wouldn't let him escape.'

He looks crestfallen. 'I was cooking us both dinner, and someone knocked on the door. I thought it was you, and it was Gary, the landlord. He'd left the downstairs open, so your cat raced out—'

I let out an angry yelp. 'LENNY.'

'Nelly...'

'Oliver, please find him.' My voice crackles.

'Let's both calm down.'

My anger spikes. 'Don't tell me to calm down when you were the one who lost—' My words fade as I spot a flash of grey inside the fence. I run to the railings and see Lenny's silver-striped feline face staring up at me.

'Lenny,' I gasp as a wave of emotion crashes over me. 'Come out of there.'

Oliver rushes to the railings. 'Oh, thank God.'

To my horror, my little cat sits down and begins to clean himself casually, like he has all the time in the world.

'Lenny, we don't have all night. Come here.' But he turns away and looks at a bird hopping about on a branch above his head.

'He's enjoying himself,' gushes Oliver.

I glare at Oliver, and he turns back to my cat. 'Lenny, mate, you need to come back as I am in a lot of trouble with your—'

'Mummy.' The word flies out of my mouth, and I instantly regret saying it.

Oliver arches an eyebrow at me. 'Mummy wants you to come home.'

The smile on his face is annoying me. 'What were you to Figgy? I can't believe you were just Oliver to her.'

He's touching his nose. 'Just Oliver.'

I think he's lying. 'I don't believe you.'

'No one has ever asked me,' he says, flicking his eyes to the pavement.

I feel victorious. 'Well? You can't mock me for calling myself "Mummy" and keep your own name to yourself.'

He's shaking his head. 'This is a bit too much for the first day of a flat share.'

'You let my cat escape. I call it a suitable punishment.'

'Will you promise not to laugh?'

I roll my eyes. 'Oliver, right now I am incapable of laughter.'

'To Figgy, I was Papa Tiger. Figgy was the little cat, and I was her... big papa cat protector.'

There's an awkward silence. I am trying my hardest not to laugh. Papa Tiger – what the hell? We can't look each other in the eye, so we turn back to look at Lenny.

'Were you in the bookshop today?' Oliver asks.

I keep my eyes fixed on Lenny. 'No, I went to visit my aunt.'

'The one who lives by the sea – right?'

'Yes.' I don't say more as I'm busy trying to tell Lenny to come home telepathically.

'Did you spend the day lazing around on the beach? The weather was amazing today. I bet you and your aunt were sipping cocktails and—'

The words shoot out of my mouth before I can stop them. 'No, I took my aunt to have chemo.'

'Oh.' Oliver goes back to staring at Lenny. The silence between us is uncomfortable, punctuated by the distant sound of a car alarm and the evening breeze rustling the leaves.

Why did I say that Aunt Polly had chemo? Did he need to know that about me?

'Do you have a key for this garden?' Oliver asks.

'Gary has my key.'

'Why does Gary have your key?'

'I don't come in here.'

Oliver is looking at me as though I've just told him the sky isn't blue. 'You don't come and sit in this beautiful place?'

I shake my head. 'I'm an inside sort of person.'

Oliver's eyes are studying my face. He turns back to Lenny. 'Come on, mate, I'm going out soon.'

To my annoyance, Lenny comes trotting over to us on Oliver's command and squeezes himself through the railings. Without hesitation, Oliver and I instinctively bend to grab Lenny at the same time, and the unthinkable happens. We bang heads.

He lets out an 'OUCH', and I yelp, waiting for the flash of white light. My chest tightens, my breath catches, and I wait.

There is nothing – no white light. No vision.

13

Oliver is holding Lenny and looking at me. 'Are you okay?'

'Yes,' I mutter, rubbing my forehead. My mind is in freefall.

When I touched Oliver, I saw nothing. No flash of light and no vision. There was no doomed love story. Just a void.

Something is wrong.

I stare down at my hands and see they're trembling. Pain is radiating out of my forehead, and my stomach has gone on a nauseating spin.

What is going on?

The ground tilts. I grip onto the railings for support. This is strange, as I have bumped heads with people before and seen a vision. My brain frantically searches for an example. Miranda's face rushes to the front of my mind. We bumped heads after I'd told her about my decision to have Oliver as a flatmate and she'd tried to give me one of her hugs. I had seen Frank and his pram. A wave of nausea washes over me. I must have a concussion. That's why I can't see anything.

'Nelly, say something,' says Oliver. 'You're worrying me.'

'I'm fine,' I say, reaching out a trembling hand to stroke Lenny. 'Totally fine.'

He blinks. 'Right. Let's get you and Lenny home.'

My legs feel like they have turned to jelly as we climb the stairs. I can't believe I didn't see anything when our heads touched. My stomach rotates, and I stop, clutching my belly. 'I can't be sick,' I tell myself. 'This is not a good start to a flat-sharing relationship.'

Taking a deep breath, I carry on walking.

Once we get back inside the flat and close the door, I can smell a gorgeous aroma that reminds me of the wholesome casseroles Aunty Polly used to cook when I still lived with her.

'Go lie down, Nelly,' instructs Oliver, pointing to the sofa. 'I'll bring you a bag of frozen peas to put on your head.'

'I'm fine,' I protest. This is a lie, but I'm curious to see what he's cooked.

On entering the kitchen, I gasp. It looks like Oliver has been cooking for half the town. The oven hob is covered in dirty saucepans, and the kitchen work surface is strewn with vegetable peelings, empty sauce cans, and bottles of herbs. The sight intensifies the pain in my head.

'I will wash and clean up,' he assures me.

I can't take my eyes off the chaos and mess. Turning my attention to the kitchen table, I let out a silent groan. It has been set for two. If I sit directly opposite him, one of his legs might nudge or kick mine under the table. I will have to sit further back from the table and hope that food doesn't topple off my fork and onto my lap.

He's looking at me. 'I know what you're thinking.'

'What?'

I watch as he glances back at the table. 'There's not much space, and with how long my legs are, we'll end up playing footsie under the table. I can't break your no-touching rule twice in the first half-hour of the flat share.'

'You remembered my rule?'

He smiles. 'I didn't when we banged heads. I'm sorry about that. You look awfully pale.'

'I'll feel better after food,' I say, optimistically.

'Let's do trays,' he suggests, and relief floods through me.

I stand behind the kitchen table while he serves. He keeps glancing over his shoulder at me. 'Do you need a bag of peas?'

'I'm fine, honest.'

'Here's your tray,' he announces. 'I checked with Miranda that you eat meat. It's a beef casserole with dumplings. All homemade.' With a smile, he picks up his tray. 'See you in the living room. Race you to the chair.'

My eyes must have glowed red or something because his smile disappears and is replaced by a look of concern. He emits a nervous chuckle. 'Only joking.'

We both devour his casserole. He's on the sofa and I am in my chair. I know he's made a mess of my kitchen, but his casserole tastes divine, and his dumplings are perfect.

After we sit for a while avoiding eye contact, I break the awkward silence. 'This meal was nice, Oliver. Thank you. How was the move?'

'Good. I only had a few boxes to carry up three flights of stairs. I'm sorry again for Lenny's escape. It won't happen again.'

'He's fine, so it's okay.'

Lenny makes an appearance and, to my dismay, heads straight for Oliver.

'I'm off out for a beer with Jamie tonight,' Oliver says. 'How's your head?'

'I've got a slight headache, but I will be okay.'

He smiles and scratches Lenny's chin. 'I'll tidy the kitchen before I go out, don't worry.'

After he washes up and tidies the countertops, he shouts goodbye and leaves the flat.

Exhaustion washes over me. 'Lenny, we're going to have an early night,' I say, lifting him off my lap. 'It's been an eventful day.'

He follows me into the hallway, and I glance down at him. 'I know you're not going to like this, but I am going to put your dirt tray in with me tonight as I don't want you escaping when Oliver comes home.'

After sorting out Lenny plus his dirt tray, I place a chair in front of my locked bedroom door. Lenny is glaring at me.

'Mummy is busy protecting us. Oliver could be the flatmate from hell and could come in here with wandering hands.'

I lie in bed and think about how I saw no vision when Oliver and I banged heads. Weird. It must have been quite a whack to my head. Lenny meows by the door but gets bored and soon comes to snuggle in with me. We both fall asleep.

CRASH. I wake up with a frightened gasp. What the hell was that noise? It's midnight. A hushed voice and a drunken giggle follow it.

With a thumping heart, I move the chair and look over at my cat. 'You stay here,' I whisper, before opening the door.

The sight in the hallway robs me of breath. Oliver is being helped into the flat by a man with short blond hair. The man looks up and smiles. 'You must be Nelly. I'm Jamie. Nice to meet you.'

I stare in horror as he struggles into the hallway with Oliver, who spots me and grins. 'NELLY,' he shouts, with outstretched arms. 'GIVE ME A HUG.'

I back away, and my horrified face makes Jamie smile. 'No

need to panic. Ollie has only had two and a half pints,' he says, chuckling, 'One sniff of the barmaid's apron and he's sozzled. Oliver has never been able to handle his drink. I'll get him into his room, and then I'll go.'

'I... hate... Rory,' slurs Oliver, falling against the wall.

'Ollie, come on, mate,' groans Jamie, helping him up and hurrying him along. Jamie looks over at me. 'He'll be fine.'

I watch them struggle along the hallway, and then they disappear into Oliver's room. An hour later, I hear Jamie leave the flat. As I pull up my duvet, I cuddle Lenny.

This won't be a regular occurrence, I tell myself. This was a one-off. Oliver probably got carried away with catching up with his friend.

There's no need to panic, Nelly.

14

There is no noise coming from Oliver's room when I wake, which is a relief. I plan to forget about the celebratory drink. He must have had fun. Normal people do that when they are not living under a curse.

My head feels a lot better, and to my surprise, there's only a tiny purple bruise on my forehead. After getting dressed, feeding Lenny and making myself some breakfast, I grab my bag and leave the flat. I call Aunt Polly, who sounds surprisingly upbeat.

'I'm feeling good, Nelly,' she says. This makes me smile, and I pray it continues.

I pass a queue of tired commuters at the bus stop. A young woman reading a pink romance book catches my eye. I recognise the cover – it's Oliver's. My mind replays Oliver and me banging heads and the strange absence of a vision. I'm not looking where I'm going when a woman rushing for the bus and talking on her phone about French lessons collides with me. A bright flash of white light zips behind my eyes. I hold my breath as the light fades, revealing her opening what appears to be a bedroom door to see a man in bed with a dark-haired woman who, it seems, lives at number forty-two on their street. Her love story ends abruptly when she discovers her husband is taking more than just French lessons.

The world becomes muffled. I reach in my bag for a boiled sweet. My head is back to normal. This is good news.

The bookshop is quiet. I'm restacking books in the young adult section.

In one of the saggy armchairs is Amber, a local teenage girl, who's seemingly pretending to be engrossed in a young adult fantasy novel but keeps glancing at me. On the table next to her is Miranda's old lava lamp and a replica crystal ball.

Amber's mum, Kate, used to be a regular at Miranda's book club. I liked Kate; she was funny and always told us hilarious stories about her three children. She was married to Ben, a local tree surgeon, and her retellings of their family life were like listening to a comedy show. The kids would always be causing some sort of chaos, Ben would be escaping up the nearest tree, and Kate would always be locking herself in the loo to read a book in peace. She was a huge fan of romance novels and would always encourage me to start reading them.

I tried my hardest to avoid physical contact with the people from Miranda's book club. They were all lovely, and I didn't want my curse to spoil things. But one evening, Kate accidentally knocked into me. I saw how her love story with Ben would end: her in a hospital bed, him holding her hand. That night I went back to my flat and cried for hours.

It wasn't a shock when, six months later, Kate came to book club and announced she had been diagnosed with skin cancer. She put up a brave fight, but sadly, the cancer was too aggressive, and she passed away two years after she got her diagnosis.

Amber's long blonde hair is twisted into a bun on top of

her head. She's clasping the book with long pink nails and fiercely chewing on a piece of gum. I often see Amber here. Miranda always says that Amber is skipping school; however, I often wonder whether Amber feels closer to Kate here. Kate used to say Once Upon a Spine was one of her favourite places.

'You okay, Amber?' I ask, while slotting a book onto the shelf.

Amber shrugs. 'Sort of.'

'No school today?'

She grins. 'I'm studying.'

I survey the book she's reading. 'I didn't know dragons were on the curriculum nowadays?'

Amber giggles. 'They're a vital part of my education, Nelly.'

I go to stand near the armchair and tidy up a shelf opposite.

'I've done something bad,' says Amber.

Every part of me tenses. 'Bad?' Oh God, at fifteen, 'bad' could mean anything; binge drinking, smoking, drug-taking, underage sex or something else like a criminal act. I turn around, and I must look panic-stricken as she laughs. 'Calm down, I haven't broken any laws.'

I breathe a sigh of relief. 'Are you going to tell me what you've done?'

'I put a message inside Mum's birthday balloon.'

'Birthday balloon?'

Shaking her head, she sighs. 'Dad does it every year to remember Mum. He gets us all to watch him let go of this balloon. It has Mum's face on it. Mum would be pleased as it's a nice photo of her. I chose it as the one Dad initially picked was her in her PJs with no make-up, and she was wearing my brother's hat as her hair was falling out. Dad said she looked beautiful. I had to tell him that Mum would not be happy with that photo plastered on the front of a balloon.' She sighs. 'Mum might not be here, but she still has photo standards.'

'Your mum loved balloons,' I say, remembering Kate telling us about how her obsession with pretty balloons always went wild on family birthdays.

Amber nods. 'This year I stuck a message inside.'

'Okay – something your mum would have liked? A verse or a poem, maybe?'

She grins, making me feel a little anxious. 'No. The message said that my dad needs a girlfriend and that I am sick of him being miserable. I hoped a suitable girlfriend for Dad would find it, contact me and work her magic with him.'

'Contact you? How?'

'Duh!' she exclaims. 'I put his name, and I said that Mum died and now he's miserable. I also wrote that he's kind, funny and grumpy in the morning before his coffee. At the bottom, I put my email address and asked any suitable woman to contact me.'

I stare at her in bewilderment. 'You put your email address on this bit of paper and stuck it in your mum's birthday balloon?'

'Yeah... I need to vet these women for Dad. If I don't do this, he'll end up with this boy called Finn's mum, who fights outside the pub.'

'Please tell me you didn't add anything else?'

She rolls her eyes. 'Duh – yeah, of course I did. I added my name and age. These women need to know they're not dealing with a child. I am fifteen, for God's sake.'

I turn back to the shelf, close my eyes, and take a few deep breaths. Kate always said Amber had her way of doing things. Anyone could find that balloon, burst it, and read her message. They could then contact her and put her in danger. I take a few more deep breaths. Realistically, the balloon will get stuck somewhere, and if someone found it, their first thought wouldn't be to burst it and then hunt for a message.

'No one is going to look inside it,' I say, my eyes still closed.

I hear a book being shut. 'You're right, Nelly.'

Opening my eyes, I turn around. 'Will you promise me something?'

'Please don't tell Dad.'

'Don't ever do this again. Call me the second anyone messages your email account who you don't recognise. Do you understand?'

She smiles and I see that she has inherited her mother's curvy lips and sparkly blue eyes. For a fleeting second, it's like I'm talking to her mother, Kate.

'Will do.' I watch her flick her eyes to the floor. 'I did it because Dad is lonely.'

As she gathers her things, I begin to lecture her about my beliefs on love. 'Maybe your father doesn't want to find love again? Life is much easier when you're on your own. Relationships should come with health warnings. In my experience, love never ends—'

Fortunately, I stop myself from telling her that love never ends well. She doesn't need to hear that. She has zoned out and is gazing at the romance book section. As she walks away, I pray the balloon is stuck in a tree and is never found. Amber doesn't need someone creepy contacting her, and her father has had enough heartbreak for one lifetime.

15

Miranda asks me to go to the till and help a woman with a book she wants to buy. As I get closer, I can see its title – *Summer Kisses at Sandcastle Bay*. The cover features a couple running barefoot through the surf, holding hands.

The woman is in her early fifties, with curly blonde hair and distinctive red-and-white square glasses. 'I'm looking for something light,' she says, gesturing towards the book. 'Is this sad at all?'

With a shrug, I say, 'I'm not a romance reader, but I will say I have heard people say good things about this author – Aimee Heart – and the books she writes.'

The woman nods. 'I used to adore romance books.'

'Used to?'

She grimaces. 'Before my divorce; I learned that love comes with legal fees.'

I watch her study the book's cover. 'It's been three years, and my friends say I should start dating again. I don't know where to start.'

The urge to tell her about all the horrible things I have seen about love is strong. I would love to go on a date without my curse spoiling it.

The woman is looking at me. 'Do you have anyone special in your life?'

I shake my head. 'Dating is not for me.'

'I wish I were like you,' observes the woman, repositioning her glasses. 'The thing is, I've started gazing fondly at couples at restaurants, in the theatre and at music concerts and wishing I had someone to lean against, someone to laugh with and someone to share my life with. Sad, eh?'

She taps her card against the card reader. 'I will read this and see what happens.'

'Good luck because... you will need it.' The last part must have come out a little too strong, as she gives me an odd look.

I serve two customers and look up to see Eva. The sight of her gazing at me sends my stomach into a nauseating spin. In my head, I can still hear her angry screams at me.

You're jealous, Nelly. I never want to see you again.

The memory of the day she moved out rushes back. Karl came with her to pack up her stuff. She must have told him about me, as on the stairs, he called me a nasty bitch.

I gulp back a wave of emotion.

Her blonde hair is styled into a shoulder-length bob. She wears a loose sweatshirt, jeans, and trainers, and as she moves towards the till, and an awkward silence descends over us both. I notice she isn't wearing any makeup, which is peculiar. When we shared a flat, Eva's desk always resembled a make-up counter at Boots. Eva was the one who taught me how to apply foundation, eye shadow, mascara, and do a bit of contouring. Maybe Karl prefers her to look natural.

'Hi, Nelly,' she says quietly.

'Hello.'

She picks up one of the pens for sale on the counter and fiddles with it. With her eyes fixed on the pen, she says, 'I need to say some things.'

My defences are rising. 'What things do you need to say?'

'Karl and I have split up.'

An uncomfortable feeling takes hold of me. Was my curse right?

She places the pen back in its box. 'Everything in my life is a mess. His and Esther's betrayal still hurts me.'

I should never question my curse. It is always right.

'I still can't believe Karl made me give up my BookTok account. But that's not what I wanted to say.' She looks at me directly. 'I'm sorry about what happened between us, and I want to be your friend again.'

I blink a few times. I'm close to accepting her apology and hugging her, but I stop myself. She could have a new man in her life, and my vision might show me their love ending. Do I want to risk touching her when my curse will surely ruin everything again?

I can't do it. After she moved out, I spiralled. It took me months to recover. I shudder with shame at all the pain and suffering my curse caused.

'Please, Nelly, I miss your friendship.'

The risk of hurting her and myself again is too high. Friendships are not for me. 'Thanks for apologising, it means a lot. I don't think we should go back to being friends though.'

'Why not?'

'My curse is too much of a burden.' Tears sting my eyes. 'I'm sorry.'

The silence between us is uncomfortable. I grip onto the till counter to steady myself. She nods and casts me a weak smile. 'Oh... well, it was nice to see you.'

I watch her walk out of the bookshop until everything goes blurry. 'It is for the best, Eva,' I whisper.

Thoughts about Eva and my curse nibble away at me as I serve the next customer.

When the bookshop is quiet, I catch sight of Henry's book jutting out of the shelf under the counter. My curiosity is peaking. I have not read Margo Lane's book. I pull out the book and read the sleeve.

> The Water Holds Me – How I Learned to Float Again. A memoir about healing and the unexpected power of swimming to pull us back to the surface, one stroke at a time.

The thought of swimming makes me uncomfortable. I haven't been swimming since the car crash. It reminds me of Mum too much.

The words 'pull us back to the surface' make me think about how, after one of my visions, I feel like I'm underwater. A memory I have buried deep at the back of my mind rushes to the front, as if carried on the crest of a wave. Mum and I are in the car travelling to my swimming practice. I'm trying to tell her about my curse. 'Sometimes when I am not wearing my gloves, I touch people, and I see...' She doesn't let me finish. Instead, she puts her hand on my arm. 'Promise me, Penelope, you will keep swimming. Now, I wonder what stroke you will be practising today.'

That was odd. I remember thinking that perhaps Mum didn't hear me. Our car was noisy. Dad used to say we had to ignore the sounds and say nice things about it, as it was old. Even though he and Aunt Polly were not close, they shared similar views on talking to cars.

My mind drifts to Henry. He said the book was for his mum. I recall his mum telling us about how she swam as a child.

'Can you tell me if my medieval history book has arrived?' I look up with a jolt to see Mrs Richards, one of our regular customers. In a fluster, I shove Henry's book back under the counter. I'm busy tapping the details into the laptop when I hear a voice.

'Excuse me.' I lift my eyes to see Mr Ellis. 'Have you managed to find my cookbook?'

'Mr Ellis, I am serving this customer—'

Mrs Richards gestures towards Mr Ellis. 'Serve this gentleman. I want to have a quick look at that new crime book on the shelf over there.'

Frustration bubbles inside me. Mr Ellis smiles. His blue eyes twinkle, and all my agitation disappears. 'I'm sorry. Once I think of Joan's chicken casserole, I can't think of anything else.'

'Barbara Plum's cookery book is out of print.'

His face lightens. 'You remembered the name of it without checking your notes. That means something to me.'

I smile. 'I will need to speak to my contacts who run second-hand bookshops.'

'Will you do that for me?' With a shaky hand, he scratches his tuft of white hair.

'Yes, I will, Mr Ellis. I have your contact details.'

He smiles. 'That cookery book is my time machine. Thank you for helping me.'

I watch him hobble away. As the doorbell rings behind him, I reflect on how he still wishes to cook the dishes his wife used to make when she was alive. Surely love doesn't live on within a recipe for chicken casserole.

16

'Welcome home,' Oliver croaks from the sofa as I enter the living room. He's sitting on the sofa with a damp flannel over his forehead and a hot water bottle against his abdomen. 'I'm very hungover. My head is throbbing and my belly hurts.'

'Yes, I saw you come in last night.'

He lifts his flannel and casts me a bewildered look. 'You saw me drunk?'

I nod. 'I also met Jamie.'

'Nelly, I'm sorry. Did we wake you?'

I don't want to moan or sound like the parent of a teenager who comes home in the early hours from a nightclub and wakes the entire house up. Oliver and I are adults. I want him to feel relaxed and that he can come and go as he pleases. Last night was a celebration, and from the look on his face, he must have partied the night away. In the end, I go for, 'Yes, but I am glad you had a good time.'

He scratches his stubbled chin before pulling the pink flannel over his forehead. 'I need to apologise. That must have been late.'

He can say that again!

I remind myself that he's paying rent. He can do whatever he likes.

'It's a bit embarrassing as I only drank...'

'Two and a half pints,' I say, finishing his sentence for him.

He groans. 'How do you know that?'

'Jamie told me.'

'I've never been great at drinking. How about a cup of tea?' he asks with a reddening face.

I nod. 'Milk, no sugar, and make sure it has a bit of colour.'

He staggers into the kitchen, clutching his aching head. After a good ten minutes, he comes back with a mug of tea. 'I'm sorry, Nelly.'

As he approaches, I survey his tousled hair, his white shirt, untucked from his faded blue jeans, and the top two shirt buttons, which are undone, revealing a triangle of tanned chest. It's a struggle to drag my eyes away and focus on him, handing over my mug of tea. A fluttering sensation in my chest distracts me, and our fingertips touch.

I wait for the light and the vision.

There is nothing.

He's staring at me. 'Are you okay?'

I blink several times. Why didn't I see a vision? I haven't banged my head again.

'Nelly?'

He makes me jolt, and I spill hot tea over my thighs. 'Ouch,' I cry, putting down the mug and rising from my chair as the heat seeps through my jeans. Oliver rushes into the kitchen, grabs a tea towel and races over to me. 'My fault,' he says, handing it to me, 'I made you jump.'

Silently, I agree with him about the spillage being his fault –

he needs to do up the buttons on his shirts when he's inside my flat.

As I wipe my jeans with the tea towel, my mind goes into freefall – why didn't I see a vision? Has my curse disappeared? Excitement takes hold of me. My twenty-four-year-old curse might have gone, and I could be free.

He's pointing to my bookshelves. 'Do you mind if I have a little browse?'

'You haven't done so already?'

'I've been so hungover. Anyway, I'm curious about what a fellow anti-romance person reads.'

He wanders over to the bookshelves. Reaching out, he points to one. '*Norwegian Wood*. Interesting but melancholic.'

'My kind of read.' I force myself sit back in my chair and sip my tea when all I want to do is get excited.

He points to another. '*Atonement*. Good but tragic.'

'It's realistic.'

I watch him point to another book. '*The Bell Jar*. It's a classic but—'

'I enjoyed the symbolism of the mental confinement.'

He chuckles. 'Nelly, we're going to be great flatmates once I stop causing accidents.'

After he returns to the sofa, I watch him place the flannel over his head and lie back. 'You need some books by a cool author I know.'

'Who is he?'

'Oliver James – you heard of him? He has terrible hangovers and needs some sympathy.'

'Not when it is self-inflicted,' I say, lightly.

'Did I say anything whilst drunk?'

'You wanted me to hug you.'

He groans. 'This is embarrassing.'

'You also were talking about how you hate someone called Rory.'

He falls silent, gazing up at the ceiling. I make a mental note of the name Rory.

My mind feels like a snow globe. When I didn't see a vision earlier, it was like someone shook the snow globe. My mind is now full of hundreds of thoughts about my vanishing curse, which are like tiny snowflakes.

His phone buzzes. After glancing at the screen, he rises from the sofa. 'Have a nice evening, Nelly.'

I watch him stagger out of the living room. He doesn't look like he can handle another night of partying, but maybe this is how he is in London? Perhaps this is normal for him?

As the flat door slams, I leap up from my chair. I get up and go to my record player. It's time to dance to Coldplay. My curse has gone. I turn up the volume and dance like crazy. Lenny gives me one of his judgy cat looks, but I don't care. This is a historic day.

After I have danced out my excitement, I sit down and think about all the things I have tried over the years to get rid of my curse. The recent attempts were from J.K. Fielding's writings and his advice on lifting curses. His book came with the bold promise, 'Guaranteed Results.' I should have been freed from my curse after his tenth herbal cleansing bath, burning fifteen sage sticks, and scattering a magic salt trail that made my flat look like a margarita cocktail rim. Instead, my curse remained, and I was left with an angry skin rash, a flat that stank for days, and no money. I had to spend a small fortune on skin creams to stop the itching and bathroom cleaning products, as my bath never fully recovered.

Lenny and I have a wonderful evening together. We sit and watch the busy street below, filled with evening restaurant-goers, groups of young people embarking on their night out, and tired workers enjoying a drink before heading home. 'I'll be out there soon,' I say to Lenny. 'Now that I'm curse-free, I can socialise like normal people.'

It takes me a long time to fall asleep as I am worked up. As part of my 'curse has vanished' celebration, I have put on my pink pyjamas, which are adorned with little grey cats. Lenny snuggles up to me as he loves my outfit. I finally drift off and dream about going to a Coldplay concert and standing in a packed music crowd without seeing any troubling visions. Just as my dream gets interesting – Chris Martin has spotted me in the crowd and by the look on his face, he likes what he sees – I am woken by the flat door slamming.

'Not again,' I wail, throwing back my duvet.

Through the wall, I can hear someone in agony or pain. 'Ouch… it bloody hurts.'

I open the door and turn on the hallway light to see Oliver on the floor in my hallway, holding up his bare foot, and Jamie bent over inspecting it.

Oliver looks up at me. 'Help, I think I have broken my foot.'

Jamie turns to me and smiles. 'Hello again. He's not had any beer tonight, but he has stubbed his toe.'

Oliver lets out a yelp. 'Jamie, I have *broken* my toe.'

Jamie rolls his eyes and looks at me. 'Oliver got frustrated about something, kicked the kerb, and stubbed his toe.'

'Will you stop belittling my serious injury?' wails Oliver, clutching his foot.

Jamie bends over and studies Oliver's big toe. 'You're moving it, so it's not broken.'

'It's shaking,' says Oliver. 'My toe is broken so bad it's trembling.'

His friend places a hand on his shoulder. 'I'll think you'll live.’ He turns to me. ‘Oliver has a vivid imagination, which is great for writing books but not so good for minor injuries.’

I suppress a smile. Oliver nods and hauls himself to his feet. ‘You don’t understand, Jamie.’ He hobbles up the hall towards me. ‘Nelly, I’m sorry for waking you again. Do you have any painkillers?’

I go to the kitchen and get him some paracetamol and a glass of water. After handing them to him, I glance at Jamie. ‘What time is it?’

He checks his phone. ‘Two thirty.’

‘I have work tomorrow,’ I groan. ‘Goodnight, both.’

‘This won’t happen again, Nelly,’ calls Oliver. ‘I love your cat pyjamas by the way.’ I turn back, and he flashes me a smile which gives me a flutter in my chest.

17

Excitement floods my body seconds after I open my eyes – my curse has been lifted. This is the start of the rest of my life.

In the shower, I mentally list what I can enjoy now without my curse turning every touch into a steady stream of tragic romantic visions: concerts, nightclubs, socialising at busy bars, public transport, and travel. Rejoicing in my newfound freedom, I apply far too much Tropical Shower Foam Burst and reflect on how my head has long been filled with the endings of other people's love stories. I will finally get to experience what it feels like to have a head full of everyday thoughts, like where I should go on holiday once I have saved some money, which bands are playing locally, and whether I should join a dating app. The latter makes me shiver. Considering what I know about love, this would require a lot of thought. The thought of being free from my curse is both exciting and a little unsettling, as I will not have it to guide me. Maybe I will just enjoy being vision-free for now?

There's no sign of Oliver. As I am feeling saintly, I leave a packet of painkillers outside his door in case he's in agony over his toe when he wakes.

Lenny must sense it's a good day as he doesn't try to escape.

Even the weather has come out to celebrate my new curse-free life. Above me is a brilliant blue sky, dotted with fluffy white clouds and a warm yellow sun.

I enter the bookshop and wave at Miranda, who looks shocked by my happy appearance. My first customer is Ken, who runs the local allotments. He's buying a book on growing tomatoes. A year ago, my curse showed me that Ken was happy being single and spent his time talking to plants on his allotment. As I slip his book into the bag, I remind myself that my curse has gone. If I touch Ken, I won't see anything. With a big smile, I hand him his paper bag and make sure our fingers brush. I groan as a flash of light hits. When it clears, I see the vision has changed. Someone new has entered his life. Ken has watery eyes, and his bottom lip is quivering. He's listening to a man tell him he's going back home to Australia and won't need his allotment any more. My heart sinks.

The world goes silent as Ken talks to me. I reach for a boiled sweet. When the sound returns to my ears, Ken is explaining how the book is a gift for his new allotment friend, Eric. My heart aches as he goes on to describe their late-night talks, sitting in deckchairs on his allotment, sipping whisky and watching the stars. As Ken walks away, I close my eyes and let out a heavy sigh. My curse has returned.

It's late afternoon. The bookshop is bustling. My curse has been busy since its blip. That's the only logical explanation I can give for its disappearance. I am trying to forget the tragic, heartbreaking visions I have seen today. I'm watching eager book customers gather around Miranda's new display table in the crime section, labelled 'Suspicious Minds & Murderous

Hearts'. Other customers browse the shelves packed tightly with spines in shades of moody blues, blood reds and shadowy blacks. The crime section has a lovely nostalgic feel, with a battered old leather armchair, a faded plaid cushion, and a table with an antique green light. Despite the murder and mayhem between the pages, it is the shop section where customers linger the longest and share theories about plot twists.

I can't stop yawning today after Oliver's toe incident.

I would love to sit in one of the bookshop's armchairs and close my eyes, but that's not going to happen.

'Nelly,' says a familiar voice. It's Amber. She's standing in front of me. 'No one has emailed me yet about the balloon.'

I am flooded with relief. 'That's good.'

She shakes her head. 'Last night, I heard Dad telling Sue from next door about how lonely he's feeling.'

'I'm sure that will pass.' My loneliness comes in bouts. It feels heavy when I am in the middle of an episode, but it does pass.

'Finn at school says his mum has got her eye on my dad.'

'Ignore Finn, he's winding you up.'

She frowns. 'He's serious. Dad *can't* date his mother.'

'Is she the one who fights outside pubs?'

Amber nods. 'I hope a nice woman finds the balloon, bursts it, finds the message and becomes Dad's new girlfriend.'

'I think it would be safer if no one found the balloon or read your message.'

She rolls her eyes. 'I must go, Nelly. I will keep you updated.'

I watch her leave and pray the balloon never gets found. Ben has experienced enough heartbreak in his life with Kate's passing; he doesn't need any more.

Miranda asks me to go to the till.

'Can I pay for this?' A man hands me a book about dogs.

'Certainly,' I say, taking it from him and scanning the barcode. 'Are you a dog fan?'

The man appears older, with short dark hair touched with grey, and pale-blue eyes. The light in his face dims. 'I never wanted a dog. I didn't like them. All the dogs I knew were always barking and were a handful for their owners. But Sandy... well, Sandy the Labrador stole my heart from the moment I held her as a pup.'

I pop his book into a paper bag and wonder what happened to Sandy, the Labrador. The man's pale-blue eyes are full of sadness, and he's clenching his jaw. I sense he's grieving Sandy's loss. If anything ever happened to my cat Lenny, I would be a mess and would be buying books about cats to try to fill the gap. I recall Oliver telling me about Figgy Pudding dying of old age. I could see from his face that he had found it hard.

'I miss Sandy terribly.'

I nod and place the bag on the counter. 'How old was Sandy when she passed?'

The man frowns. 'Sandy is alive and well in Scotland. Well, that's what my ex-wife says, but I stopped believing anything she said years ago.'

'Oh, I am sorry.'

He gestures to the book. 'This is my way of coping. When we got divorced, my ex-wife took Sandy away. They now live in Scotland with my ex-wife's new fancy man. The one she was having an affair with while we were still married.' His voice cracks.

This is a helpful reminder for me about love. When someone breaks your heart, they can stick the knife in further by taking away your beloved pet.

'The book has a big section on Labradors, and I can sit and think about Sandy,' he continues.

In my mind, I picture this poor broken-hearted man sitting in an armchair reading a book and longing for his beloved dog. He's probably surrounded by photos of Sandy and him on walks, on wind-swept beaches, and perhaps Sandy sitting by his armchair. 'That's nice,' I croak as my eyes start to fill up.

He takes the book and hugs it. 'I miss Sandy every day. I'll never forgive my ex-wife for taking her.'

'Love can be so cruel.'

'I'll never fall in love again,' says the man, shaking his head.

'Avoid love at all costs,' I say to him before he walks away clutching his book.

When I arrive home, Oliver is sitting on the sofa with a bag of frozen peas on his foot. He still looks annoyingly handsome, with broad shoulders, dark eyes housed under thick lashes, and messy hair, despite being slumped with a bag of peas on his abused toe. He casts me a sorrowful, war-hero-type expression that is probably meant to inspire sympathy, but it makes me want to smile.

'Sorry about waking you last night.'

'It's okay,' I say, trying not to get too distracted with those buttons on his shirt, which have come undone again. I head for my chair. 'What happened to your toe?'

He groans. 'Nelly, I was pissed off about something and kicked the kerb.'

'What were you angry about?'

Something flickers across his face. 'I don't want to talk about it. You know how I said I was no good at drinking – well, I am also not great at getting angry.'

I want to tell him that he's also rubbish at entering the flat without making a sound in the early hours, but I decide to keep it to myself. Tiredness washes over me. 'You need to rest your toe,' I say, after yawning. 'Maybe an early night will do you good.'

18

'We have author Rosie Flint doing some book signings this afternoon,' announces Miranda, gliding past the counter with a cardboard box. 'Rosie's new book on magic, spells, and hexes is excellent. I finished it last night.'

I meant to have a look at Rosie's book over lunch, but we were too busy. I've been wondering whether it covers curses and how it compares to J.K. Fielding's tome.

'You look tired, Nelly.' Miranda grins. 'Is he keeping you up?'

I'm too tired to reply. It's been a week since Oliver arrived, and he's woken me up every night for various reasons. After the night he stubbed his toe, he made Jamie take him to the hospital for an X-ray. Because A & E was busy, he wasn't seen until midnight and got home at three. As Jamie predicted, his toe was just bruised. Once home, Oliver slammed my door and hobbled down the hall. Since then, he's woken me for many reasons: keys at Jamie's, keys left in his coat at a bar, and a bloodied nose after an argument with a man over a taxi.

Oliver is a night owl, and I wish he'd made this clear in the interview.

It's great that I don't have to have awkward conversations with him in the living room in the evenings, but I wish he'd be quiet when he came home. I can't remember the last time I had a whole night's sleep.

Oliver and I have got into a pattern. He's asleep in the mornings before I go to the bookshop or to visit Aunt Polly. When I get home, he is always sitting on the sofa with his unbuttoned shirt looking handsome or he's cooking me a delicious meal as a way of an apology. Last night's coq au vin was exceptional, and he tidied up before he went out.

Being awakened at two in the morning every night is exhausting, and Aunt Polly keeps asking me why I am so drained when I'm with her. This is frustrating because my time with her is special, and I want to be wide awake and alert when she has her chemo, not yawning and dozing off in a chair.

Last night, in the early hours, I was woken up by voices and someone slamming the door shut. They had taken no notice of the giant piece of white paper stuck to the door, which read in capitals: *CLOSE THE DOOR QUIETLY.*

I heard Jamie exclaim, 'Your nose is bleeding, and it's going on the floor.' My irritation levels spiked and I was at my bedroom door in seconds.

Oliver had a bloodied nose and was pressing the tiniest bit of tissue against it.

'What happened?' I exclaimed, staring in horror.

They exchanged an odd look with each other before Jamie said, 'Ollie disagreed with a guy who wanted our taxi. He came off worse.'

'Who – the other guy?'

Jamie smirked. 'No, Ollie.'

I glanced at Oliver, who cast me one of his sorrowful looks. 'Punching is not one of my strengths.'

By this point, I was at the end of my exhausted tether. 'Oliver, do you think you could go out for once and not kick any kerbs, argue at a taxi rank or lose your keys? Also, could you come home QUIETLY? And not wake me up?'

Oliver hung his head and Jamie mouthed the word 'sorry' to me.

After I'd cleaned up my floor and Jamie had helped sort out Oliver's nosebleed, I managed to fall back asleep.

I look at Miranda. 'Did Oliver go out a lot when he stayed with you?'

She laughs. 'Nelly, he's a handsome bachelor. He's enjoying himself with half the young female population of this town.'

From what I've seen of Oliver, I'm not getting the sense he's enjoying himself with the ladies. He's too busy causing himself unnecessary minor injuries, forgetting his keys and making a racket in the small hours.

'He's a bit chaotic – don't you think?'

Miranda blinks in astonishment. 'Nelly, he's a bestselling author – chaos is part of the author package. Oliver can come and be chaotic with me any time he likes.' She lets out a dreamy sigh, then tilts her head to one side and gives me a serious look. I can tell she's about to offer some of her life advice. 'For God's sake, let the man live.'

I open my mouth, but she ignores me and changes the subject. 'Rosie has spent her life studying her subject. You could write what she doesn't know about magic on the back of a postage stamp.'

Rosie, the expert in all things magical, might have the solution to lifting my curse. Excitement takes hold of me, and I forget all about my nocturnal flatmate.

I crane my neck to look in the box Miranda is carrying. 'What's in there?'

'Fairy lights, bunting that I think looks mystical and glittery things,' explains Miranda. 'Readers who go to Rosie's book signing table will be in for a real treat.'

The box makes me think of Cynthia's garage.

Miranda pauses, turns around, and approaches the counter. 'In Rosie's book, there's a chapter on love pouches and spells. There are also instructions on how to make them. Last night, I made Frank a special love pouch. Nelly, I am desperate. According to Rosie's book, the aroma will seep into his brain and make him think about love.'

'Doesn't Frank have a lot of allergies? Did you check the ingredients of this pouch?'

She smiles. 'He will be fine. I have put it under his side of the mattress.'

I find something to do underneath the counter in the hope Miranda will take a hint and go away.

'It contains rosemary, flower petals and a lock of my hair. He can't be allergic to my hair.'

'Oh.' I rustle some of our paper bags to give the impression I am busy.

'That's not all, Nelly,' she gushes, the excitement lifting her voice a few octaves.

Miranda is gearing up to tell me something.

'Last night I also cast a special love spell. I lit some cinnamon sticks, whispered our names into a jar of honey and rubbed wax on my...'

Sweet Jesus! I shoot up from behind the counter too quickly and bump my head. 'Ouch – that hurt. Miranda, I don't want to know.'

She giggles. 'I will let you know if all these spells work, and you can try them on Oliver.'

I groan as she walks away with a hop and a skip.

To take my mind off my exhaustion and Miranda's attempt at a love spell, I restack the new-fiction display table and serve a few customers.

I also perform a small miracle when a woman asks me to help her find 'that book with the blue cover that was on TV last year.' It takes me a while to find it, but to my frustration, she buys another book.

* * *

It's the afternoon, and Rosie Flint's book signing is in full swing. Miranda has kept me busy, so I haven't been able to flick through Rosie's book. I'm lingering near her table, listening to her explain to an eager reader about the healing powers of crushed lavender.

Rosie Flint looks like she's spent too long in Cynthia's garage. Her mass of brown hair has been sprayed with a glittery hairspray; her ears are struggling to hold her huge moon-shaped earrings and her cheeks are covered in stick-on hearts. I'm not judging her appearance. This woman could be my heroine. I can't stop staring at her book's sparkly purple cover. Inside that book could be a set of instructions on how to lift my curse. By tonight, I could be free from its shackles.

Once the signing queue dies down, I step forward to greet Rosie. I'm not going to admit to having a curse. Instead, I am going to pretend to be helping a troubled friend.

'I have a friend,' I say as Rosie looks at me and smiles. 'She thinks she might be cursed.'

Rosie's face lights up. 'I love a good curse story – especially ones involving family mirrors. Has your friend seen unimaginable things in her family's antique mirror?'

I wish my curse were as simple as gazing into an old mirror.

My life would be a lot easier if all I had to worry about were what I saw in a mirror.

'This friend's curse is different,' I explain. 'She touches someone, and she sees how love ends.'

My eyes are glued to her face. I am waiting for some sign of recognition. I want her to tell me that she has researched this type of curse and has extensive knowledge about it.

Rosie blinks and tilts her head to one side. 'This sounds fascinating.'

Is that all she has to say? My curse is not fascinating. Irritation simmers inside of me.

'Tell me more,' says Rosie.

'My friend sees cheating love rats, lying scoundrels, fatal accidents, and tragic deaths of childhood sweethearts.'

Rosie takes out a hankie and dabs at her sweaty brow. 'That sounds intense.'

I nod. 'This friend struggles to find love as she always sees how everything ends.'

With a nervous laugh, Rosie shakes her head. 'Not all curses are real. Sometimes, they're tied to past traumas. It sounds like your friend could do with some therapy, to be honest.'

Therapy? Trust me – I have trawled Google for therapists who specialise in offering support for curse sufferers.

'My friend's life is so sad because of her curse.'

Rosie shifts uncomfortably in her chair. 'Does your friend want a free signed copy of my book?'

'Will your book tell my friend how she can remove this curse? It disappeared last week for twelve hours, but then it came back.'

Rosie casts me an uncomfortable look. She picks up a copy of her book. 'I do touch on curses, but I don't talk about how to lift them.'

My heart sinks.

Miranda appears at my side. She smiles at Rosie. 'Is Nelly asking you about your love pouches? I told her about what I made for my other half, Frank, and she was keen to know more.'

I shake my head, but Miranda ignores me. 'Nelly has a new handsome flatmate, and your love pouches will come in handy.'

My boss is a nightmare, and Rosie Flint's book will not offer me any help or guidance. I go behind the counter and sulk.

Before Rosie Flint leaves, she comes to the counter and, with a trembling hand, passes me a signed copy of her book. 'This is for your friend. I would also advise that she sticks some bay leaves under her mattress.'

Ripples of hope pass over me. 'Bay leaves?'

Are bay leaves the answer to all my troubles? I have always thought they were used to flavour sauces. I didn't realise they have potential curse-lifting properties.

Rosie nods. 'Bay leaves can be used for emotional protection and help guard the mind and spirit from those who may wish you harm or ill will. They can also banish negative energies.'

'Bay leaves – really?' I question.

Rosie nods. 'Bay leaves are very powerful.'

I thank her and open the cover and see that she's scrawled:

Sending Love and Light. Rosie Flint x

On my way home, I buy an astonishing amount of bay leaves. Even the supermarket check-out girl raised an eyebrow at the amount of bay leaves I was buying.

I'm busy stuffing bay leaves under my mattress when I hear, 'What are you doing?'

With a groan, I turn around and spot Oliver standing in the

doorway to my room. I was so quick to put the bay leaves under my mattress that I forgot to close my door.

'It's a natural remedy for a condition I have,' I mumble.

He surveys the empty boxes scattered all over my floor. 'Well, I hope it works. You'd better be careful, as bay leaves can be used to manifest love.'

'I'm not doing this to manifest love.'

'You won't catch me trying to manifest love,' he says gloomily. 'I am done with that emotion.'

I feel a twang of irritation. 'I'm not manifesting love, Oliver.'

'I'm sorry about last night. I should not have argued with... that guy in the pub.'

Did he say – pub? That's not what they told me last night. 'You said it was an argument at a taxi rank.'

His eyes widen. 'Oh, yes... you're right. The taxi rank.'

Why do I sense he's not telling me the truth about what happened last night?

He casts me a gloomy look. 'I'm off out.'

'Do you ever have a night in, Oliver? Perhaps watch TV or write something?'

An awkward silence descends upon us. He scratches his head. 'I have to put Alfie...' His words come to an abrupt stop, and I make a mental note of the name Alfie.

He clears his throat. 'Jamie is lonely. He... ummm... needs company.'

'Jamie?'

'Yes, he's struggling. I'd better go out. There's a homemade meat pie in the oven for you.' His dark eyes hold my gaze for longer than necessary.

I return to shoving handfuls of bay leaves under my mattress and mutter under my breath about annoying but handsome flatmates who cause chaos but cook wonderful meals.

19

He's gone out. The apology dinner he'd cooked for me was out of this world. His homemade meat pie had golden-brown flaky pastry and a rich beef filling. He had served it with cream potatoes and a plate of green vegetables, which were so flavoursome I devoured them in seconds. Lenny sat on the opposite kitchen chair and cast me judgey looks. He is a huge Oliver fan, and I sense that he wants me to forget about the late nights and enjoy the food.

After washing up my plate, I open up TikTok on my phone and gasp. On my For You page, staring back at me is Eva and her new book-review account. Wow – she's gone back to what she loves best. Seeing her greeting her followers makes me feel emotional. She's standing in front of a white bookcase, filled with colourful book spines, ornaments and a lush, green trailing plant.

She holds up a pink romance book. 'I have finished reading this. It was spicy, yet in places an emotionally charged read. It was so well written that I felt like I was the female lead by the end, and he was my sexy boyfriend. I will say that if he were my boyfriend, I would have to do something with his obsession with beige roll neck sweaters.'

That was posted earlier. I flick through her new profile and see that she has several new videos. I watch her first one where she introduces herself, and then I watch the rest. By the end, I am fighting back tears.

We fell out because of my curse and my big mouth. If I had kept my mouth shut about Karl, Eva and I would still be friends.

I flick onto Instagram and see that she's on there too with her book reviews and her pretty shelves. She must be back living with her mum, as I can see photos of her in a kitchen with a silver tabby cat who looks like her mum's cat, Tiddles.

God, I miss you, Eva. I stare at a photo of her smiling into the camera.

A memory comes to mind. Before she met Karl, she and I created what we called her 'Hot Rocker Manifestation Board'. She was struggling on dating apps, and one evening, we decided she needed to manifest her ideal man. As a teenager, she'd had many crushes on rock stars, so she decided that she would manifest a hot man from a rock band to date.

I brought home some old music magazines, glue, and coloured paper, and we sat at the kitchen table, drank wine, and made her Hot Rocker Manifestation Board. On a piece of pink A3 paper, we wrote down ideas about his appearance and qualities: a skilled musician, looks hot in leather, hairy chest and bushy hair. We then glued pictures of Kurt Cobain, Jon Bon Jovi and Michael Hutchence. Once we finished the board, we pinned it up in the kitchen and did a celebratory dance.

I wipe away a tear. 'I hate you, curse. I hate you so much.'

Since Oliver moved in, Lenny has become... demanding. After watching the hustle and bustle of the street below, I rise from my chair and announce that it's time for bed. Lenny looks up at me, opens his mouth and begins a protest meow that doesn't end until I comply. I pick him up. Instantly, the meowing stops. He purrs loudly in my ear as I carry him to bed, like he's royalty. I suspect Oliver is behind this, attempting to buy Lenny's loyalty with extra cuddles. This is unsettling.

* * *

It's two in the morning, and I can hear raised voices in the hallway. One of them belongs to a drunken Oliver, and the other to Jamie. They woke me up a few minutes ago after one of them slammed the door. I hope they will head to the living room, and I can go back to sleep.

BANG. THUD. CRASH. The sound of my hallway table hitting the floor is followed by something smashing into tiny pieces.

'Ollie,' cries Jamie. 'Look what you've done.'

'Mum's vase,' I gasp and shoot out of bed.

My heart is thudding away in my chest.

I can hear drunken groans.

'Ollie, help me clear this up,' urges Jamie.

'They did this to me,' slurs Oliver. 'I will never forgive them.'

'Mate, we're not talking about them. You need to get a dustpan and brush.'

He's broken Mum's vase. That's what Jamie is referring to.

Anger flares inside of me. I've had enough. This is getting ridiculous. I march to my door and yank it open. The bright light makes me blink. Oliver is sitting against the wall with his head in his hands. Jamie is crouched down low, picking up pieces of the vase.

Jamie looks up when he sees me. 'Oh, Nelly – I am sorry.'

Oliver looks up and gives me a drunken smile. 'Hello, Nelly,' he mumbles as his eyes go wonky.

I stare at the pieces of the vase. 'You've broken Mum's vase.'

'Sorry,' mumbles Jamie.

'I'll buy you another one,' slurs Oliver.

I glare at them both.

Jamie reaches down and pulls Oliver to his feet. 'Let's get you to bed.'

Oliver tries to bat his hand away. 'Leave me alone.'

Jamie shakes his head. 'You need some sleep.'

I watch Jamie drag Oliver to his feet and lead him up the hallway.

I drop to my knees and stare at the scattered pieces of Mum's vase. With a trembling hand, I reach out to pick up one of the broken pieces. In my head, I can hear her instructing me to be careful when carrying it. I used to help her clean our old living room, and I would always offer to move ornaments and this vase to a safe spot while we dusted and polished. Tears rush to my eyes and plop onto the wooden floor. This vase is like a time machine. Every time I look at it, my mind transports me back to when Mum was still alive, and everything was still whole. Now my time machine has gone. 'Mum,' I whisper and press the piece to my chest.

After going into my room, I grabbed a shoe box and carefully put all the pieces inside it.

Chucking on my dressing gown, I pad into the kitchen and make myself a cup of tea.

There's a knock on the door and I turn around to see Jamie looking sheepish. 'I'm sorry. I feel bad for the vase. He'll also feel guilty in the morning when I remind him.'

'It's okay,' I mumble.

'It meant a lot to you – the vase – yes?'

I nod and wipe a stray tear. 'It belonged to my mum. She's no longer with us.'

Jamie lets out a heavy sigh. 'He got a text message from someone who had upset him. We ended up drinking back at my flat.'

'Thanks for apologising.'

'It's no excuse, but he's going through a rough time.'

I watch my tea bag tear apart in my mug of hot water and spew its tea leaves, which adds to my frustration. This flat share with Oliver isn't working. I can't carry on like this. Maybe having a flatmate wasn't a great idea. Perhaps I should have tried to cope with my financial woes differently.

'He's a good guy – honest.'

'Is this why he's not writing?'

Jamie sighs. 'Yes. I wish he would talk about what's going on in his life as even I am getting tired of this non-stop drama.'

'Is there something I should know about?'

'Molly...' He stops. 'I am going to let Oliver tell you himself. Goodnight, Nelly.'

I sit at the kitchen table with my notebook, sipping my tea, and make a list of all the things that are not working with this flat-sharing arrangement. After jotting down all the times Oliver has woken me up, the secret cuddles he's given Lenny when I am not around and him knocking over Mum's vase, my mind wanders. I picture him and find myself writing – 'buttons undone on shirt a lot' and 'dangerous smile'.

* * *

I didn't get back to sleep until five. My eyes feel puffy, and it's an effort to haul my tired body out of bed. The pungent aroma of bay leaves greets my nostrils and makes me gag as I leave my bedroom and head for the bathroom.

Luckily, there is no sign of Oliver. As I pass his closed bedroom door, I think about Mum's smashed vase. Maybe I could find some glue and piece it back together?

Jamie's voice echoes inside my head. Who is Molly, and what has happened between her and Oliver? Is she the reason why he doesn't believe in love?

After I've showered, fed Lenny, and grabbed my bag, I head to work. Outside, I'm greeted by a bright blue sky and golden sun rays, which take away my sadness about Mum's vase.

I wonder whether the bay leaves lifted my curse. This could be the start of my new curse-free life. It's time to get a takeaway coffee and somehow touch the young barista's hand to see if the bay leaves worked. My hopes soar as he prepares my drink.

Behind him is a noticeboard with a photo of him and an attractive young woman with long blonde hair pinned up. They seem to be in the middle of a jungle, surrounded by thick green vines. Their cheeks are pressed together, and they're both wearing huge ear-to-ear smiles. I feel they are madly in love.

This is my pivotal moment. All those stinky bay leaves under my mattress must have got rid of my curse. I could touch his hand and see nothing. He and his adventurous love interest look happy together. I don't want to know how their love ends. I take a deep breath and pray that Rosie Flint knew what she was talking about when she suggested my friend stick bay leaves under her mattress. I recall Miranda telling me that Rosie was knowledgeable about hexes and magic. I am feeling confident.

I ensure our hands briefly brush as he passes me my cup, and my heart sinks. A flash of white light captures my attention.

I see him performing CPR on the young woman with blonde hair. They are at the edge of a rainforest and on the bank of a fast-flowing river. Her hair is wet, and her clothes are sodden. He has pulled her from the river. The CPR doesn't work, and I watch him start to sob over her lifeless body.

Excellent – a flat white, flavoured with disappointment at Rosie Flint's naff advice and an extra shot of tragedy.

I should never have listened to Rosie Flint. Embarrassment for believing in the magical power of bay leaves engulfs me. Why did I waste so much money on so many of them? I did the same after I'd read J.K. Fielding's book and got my hopes up about herbal cleansing baths and trails of salt. A little voice from deep inside me whispers back, *You're desperate, Nelly. You want to be normal like everyone else.*

Perhaps it's time to accept that I will always have my curse.

Maybe I am destined to be on my own for the rest of my life?

Tears sting my eyes as I make my way to work. After wiping my eyes, I take my mind off bay leaves, Rosie Flint, Oliver's late-night shenanigans, and my curse by sending a text message to Aunt Polly to ask how she is and tell her that I'll be over to see her tomorrow.

It's been a busy morning. I haven't had a chance to give Miranda feedback on today's outfit – a tiny black dress that's more like a belt. She keeps strutting past me and gesturing towards it. 'Before you ask, Nelly, Frank was too busy this morning lubricating his bike chain with WD40 to notice what I am wearing. My online stylist thinks he's a lost cause.' She lets out a fake laugh. I know she's hurting.

There's a queue at the till. Waves of exhaustion are crashing over me. I might have to ask Miranda for a nap at lunch.

The woman with the red and white glasses and blonde curly hair is at the front clutching the book she bought the other day. 'I'd like to return this.'

I look down at the book, *Summer Kisses at Sandcastle Bay*.

The cover is pristine, the spine uncracked, and there are no signs of dog-eared pages. 'Sure, can I ask whether there is anything wrong with the book?'

She smiles. 'Not with the book. With me.'

'You?'

'I can't bring myself to read it.'

'Oh.'

'Once you go through a messy divorce, you never see love in the same light.'

She should try living with my curse.

'I've lost faith in love, so I'm returning this.'

'I think that's a wise decision. Love only ends in heartbreak...'

She gives me a knowing nod. 'You're right.'

I point to the crime section. 'We have some great serial killer fiction novels on display. A good alternative to romance.'

* * *

On the way home, I decide that it's time to tell Oliver the flat share isn't working. I wish I were a wild thirty-something-year-old like him, but I am not. I have a full-time job and a sick aunt who needs my support. Being exhausted every day is not enjoyable. Lenny will hate me, but I will just have to suffer his dark moods once Oliver goes.

Oliver is sitting on the sofa when I get home. He's staring at a blank Word document. I watch as he glances up at me, leaps out of his seat and grabs something behind the sofa. He thrusts a bunch of tulips at me. 'Nelly, I'm sorry about last night.'

'You didn't have to get me flowers.'

He bows his head. 'I keep waking you up. I also smashed

your mum's vase. Jamie had a go at me earlier. It wasn't pleasant.'

'Oliver, this flat share arrangement isn't working.'

He blinks, and his jaw tightens. 'Not working?'

I nod. 'You wake me up every night when you come home in the early hours. I am so tired all the time.'

He puts his head in his hands. 'Oh, God, I'm sorry, Nelly.'

'I love it that you've got a great social life here...'

Lifting his face from his hands, he casts me a bewildered look. 'Is that what you think I am doing... socialising?'

I shrug.

He stands and runs a hand through his hair. 'Please give me one more chance?'

Those dark and intense eyes of his have found mine. They are hard to ignore. It's only the second week. Perhaps I'm being harsh?

'One more chance – okay?'

A boyish smile sweeps across his face. 'Great. I want to mend your mum's vase.'

I blink and wonder whether I heard him correctly. 'You want to mend my mum's vase?'

A smile spreads across his face. 'If you get me the pieces, I will put them back together.'

'You don't have to do that.'

He shakes his head. 'I want to.'

As I retrieve the box filled with broken vase pieces from my room, I think back to what Jamie said about Oliver and this Molly person. Is there something going on between him and Molly that is causing his erratic behaviour? Now that my curse has returned, I could use my curse to find out how his love for Molly ends.

As I hand him the box, I make sure our fingers touch.

My body flinches. I wait for the flash of white light.

Nothing.

'Nelly, why are you closing your eyes?'

I flick them open. 'Oh, I didn't realise they were shut.'

'This can be fixed, Nelly,' he says, taking the box from me as my mind once again goes into freefall. My curse has stopped working again. The living room starts to spin. What's going on? Reaching out, I steady myself by gripping onto the arms of the sofa. Why does it keep glitching? Maybe it's losing power? None of the books on curses mention a period of a curse acting like faulty Wi-Fi, but then again, I have always wondered whether the authors have ever experienced a curse. J.K. Fielding's book springs to mind.

'Nelly, are you okay? You look deathly white.' Oliver comes over to me.

'I'm fine,' I mumble. 'Just a little dizzy.'

He goes to make me a sugary cup of tea, and I sit in my chair in the living room.

Lenny comes to sit on my lap. He senses I might need emotional support. Have I been given another chance at a curse-free life?

'We're missing a piece,' Oliver says after handing me a mug of tea. 'I'll go look for it.' He studies my face. 'You've got your colour back.'

I smile while nibbling on my thumbnail.

'I'll be in the hallway on my hands and knees if you need me.' He beams.

'Oliver, you don't have to do this.'

'Nelly, I do.'

I'm busy searching Google for faulty curses when he comes back with the missing piece. 'I'll find some glue. I won't let you down, Nelly.'

I want to believe him, but he keeps letting me down.

20

I boarded the train to Aunt Polly's, wondering whether this would be my first-ever normal train journey. There would be no need to squeeze myself against the window to avoid touching anyone or any unwanted romantic visions. Excitement ripped through me.

When a handsome young man with a crooked smile, styled brown hair and piercing blue eyes asked me if the seat beside me was free, I beamed. 'Yes, it is.' He grinned and sat down, clutching his vape and an energy drink. For a few fleeting moments, I told myself to appreciate this new experience – sitting next to someone cute on a train, without an annoying curse to spoil things.

'Are you going far?' he asked, making me jolt with surprise. My heart went berserk. Not only was I curse-free, but I was also about to start an engaging conversation with someone of the opposite sex. The train jolted, and we both reached out to the seat in front to steady ourselves, accidentally touching hands.

I held my breath. My curse was gone, so there would be no more visions.

White light flashed behind my eyes, and when it cleared, I saw him sitting in a café, explaining to a heavily pregnant young woman why he was texting someone called Carrie. My vision remained long enough for me to read the text. The pregnant woman was scrolling through his phone with a look of horror on her face. 'You were hooking up to have sex with Carrie in the back of your car,' she exclaimed. 'Our baby is due any day and you're having sex with other women.'

He's shaking his head. 'Zoe, calm down, it's not what you think.'

Sadness enveloped me. My curse was back.

I silently vowed to stop getting my hopes up and accept the fact that it's either glitching like Miranda's Wi-Fi or... it's running out of cursed energy. This was a new angle. I took out my phone and asked Google for its view. Wow – according to Google, the energy behind a curse can diminish over time, although this can take years.

'Well? Are you going far?' The young man repeated his question, casting me that dangerous crooked smile of his. 'If you are, we could keep each other company.'

I let out a heavy sigh. 'No thanks, I prefer total silence.'

His phone bleeped. As he glanced at the message, I couldn't stop words flying off the tip of my tongue. 'Is that Zoe or Carrie messaging you?'

I have never seen someone change seats so fast in all my life.

I'm now sitting on Aunt Polly's sofa, flicking through her photo album. It's mid-afternoon and my aunt is upstairs having a nap. I noticed the album under the coffee table while vacuuming. Aunt Polly and I only looked at the photos of Luke and me, but I'm curious about the rest.

This morning, she was cheerful despite telling me her hair was starting to fall out. As I drove her to the hospital, she talked about her exhaustion and daily self-injections to boost her white blood cells, putting my worries into perspective: an annoying curse, a chaotic flatmate, a cat trying to escape, and a negative view on love. I'm not facing cancer or worrying about my blood count. We shared an emotional hug in the car park, and I said her bravery and positivity inspired me. She said if I'd seen her the first time she had to inject herself, I'd see her bravery differently; she cried like a small child.

Once we got home, I cleaned her bungalow and sorted through her pile of ironing while she settled on the sofa with her crossword book, her novels, and the TV remote.

After flipping through pages of teen photos, I find one of Aunt Polly and Hilary outside a lively bar abroad. The sky is clear, and everything looks bright – perhaps Ibiza. Seeing them smile together in tiny denim shorts, low-cut vests, flip-flops and Hilary's pink cowboy hat makes me emotional. I notice Aunt Polly's smile looks wider with Hilary. Turning more pages, I see a photo of them in a nightclub, holding large cocktails, with Hilary talking to a bare-chested man in a policeman's hat, probably after giving relationship advice to a male stripper with issues, which Aunt Polly joked probably saved his relationship.

I think about Hilary, her advice, which always helped my aunt and me navigate difficult times, and how she was there for us, no matter what was going on in her own life.

'Hilary,' I murmur, 'I wish you were here.'

The rest of the photo album celebrates Aunt Polly and Hilary's friendship. On the final page, they are preparing for a road trip along the south coast. Aunt Polly had recently moved to Tide-Leigh. I'd found a flat to rent and had decided not to go live by the coast. She and Hilary started their great adventure from her bungalow. It was their last holiday together. After this,

Hilary moved away to be nearer her ex-husband, Mike. She and Aunt Polly stopped speaking, and Hilary became a distant memory.

In the photo, Aunt Polly is hanging out of the passenger window, wearing a straw hat and clutching a bag full of wine bottles and packets of crisps. Hilary stands beside her, wearing giant pink sunglasses and clutching a bodyboard. I remember waving them off and shaking my head in embarrassment as Hilary turned up Bon Jovi on her car radio.

As I go to close the album, I notice there is something tucked behind the photo of them about to embark on their road trip. Upon closer inspection, I can see that it's an envelope inside the plastic wallet. I pull it out and see that it's addressed to Aunt Polly. My eyes dart to the Exeter postmark.

My heart starts to thud. I have always been curious about what happened between them. Perhaps the answer is in this letter? I know that Hilary cared a lot about my aunt, and she would want to know about the breast cancer.

An uncomfortable feeling passes over me. This letter is personal to Aunt Polly. The reason why their friendship ended is none of my business, and that's how it should remain.

I hear shuffling around upstairs. In a panic, I slide the envelope back behind the photo, close the album and shove it under the coffee table.

Later, I exit the station, and spots of rain greet me. We haven't had rain since the night my bedroom started leaking. Looking up at the sinister grey clouds above, I recall the sheets of paper Gary fixed to my ceiling. Let's hope the rain isn't torrential.

As I climb up the stairs to my apartment, I hear voices. One belongs to Oliver, while the other is a familiar female voice.

Oliver is standing in the doorway of my flat, talking to Eva. They both look up as I approach.

'Ah, Nelly, perfect timing,' says Oliver. 'Your friend is here to see you.' He smiles at both of us before disappearing inside the flat.

Eva looks at me. 'Hello again.'

'What are you doing here, Eva?'

She gestures into the flat. 'You're living with Oliver James – the romance author?'

I nod. 'He's my new flatmate.'

Her eyes widen, and her mouth opens in shock. 'When he opened the door, I nearly fainted.'

'He won't be here long,' I say with a casual shrug. 'It's temporary while his flat in London sells.'

'Why is he here?'

'He's no longer a fan of London life.'

She gives me an odd look; the same one we share when she knows something about one of my book customers that I don't. She always had a good ear for town gossip.

'Why are you looking at me like that?'

She pushes her blonde hair behind her ears. 'You know that Oliver James is his pen name – don't you?'

'Errrr. Is it?'

'His real name is Oliver Shadwell.'

My heart has ground to a halt. He hasn't told me that. 'I think he told me,' I lie.

'You know about the scandal that he was involved in – don't you?'

Air gets trapped in my throat. Eva is looking at me with what appears to be concern. 'Scandal?' I croak.

I think back to how well my day started and how I boarded

the train thinking I was once again curse-free. Since I touched the hand of that handsome sex addict on the train and discovered my curse has returned, my day has taken a downward turn. Now I'm about to hear that my troubled flatmate was embroiled in a scandal. Could today get any worse?

21

Eva nods. 'You're not a fan of reality TV – are you?'

'Reality TV?' Oh, God, is Oliver the male version of Francesca – the potential flatmate I interviewed who was going on a reality TV show where everyone was naked?

I grip onto the doorway of my flat.

'You need to look at the press stories from a few years ago. His girlfriend at the time, Molly, went on a reality TV show.' I remember Jamie saying her name.

Eva continues. 'Molly and the other contestants were flown to a villa in Ibiza, where they were given a lot of money and filmed day and night.'

'What does Oliver have to do with this?'

'Molly cheated on him on live TV. It was all over the press, and social media went wild.'

I stare at Eva. 'Cheated?'

Eva lowers her voice. 'Molly was filmed on camera with another bloke in her bed.'

'Oh, God.'

She nods. 'The press hounded poor Oliver. There were cruel

memes all over social media. It wasn't very nice. I think he and Molly split up. Then he disappeared, locked himself away and started writing books.'

'Miranda never told me this.' I think back to the lengths my boss went to to get me to take Oliver on as my flatmate. She had admitted the bookshop had not been doing well financially and having access to bestselling romance author Oliver, via me, would give her business the boost it needed. I can now see why she withheld information about Oliver's scandal from me.

'Oliver has been through a lot. I know we've had our differences, but I care about you, Nelly. If I were you, I would keep things strictly professional between you both.'

I arch my eyebrows at her. 'This is me you're talking to, Eva.'

'That man has been through something traumatic, and I've heard through my book contacts that he doesn't have the best view of relationships or love. He's still hurting, and you can see that from his appearance.'

I think about his late-night entrances into the flat, the chaos he has managed to cause in the early hours and how Jamie mentioned Molly's name. She must still be in Oliver's life.

Pressing her hands together, Eva inhales deeply. 'Nelly, I am going to fight for our friendship.'

I blink in surprise at her. I don't recall anyone ever fighting for my friendship.

Until I met Eva, friendships had been an emotional minefield. As I grew older, it became harder to maintain friendships, because most of the time I knew they were heading towards heartbreak. Over time, I drifted to the edges of friendship circles. Getting close to people meant that every day I spoke to them, I was reminded of my visions, which told me their love story would end.

Eva forced me out of my hermit-like shell. She refused to let me stay in alone night after night. As she hadn't met a red-haired man called Karl, I put my vision to the back of my mind and did something I'd not done before – I started to enjoy life. For a few cherished months, I ignored my visions. It was bliss. Eva and I became regulars at a cocktail bar in town, we joined a yoga class, we drove to the seaside in her rusty old car, and we laughed a lot. Everything changed the day I came home to find Karl in my kitchen.

'What happened to you and Karl?' I ask.

She blinks. I watch her thread her fingers together and squeeze until they turn white. 'We moved away. I left my job, and I stopped reviewing books. All for him. He swore to me he didn't fancy Esther, but that was a lie. I found them together in my bed.'

'I'm sorry.'

'Karl and I have broken up, and Esther has returned to New Zealand... for good. Please listen to what I have to say, Nelly. I didn't want to hear about Karl because deep down, I already knew he would never be faithful. Esther has no loyalty to me.' Eva takes a deep breath. 'She's done that to me before.'

'What?'

She nods. 'It's true. You told me what I didn't want to face.'

I can't believe what I'm hearing.

'Esther slept with the boy I was seeing when I was eighteen. And on top of that, when I met Karl, he confessed to cheating on his last girlfriend. I stupidly assumed I would be different.'

'You didn't tell me this.'

She fiddles with a strand of hair. 'It's not something I wanted to shout about. I still miss you, Nelly. I miss laughing so hard my belly hurts. I miss our drunken makeovers, I miss our attempts at the latest TikTok dance craze, and I miss our cocktail nights. I am also glad you have cured me of red-haired love rats.'

Something inside me shifts. I realise how much I have missed her.

'Can we start again, Nelly? Can we rewrite our friendship ending?'

'But – what if…?'

She holds up her hand. 'I don't care if you touch me and never see a happy ending with a fella. Your friendship means so much more to me.'

'Eva, I could put you off love for life.'

A grin spreads across her face. 'I'll still be your friend. That's enough.' She opens her arms to hug me.

I step back and avoid her hug. It's too soon for physical contact. To my relief she smiles.

'I'd like to be friends again, Eva.'

She pulls out her phone. 'I still have you on WhatsApp, so I'll message you and we can go out.' A huge grin spreads across her face. 'Speak soon, Nelly.'

After she's gone, I head into the flat feeling lightheaded and buzzing. Eva and I are going to be friends again.

'I'm off out,' says Oliver, striding down the hallway and putting on his jacket.

Everything Eva told me comes rushing back. If he's going out, that means I can do some internet sleuthing on Oliver Shadwell.

* * *

Someone is calling me. My phone is vibrating on my bedside table. Opening a bleary eye, I groan. My clock tells me it's three in the morning. Who is calling me at this hour?

Panic takes hold of me.

It could be Aunt Polly.

Oh, God.

Grabbing my phone, I stare at the screen. It's Oliver. Irritation courses through my veins. This is it – he will have to leave. I can't carry on like this.

I haven't had a good night's sleep as my ceiling started leaking at midnight due to the heavy rain outside. Once I'd pushed a bowl under it to catch the drops, it took me ages to fall back asleep. Now this.

'Nelly,' he says, 'I'm sorry, but I've lost my flat keys. Could you let me in?'

After I open the door and perform a merry dance to stop Lenny from escaping, Oliver enters. He's drenched. His jacket is soaked and hair is plastered across his forehead. Flicking his gaze to the floor, he bows his head. 'Nelly,' he murmurs. 'I'm so sorry.'

I am so annoyed that I don't say anything. I open the door wide, so I don't have any physical contact, and let him in. His trainers squelch as he passes me. 'Did you lose your umbrella as well?'

He looks at me and there is a ghost of a smile. But then it fades. 'I've been walking and thinking.'

'In the pouring rain?'

He gives me a sad nod and squelches up the hallway.

I think back to the press articles I read before going to bed. The ones from a few years ago, which showed Oliver's pain and suffering after photos and videos of Molly having sex on TV circulated the country.

The photos of Molly depicted a glamorous blonde young woman with long, voluminous, curly hair, dressed in a tiny bikini. In the articles I read, she chose to appear on the TV show to chase a dream of fame – and to see if she could stay loyal to her boyfriend. Some of the photos from her early days in the luxury villa showed her lying on a sun lounger while a French male model applied suntan lotion to her thighs. They must have been excruciating for Oliver to see. The French model was the man Molly fell for and she ended up in his bed on day five. One article claimed the TV crew had to turn off the cameras as things between the model and Molly became too raunchy.

In the days after the scandal, the only images Oliver was pictured in were of him going to his local shop and talking to a friend in a café. His face was chalky white, and there was a haunting look about him. He was going through hell.

What is clear is that he's still suffering. She must still be in his life, although I can't think why she would be after what she did to him.

This is a personal reminder to me that heartbreak can happen to anyone, and it manifests in various forms for years afterwards.

I do feel sorry for him, but I'm worried he needs a therapist and not a flatmate.

I can't get back to sleep, which is annoying, so I go to the kitchen to make myself a cup of tea. To my horror, he's slumped over the kitchen table and asleep. There are a series of little puddles around his chair from his wet clothes.

For a few moments, I stand at the doorway and try to stifle my agitation. Why can't he go to sleep in his bedroom?

He wakes up with a fright, and this makes me yelp.

'Nelly…' he gasps. 'Oh, God, have I been asleep?'

I nod. 'I'm awake and wanted a cuppa.'

He rubs his face. 'This is my fault. Oh, God, I will need to move out.'

'Let's talk in the morning, Oliver.'

He hauls himself to his feet and falls over the chair. Both he and the chair crash to the floor. I watch as he groans and stands up. 'This is embarrassing.'

'Go to bed, Oliver.'

'I've had a terrible night, Nelly. I'm sorry.' He scratches his messy brown hair. 'I went home with someone. Not just anyone. It was Rory's sister.'

He thinks I know who Rory is. I don't.

'I knew it was wrong, so I left her house and have spent the last few hours walking in the rain.'

'Okay, why don't you go to bed?' I point across the hallway to his bedroom.

Something flickers across his face. 'Ah – yes. You're right. I need to go to bed.'

I stand back as he squelches out of the kitchen. 'I didn't sleep with her though.'

This is now incredibly awkward. I don't want to know about his love life.

'Oliver, go to bed.'

'I told her it wouldn't be a good idea.'

Oh, God, this man is annoying. I'm so tired, and I have work in a few hours. 'Oliver – go to bed.' My voice is firm and makes him look at me.

'I just want to see Alfie, Nelly.' He rests his forehead against the wall in the hallway.

I have no idea who Alfie is, and right now, I don't care. My anger is simmering.

'Oh, God, Nelly – what am I doing with my life?' He plunges his face into his hands.

That's it – my head is going to explode. 'GO TO BED!' I yell, which makes him jump and look at me like a startled wild animal.

He mumbles, but I can't make out what he's saying.

'Oliver – it's four in the morning.'

'My life is crumbling, Nelly,' he moans. 'I don't know what to do.' His brow is deeply furrowed, and he looks like he's carrying the weight of the world on his shoulders.

I know he's struggling, but I am too. 'Oliver, I spent today with my poor aunt, who has a daily battle with the effects of chemo and every evening must inject herself.'

He nods. 'That's tough. I'm sorry.'

'I have had no sleep due to my leaking ceiling and your lost keys. In a few hours, I must go to work. Please go to bed before I say something I will regret.'

'I didn't sleep with...'

'I don't care, Oliver. GO TO BED!' I roar so loud he scurries away into his bedroom and closes the door.

22

Oliver is not up when I leave for work which is probably for the best. Before leaving I slide a note under Gary's door, which I wrote in the early hours after my dripping ceiling had awoken me. It is written in capitals, and at one point, I was so angry with him that I pressed so hard against the paper that a hole formed. There's no greeting, and I haven't even included his name. It reads:

MY CEILING IS LEAKING AGAIN. FIX IT. NOT WITH PAPER.

The bookshop is quiet, which is a relief as I am tired. Miranda is having a day at a spa which is another blessing.

The shop doorbell jangles and I look up to see Henry, my old friend from my childhood swimming club. He smiles and comes to the counter. 'Hello, I'm back here with work for a few weeks. I have decided that I will keep pestering you for a coffee until you agree.'

I feel a prickle of anxiety and grab a pencil to fiddle with. 'Maybe next week?'

His smile gets wider. 'Great, I will come in again soon. Oh, do you have my mum's book?'

Reaching down I grab Margo Lane's book and hand it to him. 'How is your mum?'

He runs a hand through his hair. 'Her best mate passed away a year ago and she's been struggling. I saw people on social media talking about this book about the healing power of water. Mum loved swimming when she was younger.'

'That's nice.'

'Do you still swim, Nelly?'

The thought of swimming makes Mum's face flash up inside my mind. My chest aches as I remember Mum cheering for me at swimming competitions and watching her glide through the water when we went swimming together. I used to wonder whether she was a secret mermaid. My shoulders and neck stiffen. 'No, I haven't been in the water for years.'

I watch as he opens Margo's book and turns to a page. My eyes roam over the words in bold text at the top.

> Every crash of a wave is an embrace.
>
> The sea carried her alone, and she realised she had never felt safer in the water.
>
> The sea greeted her like an old friend.

Henry snaps the book shut. 'I'll come in again next week, reminding you about a coffee. Remember how annoying I was when we were at the swimming club – well, I am still that little kid.' He laughs before taking out his phone. 'What's the damage for the book?'

He pays and says he will be back soon. As he leaves, our fingers touch. When the bright light clears, I can see him on the hard shoulder of a motorway. He's leaning against a car and watching a figure, who has their back to him. They have a cap on; they're wrapped in a red tartan travel blanket and looking ahead up the motorway lane and into the distance. That's a weird ending for his love story. Maybe they have broken down, and the capped figure will fall in love with whoever is coming to rescue them?

For the rest of the day, I think about Mum and the words from Margo's book. The memory of our conversation in the car comes back to me, and I remember how insistent she was that I keep swimming. It unlocks another memory: how the kids at primary school teased me for wearing gloves, and how this made me look forward to the weekly swimming lessons. Being in the water always gave me a sense of liberation. I didn't have to worry about touching anyone or other children laughing at me. The ones who made my life a misery would always be in the baby pool with floats, whereas I would be free in the adult pool.

By the time I lock up the shop, I am questioning why I have turned my back on swimming. Before I leave, I do something I have never done before – I find a second copy of Margo Lane's book in the non-fiction section and slip it into my bag.

I arrive home, climb the stairs and hear voices from my flat. Gary waves at me from the doorway. 'Bad news, Penelope.'

'My name is Nelly – what bad news?'

He grimaces. 'The ceiling in your bedroom.'

Oliver is behind him in the hallway. He's holding Lenny and casts me a sympathetic look.

'What's happened?'

Gary takes in a deep breath. 'It's fallen in.'

I stare at him as my heart grinds to a shuddering halt. 'Fallen in?'

He nods. 'It's a bit of a mess, but I have a bloke coming to look at the damage tomorrow.'

Gary steps out of my flat and lets me through. Oliver backs away, and I race into my bedroom. It's a good job Oliver is holding Lenny, as my scream is piercing.

There's a gaping dark hole in my ceiling. My bed is covered in bits of plaster and the soggy remains of Gary's sheets of paper. Anger and frustration join forces before coursing through my body. 'I told you about this problem weeks ago, and you've done nothing.'

Gary runs a hand through his greasy black hair. 'Penelope, I fixed it a few days ago.'

'My name is NELLY,' I bark, making him flinch. 'You didn't fix it, Gary, you put a few sheets of paper over it.'

He scratches his jaw. 'I've been busy. You can't sleep in here. Also, there's an odd smell in here as well. It reminds me of bay leaves.'

Tears rush to my eyes, hot and stinging. I blink them away.

'I'll be back tomorrow,' says Gary. 'I have a spare room if you need it.'

The thought of spending a night in Gary's flat makes me cringe. 'No thanks, Gary.'

He waves at Oliver and leaves.

For a few moments, I stand and survey the mess. The tears never went away. They now start to roll down my cheeks. What am I going to do? Where am I going to sleep?

'Nelly,' says Oliver. 'Don't panic. I'll sleep on the sofa, and you can have my room.'

'The sofa is designed for mice,' I say with a sob.

'Nelly, I've been a nightmare to live with, and last night was my last chance. I'll sleep on the sofa and look for somewhere else to live.'

I remain silent.

'What we both need right now is a cup of tea,' he says. 'I'll go put the kettle on.'

He returns with a cup of tea for both of us. I watch as he places it on my bedside table and hovers in the doorway.

As I clasp the cup of tea, I find the heat soothing.

'Are you sure about the bed?' I ask.

He nods. 'It will be fun, and Lenny will hang out with me.'

'Thank you.'

With a shake of his head, he says, 'No, I should be thanking you.'

'Did you manage to get some new keys?'

He nods. 'Gary helped me out with a spare set.'

I turn back to survey the devastation in my bedroom.

'Do you want a hand clearing up?' Oliver asks.

'Thanks, but I'm okay.'

'I'm going to look at some flat-sharing sites.'

I glance over my shoulder at him. He offers me one of his dazzling smiles, and annoyingly, I feel a flutter in my chest. I quickly suppress it. This man is troubled, I tell myself. Right now, he's a walking red flag. I need to remember what Eva said.

'Drink the tea, and I'll change my bedding for you.'

His room smells of cedarwood and lemon aftershave. He's changed the bedding for me but left his belongings and toiletries out on the desk. I can hear him in the kitchen, so I seize the opportunity to have a snoop. I must say that Oliver owns more beauty products than I do. His aftershave, Whispering Cedar, sounds like something out of a romantasy novel. He has a serum called Essence of Renewal, which sounds like a chapter from one of the spiritual-awakening books we sell, and his hair is styled with Alpine Meadow clay, which sounds more like a posh cheese. I bet he spends a fortune in Boots. On the desk are a few books and the board game Monopoly. I hope he doesn't ask me for a game. Aunt Polly used to say I laughed like an evil villain when she landed on one of my properties and was forced to hand over an eye-watering amount in rent. She struggled to beat me. It would not be enjoyable for Oliver to watch me bankrupt him.

I notice he's pinned a few photographs on the corkboard above the desk. One shows a younger Oliver standing with Jamie. There's another person beside Oliver, whose black shoes are visible, but I can't see any more as their part of the picture seems to have been torn off. There is a photo of Oliver and an older man, whom I assume is his father, on a beach. The third photo is of a little boy clutching a large teddy bear. He has Oliver's dark eyes and facial shape. I wonder whether this is a photo of him when he was little.

23

For the past few days, I've slept in Oliver's bedroom, and he has taken the sofa.

He's maintained his social schedule but hasn't woken me up. I've slept like the dead and feel human again. He's also cooked some excellent meals, and last night I found myself telling him that if the romance-writing career doesn't work out, he should go into food.

Today was spent with Aunt Polly. I read Margo Lane's book on the train to Tide-Leigh. It was a good distraction from the tragic visions I observed. Water was on my mind when I got off the train and spotted the shimmering blue horizon in the distance. I found myself delaying going to Aunt Polly's house and walking down to the pier. Watching the salty waves break along the shore made my hunched shoulders sink. A mischievous sea breeze raced around me, and I could feel it encouraging me to step onto the beach and head for the water. For the first time in years, I felt the pull of the sea. My mind reminded me that Aunt Polly, and her new hairstyle, were waiting, so I told the waves I would come back soon.

Thoughts of the water stayed with me like a loyal friend as I stood on the doorstep, staring in shock at my aunt's newly shaved head while she grinned. One of her friends, a hairdresser, had taken some clippers to her black hair, which was looking patchier by the day. 'I feel like I am young again,' she gushed. 'A skinhead at my age.' I was still thinking about swimming when I took her to chemo, bought her a cap because her head was cold, and when she cried in the car afterwards.

The thoughts of the sea have been stronger than those of my curse, which has been refreshing. For once, I have been consumed by something other than all the sad things about love I have seen.

I've just entered the flat. Oliver greets me from the far end of the hallway. 'I've made you dinner. Come and eat.'

As I walk down the hallway, I smell the familiar scents of bleach and furniture polish. He's been tidying up. The living room appears spotless. He has vacuumed the floor and polished all the surfaces to a shine.

The kitchen is relatively tidy for Oliver. I can see he's trying. His French chicken casserole is divine and makes all my frustration with him slip away.

I join Oliver in the living room. He waits for me to pull my chair over and sit opposite him.

'You didn't need to sort the kitchen,' I say. 'I was going to do that.'

'It's okay, I like cleaning.'

He reaches behind the sofa and brings out Mum's vase. It's been glued back together, and he's done a fantastic job. The sight of it makes my eyes water. He stands it on the coffee table. For a few seconds, the white vase goes blurry. After wiping my eyes, I inspect it. 'Oliver, you've mended it.'

'I'm glad you're happy with it.' He smiles at me, and I find myself wondering whether he's a decent guy who's just going through a tough time. 'I've seen a few flats today, and none are as lovely as this. They're either miles outside of town or are in a bit of a state.'

'Oh.'

We both go silent until he says, 'Gary came again today with a builder.'

'Did they start work on fixing my ceiling?'

Oliver shakes his head. 'They need to sort out the roof. It's a loose tile which has caused this. Once the roof is done, they need to put in a new ceiling board and plaster and paint it.'

'That's going to take longer than a few days.'

Oliver nods. 'We're talking ten days minimum. More like two weeks and Gary kept saying there was no rush.'

My heart sinks.

Oliver points to the half of the sofa he's not sat on. I can see a mound under the material.

'A spring has come loose. It happened last night and gave me the fright of my life.'

There's no way Oliver can continue sleeping in here. He's too big for the sofa, and now this loose spring will make sleeping difficult. I am very angry with Gary for not resolving the issue in the first place.

'I need more time to find somewhere to live, but we need another sleeping arrangement.'

'Yes, we do.'

He clears his throat. 'Look, this is going to sound crazy, and I will respect it if it is... but my bed is big enough for two if we share...'

My eyebrows have risen so far up my forehead they are now in my hairline.

I hope he's not expecting us to share a bed.

I have standards, and they are sky-high.

'Hear me out, Nelly. I'll be fully clothed, in full pyjamas, and I'll build you the biggest wall made of pillows. It'll be an impressive barricade.'

I think about his proposal. On two occasions, I haven't seen anything when we have touched due to my glitchy curse. At some point, my curse will show me something about Oliver, and I am not sure I want to risk seeing something upsetting in bed, which has always been one of my safe places.

I think of his nocturnal habits. 'Oliver, you are out late every night,' I exclaim. 'You typically arrive home in the early hours. What you do in your spare time is your business, but I have a full-time job, an aunt who is undergoing chemo, and I need my sleep.' I let out a heavy sigh. If I am honest with myself, the threat of my curse is my biggest issue with his idea, but I am not about to tell him that. 'Sharing a bed will be a nightmare as you will continually wake me up.'

My eyes roam over his messy bed hair, his fitted white T-shirt, which is hiding a defined physique, and his arms, which are a beautiful golden-brown colour. I lift my gaze to his dark, captivating eyes as my treacherous body silently screams, *SAY YES!*

To my surprise, he nods. 'You make a fair point.' He rises from the sofa and walks over to the large sash window. I watch him lean against it and look down at the busy street below.

'I'm not partying. I want to make that clear.'

'Oh.' If he's not partying – what is he doing?

'Coming back here has been more complicated than I expected. I won't bore you with my life story, but it's been a struggle.'

'Okay.'

Moving away from the window, he starts to pace. 'The other night was a bit of a wake-up call for me.'

Was that when he lost the keys to my flat, chose not to sleep with Rory's sister (whoever Rory is) and came home to have a crisis in my kitchen?

'I need to stop going out all the time and, as Jamie says, "causing drama". I am not going to lie, I have a lot on my mind, and I think I have been letting my emotions get the better of me. It's not just causing me issues with you but with others as well.'

I nod, and he comes back to sit on the sofa. 'Sharing a bed with you will force me to get out of this negative cycle. I'll build the wall tonight. It will be so high they will be able to see it in space.' He's looking at me. 'What do you think? I'm a decent person, and I respect your concerns about physical contact. I'm brilliant at building things. If my writing career dries up, I'll turn to food and... bricklaying.'

The words 'no way' are jostling around on the tip of my tongue, but I can't push them out.

I yawn and wonder whether this will result in me getting a good night's sleep.

He can read my mind as he says, 'No more middle-of-the-night wake-ups. I will be the perfect flatmate and bed sharer.'

I wish he wouldn't make bold claims and follow them up with that dangerous smile of his.

'If you wake me up in the early hours again this arrangement is over. I mean it, Oliver.'

'Nelly, if that happens, I will return to this sofa and sleep with a loose spring digging into my bottom as punishment. In years to come, you'll see me struggling to sit down at author events because of my injured behind.'

My face is getting warm at the thought of his rear end. 'Can you stop talking about your bottom?'

He smiles. 'What do you think?'

All want is a good night's sleep. I can't believe I am going to agree to this. 'Yes.'

A huge smile spreads across his face. 'That's great. I will build the wall. Nelly, I need something like this as I can't carry on living the way I have been, and I need to start writing again.'

'Make sure it is a high wall.'

He chuckles and gets to his feet. 'Don't worry, it will be.'

Oh, God, what have I agreed to?

24

Oliver has built an impressive wall of pillows and cushions. He has used all my lounge cushions, my two spare pillows from his cupboard, and a load of new, cheap cushions he bought earlier. I sense he's been planning this.

'What do you think?' he asks, proudly gesturing to the wall.

I nod. 'Impressive.'

'Thanks for taking a chance on me.' He holds my gaze and I can feel an annoying fluttering inside my chest.

'I need to go out,' he says softly, and I feel my heart sink. 'But,' he says, with a slight smile, 'I'll be back in about an hour so we can officially start our bed-sharing.' There's something different about his dark eyes. They look brighter and bigger. 'I promise I'll be back and there will be no stubbing of toes, bloodied noses, lost keys, the consumption of two and half pints or sad walks in torrential rain.'

I watch him leave and go sit on my chair with Lenny. 'I believe him,' I whisper to Lenny. 'I don't know why, but I sense he wants to change.' I pick up Margo Lane's book and dive into where I left off.

True to his word, he returns after an hour. 'Nelly,' he calls out from the hallway after closing the flat door. 'It's nearly time to get our pyjamas on.'

We sit in the living room opposite each other. He's reading a romance book written by one of his author friends. Tonight, he's wearing a fitted pink shirt and black jeans. His dark hair has been styled and is sporting some beautiful waves. I am trying to focus on Margo's words about how it feels to be embraced by water, but my annoying mind keeps imagining what it must feel like to be in Oliver's arms.

I have just been in the bathroom and put on my pink pyjamas which are covered with tiny grey cats. He's changed in the living room and is wearing a pair of blue pyjamas. As I enter the bedroom feeling anxious, he hands me the rolling pin from the kitchen drawer. 'Take this.'

'What?' I gasp.

'I know you're worried about sharing a bed with me, and I want you to feel safe, so take this, stick it under your pillow and feel secure in the knowledge you are armed.'

'Really?' I stare at the wooden rolling pin.

'I wouldn't dare to enter your side of the bed, but I don't want you to feel in any danger. Do it,' he beams.

His wall separates the bed into two parts. If it doesn't topple over us in the night and we don't touch, I will be fine.

We pull back the covers of our respective sides of the bed and climb in.

Even though pillows and cushions separate us, I can hear him breathing. My nostrils have detected his Whispering Cedar aftershave.

Anxiety courses through my body. What the hell have I agreed to?

Despite being tired when I got home, I am wide awake now.

The prospect of sharing a bed with Oliver has put my body on high alert.

I am lying on my side and facing away from the pillow wall.

'Nelly? If you're nervous about this new arrangement, I don't blame you. Are you impressed by my wall-building skills?' He sounds like an excited boy scout.

'It's the best I've ever seen, Oliver. You have a hidden talent.'

He's rearranging his pillows. 'I respect you, Nelly, so please don't worry. This is why I gave you the rolling pin.'

'I'm not worrying,' I lie, slipping my hand under the pillow and touching the wooden rolling pin. He better not try anything because I will use the rolling pin.

'Can you believe we're sharing a bed?'

'I blame Gary for this,' I groan.

'Gary is an interesting character,' he says. 'My thriller author friend would love to meet him.'

'Why?'

'Claire loves meeting creepy people. Gary would give her so much book fodder.'

We both giggle, and I can feel myself start to relax.

'We hardly know each other,' he says, which makes me emit a nervous laugh.

'Yes, and now we're sharing a bed,' I say with a deadpan tone.

We go silent, and I listen to the creaking pipes and footsteps on the floor below.

'Nelly,' he says.

'Yes, Oliver.'

'I know this is nosey, but I saw the book you were reading earlier. Can I ask what it's about? It has an image of seawater on the front.'

'It's about the author, Margo Lane, who turned to swimming

to process her grief. The water healed her. Can you swim, Oliver?'

'Very well, Nelly. Can you?'

I smile at his confident response. 'What's your best stroke?'

He rearranges his pillows. 'Front crawl. You?'

'I excelled at backstroke and won numerous competitions when I was eight. Although I preferred front crawl.'

'You won competitions?' he exclaims. 'When was the last time you went swimming?'

'Years ago. I stopped when…' I take a shaky breath. 'I was nine.'

He allows my emotions to settle before speaking. 'Maybe this book is a sign that you should go swimming again.'

We both go silent. I can feel him turning over, and I think he's facing the pillow wall. 'I have been meaning to ask, how is your aunt doing?'

'She's okay.' I think back to earlier when she modelled her shaved head.

'That must be hard for you both.'

I gulp back a wave of emotion. 'It is hard, but we're doing okay.'

'That's good.'

'She means a lot to me.'

'Talk to me about her,' he says, his voice soft and inviting. I hesitate. It feels unnatural to talk about my life. This is new territory. I do my best to avoid human interaction and lock myself away. But his gentle tone is coaxing me to start.

I take a moment. I have learnt that if I don't do this, my emotions get the better of me. 'My parents died in a car crash when I was nine. My aunt became my legal guardian.'

'I'm sorry, Nelly,' he says quietly.

We don't say anything else to each other. I close my eyes and when I open them again, it's morning and his half of the bed is empty.

He's not in the flat, so I assume he's gone out for the day.

After I shower and get dressed, I head to make my morning coffee, and I hear the front door close. 'Nelly, we ran out of ground coffee, so I've been to the café and bought us a takeaway coffee each.'

He stands at the doorway to the kitchen, a packet of ground coffee tucked under his arm and a cardboard tray in hand, carrying two coffee cups. His dark hair looks messy and wild. Despite all this, his captivating eyes and boyish smile make my heart beat faster.

'You didn't have to do that.'

He grins. 'It's a celebration. We survived our first bed share together.'

'Yes, we did.'

'You didn't have to use that rolling pin on me either.'

He places my cup on the table and raises his cup in a toast-like manner. 'Here's to us and many more nights of you and I bed-sharing.'

I smile and take a sip.

'It feels good to wake up at a reasonable hour and not be plagued with worries about the night before,' he says.

'Do you worry a lot?'

He scratches his stubble-coated jaw. 'I have been worrying about what you think of me and all my chaos.'

'I feel like things might be different now.'

Lenny comes into the kitchen and meows at Oliver. Reaching down, he scoops up my cat, who is purring loudly. I watch Lenny brush his head against Oliver's chin. 'Life in this flat is going to be different – isn't it, little fella?'

The sight of my little cat giving him a lot of feline love makes my heart melt for the first time.

Oliver lifts his gaze to me. 'Did I mention that I'm coming to the bookshop today?'

'What?'

He nods. 'Miranda's been begging me to visit Once Upon a Spine.'

Inwardly, I groan. I will have to spend my time at work with Miranda, who will be in a state of emotional hysteria. With Oliver in the bookshop, she'll be chaotic, hormonal, and loud.

'Wow – you look over the moon at hearing I'm coming to the bookshop,' he says, casting me a bewildered look.

'It's not you, it's Miranda.'

He smiles before taking a sip of his coffee. 'I'm sure she'll be okay.'

'You don't know what it's like to work with Miranda.'

25

When I arrive, Miranda is twirling around the romance section. Thankfully, the shop has not yet opened. 'Morning, Nelly,' she coos, stopping by the display table and stroking the spines of Oliver's latest book. 'He's coming in today.'

'I know.'

She dances over to the counter where I'm standing. Today, she's dressed in a green vest and trousers, both adorned with a bold tropical plant print.

'How's life living with Oliver James?'

'Okay.'

Her pencilled eyebrows rocket up her forehead. 'Okay? Nelly, you are living with publishing's hottest romance author, and you say he's... okay.'

'What do you want me to say?'

She leans in closer. 'Have you seen him fresh from the shower yet? Maybe with a tiny towel wrapped around his waist?'

'Miranda!' I exclaim.

She giggles. 'I know he's a bit rough around the edges nowadays, but I think he still looks divine.'

'How's Frank?'

Her groan is loud and dramatic. 'I think I might be invisible. My fashion stylist is shocked he still hasn't said anything about my outfits.'

'Maybe you need to change fashion stylists?'

She casts me a horrified look. 'That young woman is worth every penny.'

'Shall we open up?' I ask, trying my best to distract her.

'Of course.' She giggles, before hurrying over to the doors.

After serving a customer and observing a vision about how the love for his girlfriend will end when he catches her in bed with his... twin brother, I suck on a boiled sweet and wait for the sounds of the bookshop to come back.

I hear a familiar voice. 'Hello.' It causes a fluttering in my chest and compels me to glance up from tidying up the pens and notepads on the till. Oliver is here and is standing in front of the counter.

His hair has been tamed, his stubble has been tidied, and the beard has been removed. He's swapped his T-shirt and worn-out jeans for a fitted blue shirt and beige trousers. He looks almost polished.

Miranda spots Oliver and squeals. She rushes over to greet him. He smiles and gives her a huge hug. I turn away as seeing others hug is difficult for me.

'How's my favourite bookshop owner?' he exclaims as they break apart. Wow – he knows how to light Miranda up. She casts him a coy look and twirls her brown hair around her finger. 'All the better for you seeing you, Oliver James.'

Two young women in the romance section look in our direction. Oh, God, they must have radars for ears. I watch as they hurry over. 'OMG, it's Oliver James,' cries one, nudging the other who's rummaging inside her bag. 'Where is my sodding phone?'

Miranda slips her hand through the crook of Oliver's arm. 'He's better in the flesh – isn't he, ladies?'

The two women gaze adoringly at him, like he's the lead singer of a boy band.

'Oliver, come and see your books,' says Miranda, dragging him away.

After taking a step, he turns back and does something I was not expecting – he smiles at me and not at the two women. My heart performs a somersault.

Miranda's playful squeals and exuberant laughter echo throughout the bookshop. I can't believe Oliver's jokes are that funny.

I try to ignore what's happening in the romance section and get on with my work.

'Hello again.' I look up to see Mr Ellis. He's smiling at me. I haven't even started hunting for his cookery book. 'I'm still searching for your book, Mr Ellis.' It's a lie because I don't know what else to say to him, and I'm still unsure about whether a copy of his wife's beloved recipe book will help him.

'Ah – good. I was walking past the shop and thought I would pop in.'

After he walks away, I write down his name on a scrap of paper and slide it into the back pocket of my jeans.

'Excuse me,' says a woman. 'My name's Alice. I've moved into the cottage next door. I've only been living here a few weeks.'

'I'm Nelly. Nice to meet you, Alice.'

Alice looks like she's around my age. She has dark hair pulled back into a ponytail and almond-shaped brown eyes.

She surveys the bookshop. 'This is a beautiful place. Living next door to a bookshop is going to be terrible for my bank account, as I love books. Are you the owner?'

'No, Miranda is the owner, and she's busy. Can I help at all?'

'Do you live locally?'

I nod. 'Yes, I do. Why?'

She points to the plastic bag she's carrying. 'I found this balloon in my garden last night.'

'Balloon?' I think of Amber.

'It's in bits.' Alice removes a piece of the balloon. 'I think there must have been a photo on the front.'

I remember Amber telling me it had a photo of Kate's face on it. 'Yes, it had a photo of a local woman, Kate, who sadly passed away. Her family commemorate her every year with a special balloon.'

Alice touches a piece that looks like the photo's corner. 'That's nice.' She puts the piece back in the bag. 'Kate's balloon was stuck on a branch. I tried to free it, but it burst. It was then that I noticed a curled-up piece of paper, which must have been inside.'

She passes me a slip of pink paper.

To whoever finds my mum's balloon, her name is Kate. She passed away eighteen months ago, and my dad, Ben, needs a girlfriend. He's been miserable ever since Mum died, and as I am an adult (15 years old), plus the oldest daughter, I have decided to take control of this situation. Dad is 39, kind, funny, always wins at Monopoly, likes books, and he's grumpy in the mornings before coffee. If you want to apply to be his girlfriend, please email me – AmberBright@Outlook.-com. You do need to like kids – he has three! Amber x

'Do you know Amber?'

I nod. 'Yes, I do, and I'm relieved you found this, as Amber confessed to putting this message into her mother's birthday balloon the other day.'

'Do you think I should give it back to her? It doesn't feel right to put the balloon pieces in the bin.'

'Amber comes in here a lot. I can keep it behind the till. Do you want me to watch out for her?'

Alice's face lights up. 'That would be great.' She gestures to the message. 'I love Monopoly, books, and I am grumpy in the mornings too. If only I were dating again...'

I find myself imagining what it would be like to play Monopoly with Oliver. Those dark eyes and that dangerous smile of his would distract me from hoarding those little houses and hotels. I glance over at him and see that he's looking at me too. He holds my gaze as Alice says, 'I've had my heart broken too many times. I've vowed to remain single.'

Her words pull me out of my trance. I tear my eyes away from him. What am I doing? Hasn't my curse taught me that love is something that should be avoided at all costs? I have also had my heart broken, and I am still glueing mine back together. Sam's face flashes in front of my eyes. I also still haven't seen anything when I touch Oliver. The light in Alice's face has dimmed and she's rubbing her chest. I give her a knowing nod. 'Love never ends well.'

'100 per cent agree,' she says. 'It's not worth it.'

She's staring at Amber's message. I wait for her to speak again.

'Do you know the family well?' she eventually asks.

She might be wavering. I need to help her stay firm. Love only leads to heartbreak. 'Yes, I do, and I knew Kate well. The kids are a handful, and he's—'

She stops me. 'I have heard enough. I'm going to stay single.'

Alice says goodbye after handing me the plastic bag. I watch her walk away and I tell myself that making sure she didn't waver was the right thing to do.

'Excuse me,' says a female voice. The voice belongs to an older woman with wavy brown hair. Behind her are her three teenage children, all busy on their phones.

'Do you have any books by the Spanish author, Miguel Diaz?'

'I can have a look.'

The woman smiles. 'I'm looking for a romance book he's written where the Spanish male character tracks down his British female pen pal from when they were kids, and when they meet up, he realises she's the love of his life.'

'Oh, I see.' I type his name into the laptop to see whether his books are in stock.

'I can't find his name on our database.'

Her face falls. 'That's a shame. Could you order one?'

I can see the book is on one of our distributor sites. 'Yes, I could do that.'

She smiles, and I notice her cheeks are reddening. 'Miguel and I used to be pen pals when we were younger. We were more than pen pals at one point.'

'Mum,' exclaims one of the teenage boys, 'You promised us you wouldn't be cringe.'

She turns to her son. 'I am not being cringe.' All three children look up from their screens and raise their eyebrows at her.

'What's all this talk about being cringe?' jokes Oliver, coming to stand near the counter.

The woman blushes. 'My Spanish pen pal has written a romance book about me, and I want to read it. I have another friend who is also Spanish, and she knows all about Miguel and me. Well, she read this book and has been insisting I get a copy. Miguel has mentioned in the acknowledgements that he still thinks about the girl from the UK with the big hair and blue eyes, who used to sing Spice Girls hits down the phone to him. That was me.'

Her three teenage children groan and look away. With a dreamy sigh, the woman leans on the counter and stares into the distance. 'One day I will go to Spain to track him down. Miguel and I could be soulmates after twenty-five years apart.'

I let out a silent groan. This is yet another example of rational people making delusional choices when they get carried away by the promise of love. I glance at Oliver, who looks captivated by the woman's story. 'I love this.' He turns to me. 'We must track down the book. Is Miguel not on social media?'

Her face falls. 'He's not on social media.' She sighs. 'I do worry that he could be happily married with kids over in Spain and I am wasting my time.'

Oliver shakes his head. 'You must try, or you will regret it for the rest of your life.'

She nods. 'I know all about regret. I told Miguel we would only ever be pen pals. That was the biggest mistake of my life. I went on to have three kids with my ex-husband, and throughout my marriage, I always wondered what would have happened if Miguel and I had made it work. Recently, I have been getting little signs. The place where he still lives, Frigiliana, came up on the TV the other night, and I have seen his teenage face in crowds.'

This is madness. I want to touch her and see how this love story with Miguel ends. I could tell her to stop wasting her time, but Oliver is staring at me. Those eyes of his are hypnotic. He leans in closer to me. I can feel his warm breath on my neck.

'Let's help her, Nelly,' he says softly. 'She can prove to us that true love does exist.'

Words queue up on my tongue. The urge to tell him that true love is a myth is strong, but his intense stare is more powerful. Before I can think about what I am doing, I am taking down her name, Juliet Armstrong, and promising her that I will find Miguel's book. She's now emotional, and Oliver has offered to hug her. Her teenage children look horrified.

Once they leave the shop, Oliver tells me he has got some errands to do in town. 'See you later, bed partner.' My heartbeat accelerates.

Frank, Miranda's partner, enters the bookshop. He comes to the till.

'Nelly, where's Miranda?'

Frank is the antithesis of Miranda. He's a quiet man who seems to long for a peaceful existence and always wears gloomy attire. Miranda often remarks that her online fashion consultant is eager to transform Frank's wardrobe.

'She's in the romance section.'

He drums his fingers on the counter. 'I need to speak to her.' I point in her direction, and he marches off.

I serve a few more customers. 'Excuse me,' says a man. 'Your free Wi-Fi isn't working.'

For goodness' sake, what is Miranda paying for? This Wi-Fi is glitchy – like my curse. I ask him to give me two minutes as Miranda looks like she's having a heated conversation with Frank in the romance section. I run out to the back and switch the Wi-Fi off and on again.

Once it's back on, I give him a thumbs-up and go back to the till. I'm distracted by loud sobbing. Turning around, I gasp. Miranda is sitting behind the till.

'Miranda,' I gasp.

'It's Frank,' she croaks. 'He's going to be a father in a few weeks, and before you ask, I am not pregnant.'

26

When I arrive home, Jamie is sitting in the living room with Lenny curled up on his lap. Oliver is in the kitchen.

'Hello, Nelly.' Jamie beams. His blond hair is spiky at the front. He's wearing a navy shirt, jeans and polished brown shoes. I'm sensing he's off out after as the air is thick with his citrus heavy aftershave. 'It's nice to see you in the daytime. Ollie is in the kitchen making something.'

'A mess knowing Oliver.' I give Jamie a wry smile, and he chuckles.

'How was your day?' Jamie asks as Oliver comes into the living room, carrying two plates of pie and chips.

'Dramatic.'

Oliver hands me a plate. 'For you. I made the pie myself.'

Our fingers touch, and I wait for the white light. There's nothing but silence. This is strange. It was working earlier when Miranda forced me to hug her as she was emotional about Frank.

'Nelly – are you okay?'

I blink several times and nod before taking my plate to my chair. 'You didn't need to cook for me.'

He casts me a sheepish smile and hands Jamie a plate. 'I do, Nelly. I have been the world's worst flatmate.'

Jamie laughs. 'Nelly, take what he's offering and milk more out of him.'

I smile but I am only half-listening. A thought has rushed to the front of my mind and requires urgent consideration – what if my curse doesn't work on Oliver? Beads of sweat have gathered on my brow, and my heart is hammering inside my chest. Every time I touch Oliver, I don't see a vision. He's the only person my curse goes glitchy on. After putting down my plate of food, I reach into my bag and take out a pencil and the notebook I used when I went to see Cynthia and when I interviewed Oliver. The front two pages are filled with the questions I wanted to ask my parents when Cynthia contacted them in the afterlife, and the next page is Oliver's interview assessment, which is a sea of ticks. I flick to the empty fourth page and write:

Theory – my curse doesn't work on Oliver.

I loved science lessons at school. I loved making chemicals react, and I also enjoyed undertaking experiments where you had to prove or disprove something. I look at my theory. Now, all I need to do is start conducting mini experiments.

Jamie catches my attention by gesturing towards a beanbag on the floor. 'I bought Ollie a housewarming gift. It'll keep him away from your chair. He has told me all about it, and you do have an impressive set-up there. I don't blame you for guarding it.'

I smile. 'Thank you. Oliver did try to bribe me with a signed copy of one of his books to sit here.'

Oliver enters, carrying a plate of food for himself. 'I thought it was a good deal.'

Jamie laughs. 'Nelly, I would have refused that crappy deal, too.'

Oliver grins and sits down on the beanbag, resting the food on his legs. 'Nelly, tell us about what's going on with Frank and Miranda. Dad texted me to say Frank has had to take emergency leave. He's got someone pregnant, and that person is not Miranda.'

'Eight months ago, Frank had a one-night stand with his ex-girlfriend, whom he bumped into on a night out,' I explain, after swallowing my first mouthful of Oliver's homemade pie. It's delicious, but I dread to think what my kitchen looks like.

Oliver gasps. 'Frank and his ex-girlfriend? How many years has he been with Miranda?'

It's hard to believe. Even though my curse has always shown Frank pushing a baby's buggy, I have never thought it could have been from a one-night stand. I never envisioned he'd end up fathering a child.

I recount what Miranda told me. 'Frank and Miranda have been together for fifteen years. He left his ex-girlfriend after meeting Miranda at a cocktail party. He was out for a darts club night out eight months ago, and his ex-girlfriend was in the same pub. Apparently, she thrashed him at darts, made all his mates laugh and then invited him back to hers for a nightcap. Frank never told Miranda as he claimed it was "just a blip" and didn't think she would ever find out.'

Oliver and Jamie exchange bewildered glances.

'He left his wallet under her bed and told Miranda he lost it. His ex-girlfriend turned up at his office last week to tell him she's pregnant. The weird thing is that before they split up, they were trying for a baby. Nothing was working. Fifteen years later she's pregnant with his child. He's told Miranda a child won't change his life. He claims he still loves her, and that they would be silly to throw away fifteen years of a relationship.'

'It will change him,' says Oliver in a serious tone, which makes me glance in his direction. He bows his head.

'Nelly,' says Jamie quickly. 'I hear you and Ollie are sharing a bed, and he's built a pillow wall.' I sense Jamie is trying to change the conversation. I look at Oliver, who is still staring at the wooden floor. Something is going on, and I intend to find out.

'Yes, Oliver is a man of hidden talents.'

Jamie chuckles and tucks into his meal.

For a few minutes, we all devour Oliver's food in silence.

When he finishes, Jamie looks at his phone. 'I'd better get off as I have a first date tonight. She's called Nia, likes paddle-boarding, chess, and sushi.'

I smile and hope she likes his aftershave. 'Good luck.'

He nods. 'Fingers crossed. I've not had much luck when it comes to romance.'

'Join the club,' scoffs Oliver, shaking his head.

I watch as Jamie glances at Oliver. 'Will you be okay tonight?' he asks with a concerned look. I recall Oliver telling me he had to go out so much in the evenings because Jamie was lonely. That wasn't true. My curiosity has piqued. What are these two hiding?

Oliver checks his phone. 'I need to go out too now.'

'You can phone me if things don't go to plan,' says Jamie.

'Are you going anywhere nice?' I ask Oliver.

He shoots me a strained smile. I can see his jaw is clenched and his face is taut. 'I have to go see someone.' He gets to his feet and heads for the kitchen. I notice his phone is lying on the floor. I'm about to pick it up when Jamie casts me a worried glance, which throws me off track. What is going on with these two? What is Oliver up to?

'See you, Nelly. I'll walk Ollie out.'

I hear them walk down the hallway, open the door, and I hear Oliver shout, 'LENNY!'

With a groan, I rise from my chair. As I race towards the hallway, I pray they haven't let him escape. To my relief, Jamie is holding Lenny. He strides up the hallway towards me, carrying my cat. As he approaches, I remember my theory. This will be my first experiment. I make sure our fingers touch. There's a flash of white light, and I can see Jamie standing, talking to a young woman with long brown hair. She's telling him that she wasn't playing chess the other evening; she was in bed with her ex-boyfriend, who also happens to be her paddle-board instructor. Poor Jamie. I can now say my curse works on him.

Jamie laughs as he hands over my cat. 'Lenny is a menace.'

'I've forgotten my phone,' says Oliver, still by the front door. He races up the hallway, smiles, and as he passes, I make sure our hands touch. 'See you tonight, bed partner.' He chuckles.

I wait for the white light. There's nothing but silence: no white light and no vision. I gulp. My curse doesn't work on Oliver.

This is odd. My head is bubbling with thoughts. I can't just do one experiment on each of them. I need more validation.

'Jamie,' I say, thinking of an excuse to touch him. Spotting my loose lace, I ask, 'Will you hold Lenny while I tie my shoelace?'

He comes over, grabs Lenny and in doing so, our hands touch. There's a flash of white light, and the same vision I saw earlier. This validates my thinking. My curse works on Jamie.

After tying my shoelace, I take Lenny back, who is now

casting me one of his evil feline stares. If there is one thing Lenny hates, it is being passed around like a hot potato.

'I'm sorry,' I whisper.

As Oliver walks back down the hallway with his phone, I smile and once again make sure our arms brush. Nothing happens. No flash of light. No vision showing how love ends for him. My theory is confirmed.

Why is my curse not working when I touch Oliver?

The sound of my flat door closing behind them triggers an avalanche of thoughts inside my head. I put Lenny down, and he scowls at me before hurrying away.

What is going on with my curse? Why does it stop working with Oliver?

I go to my chair and take out my pencil and notebook. On my page I mark down Jamie's name and put a line through it. I then circle Oliver's name. Chewing on the end of my pencil, I decide that I need to undertake more experiments with different people. The thought makes me gulp. I am going to have to touch people intentionally.

On a separate page, I brainstorm some reasons why I can't see anything when I touch Oliver:

He's magically protected against curses.

He can't experience love any more due to heartbreak.

He has written so many happy endings that he's developed curse immunity.

I sit and stare at my ideas. None of them stand out. I'll keep this list in case any more ideas come to me.

The kitchen is messy. He didn't get a chance to tidy up before he went out. I decide to sort it out and restore my high standards of kitchen cleanliness.

To my surprise, an hour later, I hear the door to my flat open and close. I gasp as Oliver walks up the hallway and strides into the living room. He smiles. 'I'm back. It's our second night in the bed share. I wouldn't miss it.'

He sounds like he's trying to make a go of our new agreement, which is nice. I watch him closely as he removes his jacket and runs a hand through his hair. He pops his head into the kitchen. 'You cleaned up. Nelly, I was going to do it.'

'I like cleaning.'

'If I make a mess, you need to leave it as I will sort it. I feel bad when I see you've tidied up for me. Will do that for me?'

'I promise.'

He watches a film on his iPad while I read more of Margo Lane's book. The urge to ask where he went is strong, but I refrain and see whether he gives me any clues. He's wearing his fitted white T-shirt, and I find myself sneaking a glance at how it skims his broad shoulders and clings to every hint of muscle. Oliver has turned something ordinary, like a plain T-shirt, into something dangerously distracting. He catches me staring at him and heat rushes to my cheeks. I remind myself that Oliver is a walking red flag for several reasons: I can't see anything when we touch, he's hurting, and he's a romance author.

Eva sends me a WhatsApp to say hello, and we engage in a bit of friendly banter about the books she's been reviewing, the trials and tribulations of living with her mum, and how I am getting on with Oliver. While he sits opposite me on the sofa, engrossed in a film, I explain to her how my curse doesn't seem to work on him. I also screenshot my reasons why it's not working and send them to her. Her response is interesting. She thinks the idea of Oliver developing immunity through his romance books is funny. She makes me smile by saying that every kiss scene he writes adds an extra layer of curse protection, and that he probably finishes his manuscripts during a full moon. Out of all my ideas, she thinks the heartbreak one is perhaps the most likely and reminds me how much Molly hurt him. I notice that she's not told me to stay away from him like she did outside my flat door.

It feels nice to be chatting to Eva again, and we both agree to meet up for a cocktail soon. I go to bed early as I am tired. However, annoyingly, I lay awake waiting for him.

27

'Have you still got your rolling pin, Nelly?' Oliver says as he climbs into his side of the bed.

I reach under my pillow. 'My rolling pin is ready. I'll be watching out for any attempts at knocking down the wall.'

He chuckles. 'On the way home, I was thinking of good conversation topics. Are you sleepy?'

The second he lies down, my body wakes up. My nostrils go wild at the scent of his aftershave, and my heart beats faster every time he repositions his pillow or shifts to get comfortable. My mind replays the memory of him in his fitted white T-shirt, his toned physique. I am glad a pillow wall separates us and that it's dark, because I am bathed in a light sweat.

'Are you okay, Nelly?'

'Yes, why?'

'You're breathing very fast.'

Damn my traitorous body! I need to change the subject. This could be a good opportunity to find out what he's hiding. 'How was your evening?'

'Fine. I enjoyed hanging around the flat tonight as opposed to staying out.'

'Did you meet your friend?'

He goes silent, avoiding my question. I listen to the rain ticking against the window, the strange creaks of an old house, and a peal of laughter from the floor below.

'This place comes alive at night,' says Oliver, breaking his silence. 'It's relaxing to lie here, listen to the rain and hear the fun that is going on downstairs.'

'It's one of the many reasons why I love this place.'

'Do you ever lie here and think about the servants who once lived in these rooms?' His words light me up inside.

'All the time.'

'I would have been a footman,' he gushes, 'Opening doors, carrying all the coal upstairs and cleaning the silverware.'

I smile. 'I would have been in my scullery maid era, scrubbing the floors and washing dishes.'

He chuckles. 'I would be good at bowing and saying, "Yes, ma'am." I also would have made sure you were doing your job properly.'

I giggle. 'I would not take orders from you, Oliver.'

'You would look good in one of those maid caps.'

'Careful.'

'Let's talk about our favourite music,' he says, changing the conversation. 'I'm a huge Coldplay fan.'

'Wow – me too,' I say, in shock from behind the pillow wall. I can't believe we like the same band.

An hour later, we are still talking across the pillow wall about albums and our favourite Coldplay songs. We have both agreed that *Parachutes* is our favourite comfort album; the song 'Clocks' is a timeless classic, and we had a lively debate about the best order for an imaginary Coldplay playlist.

Our Coldplay discussion comes to an end, which makes me feel sad. I hope we can carry on talking.

'What shall we talk about now?' he asks, making me feel like an excited child who has been allowed to stay up late.

This is an opportunity to find out more about him.

'Miranda tells me your father lives in Cornwall…' I remember her also telling me about his wealthy father and his playboy lifestyle.

'Yes, Dad loves Cornwall. He and Mum used to go there a lot on holiday… before she got sick.'

'I'm sorry, Oliver.'

'She's been gone a long time, but I still miss her a lot.'

Mum and Dad's faces appear in my mind. 'I can relate to that.'

'It's not easy losing a parent.'

'How is your dad?'

Oliver chuckles. 'Dad is doing great. He still can't surf properly, and he's terrible at paddleboarding, but he's good. He does a lot of work for charity when he's not working.'

'Has he found anyone special?'

'He says his marriage to Mum was enough for him. He has a lot of women who are friends, but there's no one special.'

This is different from what Miranda told me. Perhaps relying on Miranda to tell me the truth about a situation is not a good idea.

'It was Mum who got me into writing,' explains Oliver. 'She was a novelist.'

'Really?' I wasn't expecting that.

'She wrote under the pen name of Penny Groves.'

I stare in shock at the pillow wall. She was a prominent romance author in the nineties. I always noticed her book covers in shops when I went shopping with Mum. Penny wrote

Regency romance, and her covers were always dramatic, showing a man on horseback rescuing a pretty woman in distress. Mum hated romance books and always mumbled things under her breath when I pointed them out to her.

'Your mum was Penny Groves?'

'Yes, that was her. When she died, I decided to carry on the family tradition of writing romance novels.'

'That's nice.'

'I hope she's proud of me.' His voice wobbles ever so slightly.

'Oliver, I am sure she's proud of you.'

He sniffs. 'I wish she were here. I've lost faith in what I write, Nelly. How can I write romance novels when I've stopped believing in love?'

'I don't believe in love either.'

He chuckles. 'This is why we're two perfectly matched bed sharers.'

I smile.

'How do you cope working in a bookshop surrounded by romance novels?' he asks.

His question makes me laugh. 'It's bloody hard. I try to spend as little time as possible in the romance section.'

'I have newfound appreciation for you, Nelly.'

'Thanks.' It's then that I notice the time. I groan. 'We'd better get some sleep. Oliver James, you are a bad influence on me and my sleep.'

'This is better – isn't it?'

'What is?'

'Us talking like this.'

I fall asleep with a smile on my face.

In the night, I'm woken by him talking in his sleep. He's mumbling but I can make out the name Alfie. I close my eyes and go back to sleep.

28

Oliver has been in the bathroom for far too long. I woke up over an hour ago because I wanted to wash my hair before work, but he was already in there.

While I waited for him, I made myself a coffee, prepared some toast, and fed Lenny. I even sat at the kitchen table with Lenny on my lap and reflected on our second night sharing a bed, which was quite pleasant. As I thought back to one of our Coldplay debates, I felt a fluttering sensation in my chest, but I remembered my experiments yesterday and how my curse doesn't work on Oliver. That put an end to the chest flutters.

I glance at the clock. He might be an oddity, but he is still in the bathroom. My agitation levels are rocketing. Is this his new routine?

I'm now standing with my ear pressed to the door. The shower isn't on. What is he doing in there?

The bathroom door opens, making me yelp. I leap out of the way and flatten myself against the wall so there's no way he can touch me.

He steps out in a grey robe. His hair is wet and flops over his face. He beams at me. 'Morning.'

Half of me wants to forget the time he spent in the shower, while the other half wants to speak up. I am feeling prickly. The latter wins. 'You were a long time in there.'

He grins. 'I do my best thinking pre-conditioner.'

I blink a few times. 'You've been in there all this time... thinking?'

He laughs and walks back to his bedroom.

I hope this is not a regular occurrence.

After showering and washing my hair, I get dressed, say goodbye to Lenny and grab my bag from the hallway. Seeing Mum's vase back in its place on my little table makes me smile.

I hear Oliver shout, 'Have a good day, Nelly.' He follows this with, 'I won't sit in your chair today as I have my new beanbag.'

'If you sit in my chair, you're out.' He shouldn't have made me wait for the bathroom. I hear him chuckling from down the hallway, which, to my surprise, makes me smile.

The warm rays of a golden sun greet me as I step outside. On my way to the bookshop, I grab a takeaway coffee, and I'm about to turn onto the cobbled street where Once Upon a Spine is located when I spot a white handkerchief on the small wall. Someone must have found it and placed it there. The cluster of pink embroidered flowers on one corner and the stitched initials, J.C.E., make me stop. That belongs to Mr Ellis. The handkerchief belonged to his wife. He must be upset about losing this.

I pick it up and put it in my bag. When I get to work, I find his telephone number and call him. I don't want him worrying.

'Mr Ellis, it's Nelly Blake from Once Upon a Spine bookshop.'

I hear a cough and a sneeze. 'Hello, Nelly,' croaks Mr Ellis. He sounds terrible.

'You don't sound well,' I say.

He coughs again. 'I've been poorly.'

'I am ringing to say I've found your handkerchief.'

'Oh, Nelly,' he croaks. 'I lost it yesterday on my way to the pharmacy, and I've had a sleepless night.'

'Let me know your address and I'll drop it over later.'

He erupts into a sneezing fit. After his sneezes have subsided, he provides me with his address and asks about the book. I feel a twinge of guilt. Mr Ellis has been here several times, and I've been so absorbed in my curse and Oliver that I haven't even started searching for it. I need to do something to help him.

'I am going to find it, Mr Ellis.'

We say goodbye, and I get to work searching for it. The bookshop is quiet, and Miranda isn't coming in until this afternoon, so I have time to hunt for *Barbara Plum's Family Cookbook*.

It's mid-afternoon, and I haven't had any success. None of my usual contacts in the local second-hand bookstores carry a copy. I'm beginning to lose hope.

Besides searching for the book, I've also been courageously reaching out and touching as many people as I can. My list of those affected by my curse is long, yet Oliver remains the only person whose interactions cause it to malfunction.

The doorbell jangles, and in walks Sam and his new wife. He grins at me as they head for the romance section and I watch as he places his hand on the small of her back, which makes her giggle. My heart aches. That could have been me with him if he hadn't have kissed her behind my back. While his new wife browses the display table, he looks up at me and holds my gaze.

What does he want?

I need to ignore him.

Luckily, a woman asks me to find a copy of a travel book on Athens. After guiding her towards the travel section, I notice he's still looking at me. His new wife is busy flicking through a book, unaware.

A familiar face appears at my counter and distracts me. It's Rosie Flint, the author who came in here to do a talk on her book on magic, and it was her who gave me the bay leaf advice.

'I saw you at the till and thought I'd pop in to see if the bay leaves worked for your friend... the one with the curse?'

I'm about to tell Rosie Flint the truth about how the bay leaves didn't work, that my friend is still struggling with her curse, and she needs to rethink her magic advice, when Miranda rushes over to the counter. She arrived an hour ago looked flustered.

'Rosie, I'm sorry to hear about your husband,' she says. 'How is he doing?'

Rosie smiles. 'He's still in the hospital, but we think he can come home in a few days. It's been a stressful time for us all.'

'I'm so pleased,' says Miranda. 'I did worry when I heard about his accident.' She surveys the bags Rosie is carrying. 'They look heavy.'

Rosie nods and drops the bags to the floor with a thud. 'I've been sorting out his late mother's house. She passed away a few months ago, and he's been meaning to take things to the charity shop for weeks but never got round to it. I was at a loose end, so I thought I'd make a start.'

Sam is heading for the counter. Oh, God. 'Can you help me find a book, Nelly?' he asks.

Miranda gestures for me to help him as she's busy talking to Rosie.

An uncomfortable feeling passes over me as he smiles,

continuing, 'I've forgotten where the psychology books are in here. Could you show me?'

I point to the far end of the shop. 'On the back wall.'

He shakes his head. 'Take me there.' To my surprise, he leans closer and whispers, 'I want to talk to you.' He glances back at his wife, who has her back to us. She's engrossed in the sports romance books on Miranda's latest display table, which bears the sign *Romances with hot, athletic people*.

I'm sensing she isn't aware of what he's doing.

'Hurry, Nelly, I don't have much time. There are things I want to say.'

I blink at him, and he gestures for me to follow.

'Come on,' he whispers.

Reluctantly, I step out from behind the counter and, without looking where I'm going, fall over one of Rosie Flint's charity bags. It tips over and spews its contents, a load of old books. 'Sorry, Rosie, I'll get them for you.'

I bend down to pick them up, and so does Sam.

'I still find you attractive, Nelly,' he whispers. 'I'd love to see you... sometime.'

'You're married,' I hiss.

He grins. 'That's never stopped anyone.'

I look at him, and something shifts inside me. I think about how much time I've wasted daydreaming about him. He will always be a cheat.

This is a helpful reminder to me that once you're married, your other half can still think about straying while you have your head in a spicy romance about two horny ice skaters.

I'm about to tell him where he can shove his idea when I catch sight of an old cookbook within Rosie's books. My chest tightens as I see the name of Barbara Plum on the spine. I grab it, clutching it to myself, my fingers curling around the worn cover. This is a miracle. I had almost given up hope. I can smell the vanilla-scented pages and faint trace of something baked with cinnamon long ago. Mr Ellis will be overjoyed. The thought of seeing him happy makes my heart swell.

Sam is watching me, with a confused look.

He's waiting for me to say something.

'Sam, go back to your wife. I'm not interested in married men.'

I stand up and smile at Rosie. 'Are you giving this book to charity?'

She nods. 'It was his mother's favourite. Why do you ask?'

Mr Ellis's face appears in my mind. 'I know someone who would love this.'

'Be my guest,' says Rosie. 'I hope it gets a new home.'

Sam and his wife leave soon after, and I know he won't be in here again. 'Goodbye, Sam,' I whisper, and to my surprise, there's no ache inside my chest.

29

The cover of *Barbara Plum's Family Cookbook* is a bit faded now. It was once a bright orange and avocado green, but its tones have softened with age. Barbara Plum's image is front and centre. She's in her late thirties with a feathered blonde bob and oversized tortoiseshell glasses. I like how she's smiling knowingly at the reader as if she's about to tell them a secret. She's standing in her avocado-green kitchen with copper pots hanging behind her, and she's holding what looks like a tasty quiche that she's just made.

Leaning against the counter, I flick through the pages, which have softened at the edges, curling slightly. The once crisp white paper has mellowed into a warm vanilla. On each page, there are faint freckles of splattered gravy, coffee, or casserole. The spine of the book has loosened from years of being laid flat on a flour-dusted surface.

An idea pings into my mind. Mr Ellis sounded unwell, and he doesn't need to trek outside tomorrow to buy the ingredients for Barbara's chicken casserole. I'm going to drop off the book and the handkerchief, but before that, I'll buy the ingredients.

Tomorrow, when he feels better, he can make the casserole, and he won't need to go to the shop because everything he needs will be in his fridge.

I'm at the self-serve till in the mini supermarket when I hear a familiar voice. 'Hello, Nelly.' I look up to see Oliver. 'Are you cooking tonight?' he asks, surveying my shopping. He looks so handsome. His hair is tousled, his dark eyes are shining, his white shirt is untucked, and the top two buttons are undone, which means I can see the top of his tanned chest. My heartbeat has quickened. I need to suppress these thoughts.

'I'm going to do a good turn for someone.'

'Tell me more.'

I explain about Mr Ellis, the cookbook, the lost handkerchief, and my idea.

To my surprise, Oliver points to the book, which is tucked under my arm. 'Can I help you with this good turn?'

'You?'

He laughs. 'Yes, me. Which recipe is it?'

I pass him the book. He flicks through it and finds Barbara's recipe for her wholesome chicken casserole. 'This sounds nice. I'll come with you to drop this off.'

'Are you sure?'

'Yes, I am sure.'

We walk to Mr Ellis's cottage. Oliver tells me about his day, which involved staring at a blank screen, doomscrolling on social media and lying to his agent about his next book, the plot for which he hasn't even thought of yet.

Mr Ellis takes a while to come to the door. He opens it, and I can instantly see how unwell he is. His skin is chalky white, his sad blue eyes are encased in two purple circles, and his nose is bright red. He coughs and then sneezes into a handkerchief. Seeing him so poorly makes my chest ache.

'I found your book,' I beam.

Mr Ellis's face lights up as Oliver holds it aloft. The excitement overwhelms him, making him unsteady on his walking stick. Oliver catches him and prevents him from falling. Once he regains his composure, I notice Mr Ellis's eyes have become watery. 'This is a wonderful day,' he gushes.

We follow him inside, and I get him seated in his armchair. I place the book on his lap, and he begins to sob as he flicks through the recipes. The sound of his emotion moves me.

'Don't cry, Mr Ellis.' I dab my eyes with my sleeve.

He shakes his head. 'I'm crying because I am so happy. I can make her casserole.' I let him reach out and touch my arm. Once the light clears, I see him spending his days sitting in his chair, flicking through Barbara Plum's cookbook and running his fingers over the faded photos of her recipes. I make a mental note to add Mr Ellis's name to my list.

'We can do one better than that,' says Oliver, standing by the kitchen door. 'Mr Ellis, would you allow Nelly and me to make your wife's favourite casserole?' He holds up the bag of the ingredients. I stare at him in surprise.

'We can cook it tonight.'

A huge grin spreads across Mr Ellis's face. 'Would you both do that for me?'

'Yes, we would, Mr Ellis.'

I can't believe Oliver and I are preparing Mr Ellis's wife's favourite casserole recipe. Oliver has taken charge of the cooking, which I am happy about since he is a great cook. I'm busy finding Tupperware dishes to store the casserole in. It's not a complicated recipe, and Oliver soon has it in the oven. He sets the timer on his phone.

'I need to pop out, Nelly, but I'll be back before it needs to come out.'

'I can sort it if you're busy.'

He shakes his head. 'I want to be here when it's ready.'

I sit with Mr Ellis in his living room when Oliver leaves. Mr Ellis looks overjoyed to have company. I make us both a cup of tea, and he talks about Joan. His mantlepiece is littered with framed photos of them together. He talks non-stop about her, and I can see his blue twinkling eyes have returned. As he tells me about her love for cooking, I can see that he's still holding on to something. There is a glint in his eyes. It startles me. The love for her hasn't left him. I can feel a tiny ball of warmth shoot up my spine. His love for Joan has embedded itself in his eyes. Love carries on even after someone has passed away.

Oliver appears a minute before the casserole is due to come out of the oven. He smiles at me as I pass him the oven gloves. 'I can't wait to see this.'

The casserole smells and looks delicious.

Mr Ellis hobbles into the kitchen, and the sight of the casserole makes his emotions return. He lets out a loud sob. 'It's like my darling Joan has cooked it and gone to see a friend.'

'Do you want some, Mr Ellis?'

The old man beams. 'I have been waiting a long time for this. My children would tell me off for eating late at night, but I don't care. I want to taste it and imagine Joan is still here.'

I take him a small bowl of casserole and cutlery. He takes a few mouthfuls, and I spot a tear trickling down his face. 'Ah,' he sighs, 'I don't think I have been this happy for a long time.'

We serve it into microwavable Tupperware dishes and give them some time to cool before we slot them into Mr Ellis's fridge. Oliver writes down how long they should be cooked in the microwave.

By the time we leave Mr Ellis's cottage, it is late, and Mr Ellis is weary. 'Thank you, two wonderful people,' he gushes. 'You've made an old man very happy.'

* * *

Oliver and I are lying in bed, divided by our pillow wall. I don't know about Oliver, but ever since we left Mr Ellis's cottage, my body has been flooded with warm tingling sensations. We shared a bowl of casserole while we waited for the food to cool. It was delicious and comforting.

'That felt so good, Nelly.' His voice in the darkness makes me smile. 'He was so happy.'

'I still can't believe you suggested cooking the casserole for him.'

'Mr Ellis was poorly. That cough sounded nasty. I felt sorry for him.'

I turn to face the pillow wall. 'Mr Ellis has so many casserole portions in his fridge.'

'It will do him good.'

'Yes, it will. He can also sit and look through Joan's favourite recipe book.'

We both go silent for a while. I think back to Mr Ellis talking about Joan and telling me all his favourite memories of her.

'I needed to cook that meal for Mr Ellis tonight,' says Oliver. 'It got me out of my head.'

'Are you in your head a lot?'

'Yes, I am.' He quickly changes the subject. 'The wall of pillows hasn't let us down, Nelly.'

'There's still time for me to use my rolling pin. All it needs is a stray arm or a wandering leg calf.'

He chuckles before saying, 'I'll keep my wandering leg calves to myself.'

'We made a good team in Mr Ellis's kitchen earlier.'

'We did. Let's hope we can do something similar for Juliet Armstrong and her Spanish love.'

I remember Juliet, her three teenage children and her desire to get back in contact with Miguel, the author of the romance book she was trying to track down. I wished I had touched her when I had the chance. 'It's been years. She could be wasting her time.'

'Nelly, you and I need to start giving love a chance,' says Oliver.

His words make my body tense. 'But we know what—'

He interrupts me. 'We both need to heal, and I believe helping people like Mr Ellis and Juliet will be good for us.'

I think about Juliet and how she's had no contact with Miguel for twenty-five years. 'Oliver, it's been years since she saw Miguel.'

He pauses and then says, 'Love has a way of lingering. Years pass; lives change but our hearts still remember.'

I think of Mr Ellis and how the love for his wife has lingered. It's still in his eyes and between the pages of Barbara Plum's recipe book. 'You might have a point.'

'Are you going to see your aunt tomorrow?'

'Yes, she has chemo.'

'What's her name?'

I smile into the darkness. He wants to know my aunt's name.

'She's always been Aunt Polly to me.'

I can feel Oliver turning over. I think he might be facing the pillow wall. 'Does Aunt Polly live on her own?'

'Yes, she does – in Tide-Leigh which is on the coast. Years ago, she lived with her girlfriend, Sandra, but they split up.'

'Oh, I see. Did you like Sandra?'

'She had hair like Rapunzel. That was the only good thing

about her. She was seeing the woman across the street behind my aunt's back.'

'I don't like Sandra now either,' he says, making me smile. 'Tell me about Aunt Polly.'

'She's Dad's sister and became my legal guardian when I was nine. I barely knew her before the crash.'

'Wow – so she raised you?'

'Yes. She's sweet, lovely, and funny.'

I can hear him turning over his pillow. 'Is there anyone special in Aunt Polly's life?'

'Not romantically.' I think about Hilary and the letter tucked inside the photo album. 'My aunt had a best friend called Hilary who was terrific. She and my aunt fell out ten years ago and they haven't spoken since.'

'That's sad. Do you know why they fell out?'

'No idea. I wish I knew because I know Hilary would want to know Aunt Polly's having chemo. My aunt used to call Hilary her fourth emergency service.'

I hear him chuckle. 'I need a Hilary in my life.'

Happy memories of my aunt and Hilary deluge my mind. 'The two of them were always going on holiday and having wild times. They were the best of friends, and no problem was ever too big for Hilary to solve. My aunt would call Hilary and six minutes later we would hear a screech of tyres, a car door slam and the sound of Hilary's heels coming up the garden path. Hilary was like our version of the cavalry.'

'Hilary sounds like a legend. Have you ever thought about tracking her down?'

'I think my aunt would be cross. Every time I mention Hilary, she looks like she's angry with me. What I don't understand is why she's decorated her hallway with photos of them when they were younger.'

I explain about how I found a photo album, and behind one of the photos was an envelope containing a letter from Hilary.

He gasps. 'Oh. Did you look inside?'

'No, I felt like I was invading Aunt Polly's privacy.'

He pauses before saying, 'I would have looked inside. In that envelope could be a clue as to why they fell out.'

'Would you?'

'Yes. They could have fallen out over something insignificant and now be too stubborn to apologise. I already feel strongly about Aunt Polly, and she needs all the support she can get right now.'

'You might have a point.'

'If I had someone as special as Aunt Polly in my life, I would move mountains for them.'

I lie awake for ages thinking about Aunt Polly, Hilary, and what he said earlier about healing. The word 'healing' makes me think of Margo's book.

Once again, I hear him talking in his sleep. This time, he's murmuring something about big red trucks. I lie awake for a few moments and wonder whether he is a fan of them. He's never mentioned this. I make a mental note to ask him.

30

There's a time and a place for Oliver James's dazzling smile, and seven in the morning, after he's spent over an hour in the bathroom, is not it.

'Good morning, Nelly,' he chirps.

I've been waiting outside the bathroom door like a Dickensian orphan, listening to him apply a hair mask and talk to himself about how long his bout of writer's block will last.

My eyes are puffy, my patience is wearing thin, and he's standing there dripping, fresh from the shower, his damp hair cascading down his forehead like he's stepped out of a romantic comedy. His dressing gown slips slightly. Just enough to reveal a triangle of tanned skin on the chest. Something inside me stirs. It looks divine. I try to suppress it. I tear my eyes away, my cheeks flushing.

'Everything okay, Nelly?'

'Yes,' I mumble, and he walks away whistling.

'Oliver, last night you were talking in your sleep...?'

He stops. 'Did I say anything interesting?'

'You talked about your love of... trucks. Big red trucks.'

Something flickers across his face. 'I've no idea where that came from, Nelly.' He gives his damp hair a flick. 'You also talked in your sleep.'

I blink in surprise. My heart has started to pound inside my chest. I am now praying I didn't mention my curse. 'Me? What did I say?'

'Water,' he says. 'You said something about it being your friend.'

Relief spreads through me. 'Margo's book. It was on my mind before I fell asleep.'

The memory of him fresh out of the shower stays with me and, to my frustration, is still on my mind as I board the train to Tide-Leigh.

As I leave the station I catch sight of the sparkling blue sea beyond the pier. On my way to Aunt Polly's, I pass a little beach shop. In the window is an array of swimming costumes and caps. There is a navy-blue one-piece costume which catches my eye, and a pink swimming cap which makes me think of Mum. Without hesitation, I go to the shop and buy them both. After stuffing them in my bag, I head for Aunt Polly's house.

'Hello, Nelly.' She casts me a weak smile and pulls her dark grey cardigan around her. Today she's sporting a black woollen hat. 'I didn't like the cap, so I bought this.'

I smile. 'You look good in both. Are you okay?'

'I'm feeling a bit tired. Nothing we can't handle.' I reach out and squeeze her hand. The same vision featuring the little silver chain with the padlock remains unchanged.

I drive her to the hospital, and Nigella is her usual difficult self. At one point, Aunt Polly tells me off for muttering bad things about the car under my breath.

Aunt Polly's chemo day at the hospital is lengthy but event-free. We play cards, discuss celebrities in a gossip magazine someone left behind on a chair, talk about the novel she's reading, struggle over a crossword and talk to the nurse.

After I drive us back, Aunt Polly tells me she wants to sit on her bed. I get her settled, and I even manage to get her TV working, which makes her happy, as it's been playing up.

'I'll be downstairs,' I explain. 'Shout if you need anything.'

She reaches out for my hand and gently squeezes it. I smile as I see the padlock on the bracelet. Reaching into my pocket, I grab a boiled sweet and suck on it until the sound returns.

Aunt Polly is smiling at me. 'Thank you, Nelly.'

'We're family, this is what we do.'

'We are family.'

I notice her cheeks are damp. 'Hey, you're not allowed to get upset on my watch.'

I grab her box of tissues and hand her one.

'I feel rotten, Nelly,' she sobs. 'I'm struggling.'

'It's understandable, but you're doing so well. Come on. Dry your eyes.'

She smiles. 'I don't know what I'd do without you.'

'I'm not going anywhere.'

I watch her sink back into her pillows. 'Ignore me. I'm having a moment.'

'I have had many moments over the years. I think you're allowed to have some now.'

She nods. 'I'll be okay.'

'On Sunday, I think we need to go to the Sailing Boat Café and eat cake.'

We laugh, and I kiss her on the cheek.

I go downstairs with a heavy heart. To distract myself from worrying about Aunt Polly, I tackle the pile of laundry, clean the kitchen, and water all her plants on the patio. I'm about to tidy her living room when I catch sight of the swimming cap sticking out of my handbag. Something inside me shifts. I can hear Oliver talking about healing and I recall parts of Margo's excellent book. The urge to get into the water is strong.

'I'm just popping out,' I shout up the stairs to Aunt Polly.

Before I leave, I put my new costume on under my clothes and grab a towel.

Time slows down as I hurry to the beach. I dump my clothes behind a rock and find a quiet spot to enter the water.

Waves rush over to say hello as I step in. My heart is hammering inside my chest. Will it bring back painful memories of Mum? The water is cold, but it's not freezing. Am I brave enough to do this? A little voice from deep inside me answers. It says yes, and this was what Mum wanted me to do.

Once fully submerged, I lie back in the water and float. The sea nurses me. Its waves massage my legs and arms. Even the coldness has a therapeutic quality. For a long time, I let it carry me. The sky above me is a cloudless blue, and the sun's golden rays dance on top of the water.

This is heavenly. The water and I greet each other like we're old friends. I can be alone here. There's no pressure to explain myself, to talk about my curse or question why it exists. Whatever happens in my life, I will always have the water as a friend.

I feel liberated from my worries about Aunt Polly, my curse and my thoughts about Oliver.

31

When I get home, the flat is empty apart from Lenny. Oliver must be out. I'm looking forward to another night of sharing a bed with him. I want to tell him about my swim. I wish I could say that after my unexpected dip in the sea, all my worries were washed away, and when I emerged, I gained a new perspective on life. However, that's not what happened. I was so cold that I couldn't stop my teeth from chattering; it took me over an hour to warm up, and every part of me ached. As I trudged back to Aunt Polly's, my shoes squelched and I questioned whether going swimming had done me any good. What I didn't expect was Aunt Polly's reaction when I told her. She pulled back her bed covers, hauled herself up and pulled me into the biggest hug ever. As the padlock vision returned and my world became muffled, I let my body relax in her warm embrace. 'Nelly,' she said when sound had returned, 'I am so proud of you for doing that. This is the first step towards healing.'

I noted the return of that word.

By the time I go to bed, Oliver still isn't back. I lie on my side of the pillow wall and wonder whether he'll break our agreement of not waking me up. My heart aches at the thought. I try to stay awake for as long as possible. Eventually, sleep finds me.

In the morning, when I wake, his side is empty.

My mind begins to consider possible reasons why he didn't come home. Maybe he met someone and went home with her. Maybe Rory's sister made a reappearance. This unsettles me. I tell myself that Oliver is a single man, and he can do whatever he wants. Just because we happen to have a bizarre bed-sharing agreement doesn't mean he has to live the life of a monk.

I get up and get myself ready for work.

On the way to the bookshop, I look for a suitable song to soothe my anxious mind – the trouble is, there are zero songs about sharing a bed with your handsome male flatmate due to a plumbing leak – while also wondering, purely hypothetically of course, if he's seeing other women.

'Hello, Nelly,' says a familiar male voice. The bookshop has been quiet. Miranda is coming in later after she's talked to Frank, so I am sneakily trying to finish Margo's book behind the counter. I look up to see Ben, Amber's father, standing by the till.

Ben has always looked as if he has been carved straight out of the wild. He's built like he could lift a fallen tree and yet possesses a surprising gentleness. Kate used to say that her husband talks to trees as if they were old friends. He's been known to talk terrified cats down from the highest branches, which always earns him a tick in my book.

'Do you have any maths books for primary school kids?'

I go to show him where the educational section is. I'm about to step out from behind the counter when the doorbell jangles and in walks Alice. She's wearing wide-legged denim jeans, a white T-shirt and sunglasses perched on the top of her head.

I glance at Alice and then at Ben, who looks mesmerised by her. It's like he's witnessing a miracle unfolding before his eyes.

'Do you want to follow me?'

He's still staring at Alice, and she's gazing longingly at his giant forearms, built through years of scaling trees.

'Earth to—'

'Uh... Oh yes. I need a maths book for an eight-year-old boy who doesn't like maths.'

Alice hears this and giggles at Ben. 'That's a tall order.'

He smiles and gestures to me. 'I have faith in Nelly.'

'Do you want me to show you where the educational books are?'

Ben nods. As we walk past Alice, she grins. 'Good luck.'

I look back to see if he's still following me and he's stood staring at Alice. After an impatient sigh from me, he catches up. 'Who was that, Nelly?'

'That's Alice.'

He seems distracted when I point to the education section.

'Is she new? I haven't seen her around.'

'She's just moved here.'

I remember the bag behind the counter. I could tell him that someone has found the balloon and miss out the part about Amber's message.

He spots the maths books and bends down to get a closer look.

Once he picks one – which makes the bold claim that it can get any child interested in maths – we walk back to the counter. I glance back at Ben, who's still surveying the bookshop.

'You okay there?'

'I'm looking for Alice. Is she still here?'

Inwardly, I groan. The last thing this poor man needs is romance. 'She's probably got somewhere else better to go.'

He pays for the book, and before I get a chance to give him the bag with the balloon inside, he has hurried away.

I think about Alice and what I said about Kate's kids. Was it wrong of me to say they were a handful? I shake off a twinge of guilt as I recall both Alice and Ben's faces earlier when they saw each other for the first time. They couldn't stop looking at each other. There was a definite spark of attraction. I recall what Oliver said about giving love a chance. No, I can't do it.

Henry enters the shop at the same time Miranda appears to relieve me for my lunch break. 'Good timing,' he beams. 'How about that coffee now?'

Half of me wants to make an excuse but the other half of me wants to have a coffee with an old friend. 'Let me grab my bag.'

As we leave the book shop, I think about my theory, and I make sure my wrist brushes Henry's hand. The vision featuring him watching the person wearing the cap on the hard shoulder of a motorway remains unchanged. I can add Henry's name to my list.

We sit by the window in the café, which is off the main high street. He sits opposite me, and I find myself comparing him to Oliver. Henry's mass of unruly black curls is striking to look at, but they don't have the same pull as Oliver's wavy brown hair. Oh, God, what is happening to me? I am becoming obsessed with Oliver James. This must stop. Our coffees arrive, and I notice Henry is staring at me. His blue eyes are warm and friendly, but they don't hold the same intensity as Oliver's dark eyes.

Henry lives in West London but works away a lot, and his job involves data and things I will never understand. His mum lives nearby in London, and what makes me smile is that he's still close to his nan. He always used to talk about his nan when we were at the swimming club. Back then, she had a motorbike and many tattoos, which Henry thought was cool. He asks me about life in the bookshop. I talk about Miranda and what it's like to work for her. He chuckles often. 'You haven't lost your sense of humour, Nelly. Miranda sounds like an interesting person. Can I ask what made you change your name?'

My chest tightens and I take a breath. Henry listens intently as I tell him about how my parents died and how I went to live with Aunt Polly, how Mum and Dad called me Penelope and how I found life easier being called Nelly after they died. For a moment, he doesn't speak or blink; he just stares at me. 'Nelly, I'm so sorry,' he says, softly. 'That must have been so hard for you.'

'My aunt was amazing. She was my rock.' I sense I need to lighten the tone as Henry looks like he's on the verge of tears. 'She also made me throw away my little gloves.'

He smiles. 'I liked your white gloves. You should have said you had a calling to be a mime artist.'

We both giggle. The conversation lightens when Henry talks about his memories of the swimming club. We laugh at our younger selves and how we thought we were amazing at crawl.

'You were much better than me at crawl,' says Henry, before sipping his coffee. 'I remember wondering whether you were half girl, half fish.'

I smile and think back to how good it feels to be swimming again.

'Do you remember when you beat that girl in a race – the one who we hated?' he asks. 'She was in our group and had short black hair. Was she called Suzie? She teased you about your gloves in the café afterwards?'

The memory of Suzie making everyone laugh at my gloves makes me feel uncomfortable.

'Why did your mum force you to wear them?'

I fidget in my chair. 'A skin condition on my hands.' I check my phone and realise I need to get back to the bookshop. Henry nods as I get to my feet.

'I'm sorry about what happened to your parents. I will tell my mum, and I know she will be upset. She and your mum had a terrible argument which I know she now regrets.'

I recall him saying this when he first came into the shop, but I was too mixed up with everything to notice. 'What was the argument about?'

Something flickers across his face. 'Dad was having an affair with someone from his office and your mum knew about it.'

How did Mum know about this? I blink several times. 'Really? How did my mother know your father? He never came to watch you swim.'

He shakes his head. 'That was the odd thing. Your mum had never met my dad. It was a shock. I mean, you can imagine my mother's reaction when someone who didn't know our family started saying these things...'

I gulp as the café goes on a nauseating tilt. Reaching out, I grab onto a chair. Why does this sound familiar? Did Mum have my curse as well? Surely she would have said something. Mum loved me. She wouldn't have let me battle my curse alone. No, she did not have my curse. I shove the idea to the darkest depths of my mind.

'Nelly, are you okay?' Henry looks concerned. 'Have I said something to upset you?'

I shake my head. 'No. I need to get back. Thanks for the coffee.'

We say our goodbyes, and he promises to call into the bookshop again. I hurry back to work, telling myself repeatedly that Mum did not have my curse.

The bookshop is busy and the afternoon flies by. When I get

home and enter the living room, Oliver is sitting on the sofa. He looks up as I walk over to my chair.

'Hi, Nelly. How are you?'

'Good,' I say, which is a lie. Ever since my coffee with Henry, my mind has been awash with thoughts about Mum and my curse. I need to lock them away at the back of my mind and perhaps mention what Henry said to Aunt Polly.

He rubs his face. 'I fell asleep on Jamie's sofa. When I woke up in the middle of the night, I thought about coming home, but I didn't want to break our agreement, so I stayed where I was.'

At least he's now thinking of me and being considerate. I am also a little relieved that he didn't go home with another woman.

'Oh, okay, thanks.'

He passes me the book which is balancing on his knee. 'It's Miguel's book.'

I gasp. 'How did you get a copy?'

'I spoke to my editor, who is Spanish, and she managed to get hold of a copy.' His face lights up. 'We can help Juliet. I will say this is my gift to her.'

'But what if Miguel is happily married and…'

He stands up. 'Nelly, we have to give a love a chance.'

His words echo inside my head. *We have to give love a chance.* This still sounds alien to me.

His dark eyes hold my gaze for longer than necessary. A fluttery sensation takes over my chest.

'I'm going to cook some tea,' he says softly. 'Do you want some?'

'What are you making?'

He smiles. 'I took a screenshot of Barbara Plum's chicken casserole and I have the ingredients.' My heart swells.

32

We're lying in bed, divided by our pillow wall. Our bellies are full of Barbara Plum's chicken dish, and we have both agreed she achieved high standards of casserole-making greatness.

Through a gap in the curtain, I can see that it's dark outside and there's a sprinkling of stars.

'I look forward to our chats over our pillow wall.' The sound of his voice makes my heart beat faster. It gives me a rush of tingling sensations. Why do I feel like my body is being traitorous again?

A smile spreads across my face. 'Me too.'

He sighs. 'I'm sorry I missed this last night.'

Oh, God, his words are lighting me up inside. I'm surprised I've not turned into one of those lava lamps from the nineties.

I think he's facing the wall. His voice sounds closer.

'While I was making our tea, I wrote down a few ideas for a book.'

'Really?'

'This old house has given me some ideas.'

He needs to return to writing. It will do him good. 'That's great news,' I say.

There's a long pause, and I wonder whether he's fallen asleep. 'I'm struggling a bit at the moment, Nelly.'

'I know.'

He stays silent for ages. I don't try to fill the gap.

'Do you know about what happened to me a few years ago?'

'I know about the reality TV show.'

'Oh.'

'That must have been incredibly tough for you.'

'It was.' He sighs. 'I feel like I am in a revolving door of pain right now. Coming back here was a bad decision.'

'Why *did* you come back here?'

'Molly, my ex-girlfriend, grew up near here. She's moved back to be nearer her parents.'

I stay silent.

'She's living with Rory, my ex-best mate.'

'I'm sorry.'

Ah, so that's who Rory is.

There's another lengthy silence. 'The day before Molly went on that reality TV show, she told me she was pregnant.'

I stare in horror towards the pillow wall.

'It was early in the pregnancy, like five weeks, and not something we had planned. She told me that while she was on the show, she would consider what she wanted to do.'

He sniffs, and I wonder whether he's getting emotional. 'When she came off the show, she had to go into hiding because the public turned on her after the way she'd treated me. Even though she'd done that to me, I stood by her as she was pregnant with my child.'

I can't believe what I am hearing. Nothing that I read online mentioned a child. That was so brave of him for standing by Molly.

His voice is cracking. 'We broke up before Alfie was born.'

The name Alfie lights up my mind. Alfie was who he was talking about in his sleep. 'You have a son. That's amazing.'

'Yes, he's two years old. He's fantastic and he loves his teddy and big red toy trucks.'

The jigsaw pieces of Oliver are starting to fit together in my mind.

He sniffs. 'I've moved back here for him and to help Molly with co-parenting. I didn't want to be a father who lives in London and sees his son only on weekends. I want to do the school picks up, homework and watch his class assemblies.'

Hearing him talk about his plans for Alfie makes me smile. I can hear the excitement in his voice.

'You sound like you are going to be a great father.'

He blows his nose. 'I moved here to be closer to Alfie. Going over to Molly's new house to read my son a bedtime story while my ex-best mate plays happy families with my ex-girlfriend and my son has been excruciating. Sometimes Rory goes out while I do bedtime, which is Molly's idea. It works; however, after I put Alfie to bed, I head into town, and I always end up bumping into Rory. We like the same sort of pubs. He tries to talk to me, which makes me angry. It was Rory who punched me when I started shouting at him in a pub. Sometimes he's in the house, and I get frustrated when I see him with my son. That's what happened when I kicked the kerb.'

I hear him get emotional.

'I've found it so hard, Nelly.' He breaks into a sob. It isn't loud, but it sounds like one of those cries you let out when you've reached the bottom of your barrel. 'She broke my heart once with that French model, and now I feel like she's doing it again with Rory.'

Oliver has been through hell. 'I'm sorry you're going through this.'

He sniffs. 'When I heard Rory was moving in, I stopped writing. That was when my writer's block began.'

I can see now why he's struggling to write his romance books. 'I'm not surprised.'

'Rory betrayed me, and I will never forgive him.'

'How do you feel about Molly?'

He pauses. 'She's the mother to Alfie, and she's good with him.' There is another silence. It's longer and I wonder whether he wants to be alone with his thoughts.

I hear him sniffing and my heart aches. 'I don't love her any more,' he croaks. 'There's only so much my heart can withstand. I've said too much. I should get some sleep.'

'You can talk as much as you want.'

'I worry I'm keeping you awake with my oversharing.'

'I don't mind.'

He turns his pillow over. 'We've kept Alfie a secret. Molly is still paranoid about bad press. I'd had several books published with smaller presses before the reality show. Around the time of her reality show, I got a big book deal, and that's when I decided to use a pen name. I never mention that I'm a father.'

'That must be hard for you. You sound like the sort of father who wants to talk about his son and tell the world how proud you are of him.'

'Nelly, you're one of the few people in this world who have said that. Everyone thinks about Molly's needs, and mine get disregarded. I would love to shout about my son.'

We both go silent for a while. I think about everything he's been through. I am not surprised he's been acting chaotic living here.

* * *

When I wake up and head to the bathroom, I find it empty. I check the kitchen and the living room, but there's no sign of Oliver.

As I make my morning coffee and feed Lenny, I hear the front door slam shut.

'Morning, Nelly,' Oliver calls, grinning as he walks up the hallway and stands in the doorway to the kitchen. I blink. He's in a white T-shirt that clings to his chest, blue running shorts and trainers. His hair is damp with sweat, and his arms are flushed with exertion.

I immediately pretend to need something in a drawer.

A moment later, he's leaning casually in the doorway, his chest rising and falling, and his cheeks pink. The sight of him sends my brain into a mild meltdown. I try to stamp out the flutters and warmth that's coursing through my veins, but I can't.

He lifts his T-shirt to wipe his brow, and I look up. Oh, God, he has defined abs.

'How are you?'

I'm trying to erase the image of his tanned abs from my mind.

'Nelly?'

'I'm fine. How are you?'

He smiles. 'Thanks for listening to me last night. I woke up this morning and felt lighter. This bed-sharing arrangement will help me.'

'That's good.'

'I woke up early and thought I would go for a run.' He wipes his sweaty forehead with his T-shirt, and once again I get to see those delicious abs.

I can feel my face reddening.

'I need to get ready for work.'

As I pass, he steps out of my way. 'I'm looking forward to tonight. Bed-sharing is becoming the highlight of my day.'

I glance back at him, and he shoots me a dazzling smile. It takes my heart a long time to recover.

33

'Frank's ex-girlfriend has gone into labour,' Miranda announces as she arrives later than usual. 'Her waters burst in the early hours.'

'Oh – is she okay?'

'She's fine but doesn't want Frank present at the birth. He's at home frantically trawling Google for articles on how to be a father. While he was locked away in his study, I had to make his mother her soft egg and make sure she took the right medication.'

I watch Miranda dump her handbag on the till counter and let out a heavy sigh. It makes me recall my vision on her: how her love ends with Frank pushing a baby in a buggy. She's been with Frank for over fifteen years, and this must be a shock. Even though she's a nightmare boss, shares far too much about her love life, and acts like a lovesick schoolgirl when Oliver is around, she's still human. Endings are painful and messy.

'Are you okay, Miranda?'

She turns to me, and I can see her eyes are pink and watery.

'I don't want to be a stepmother, Nelly. I have never wanted kids, and this situation with Frank has not changed my view.'

'Have you spoken to Frank?'

She nods. 'He keeps saying that when I see his new baby, I will melt and have an urge to buy baby clothes, change nappies and stay up all night singing nursery rhymes.'

I know she keeps questioning what goes on inside Frank's head, but I now find myself having the same thoughts. Miranda and small babies do not mix well. The other day, a woman had a baby in a buggy, and she couldn't get it to stop crying. After five minutes, Miranda had to go lie down in the back room, as she claimed the noise had given her a migraine. If she doesn't get her full eight hours' sleep, she's evil and hates getting her hands dirty.

'I'm sorry, Miranda.'

A tear travels down her cheek, and she wipes it away. 'I'll be in the back room today. I have paperwork to do.'

I watch her walk away, shoulders stooped and head bowed. It's bad enough seeing visions of heartbreak, but watching them play out before my eyes is harder. I sense that Miranda is going to unravel.

'Hello,' says a female voice. 'I'm just wondering whether you have managed to locate my book.' I turn to see Juliet standing by the counter.

'Ah, I have a surprise,' I say, reaching down under the counter. Earlier, I'd placed Oliver's copy of the book there as I was going to call her later.

I lift out the book, *Cartas del Ayer, Amor de Hoy*. I googled the translation, and it means 'Letters from Yesterday, Love from Today'.

Juliet's face lights up as she studies the cover. 'Wow – I can't believe it's his book.'

'I take it you read Spanish?'

She smiles. 'I've been taking evening classes for years, and I even have an A level in Spanish, so this will be a good read.'

'Are you still planning to visit him?'

She nods. 'Next month. It's booked.'

The urge to touch her is strong but I hear Oliver's words in my head: *Give love a chance.* If I touched her hand and saw something upsetting, I'm not sure I could refrain from telling her something. Perhaps I should leave it up to Juliet. She needs to discover how love ends for herself.

She smiles. 'How much is the book?'

'It's a gift from Oliver James, the romance author.'

Juliet's eyes travel to the display table, piled high with Oliver's latest. She gasps. 'Was that Oliver James who was in here the other day?'

'Yes, he has paid for your book. Your story touched him. You must let him know how your trip to Spain goes.'

She hugs Miguel's book. 'Please thank Oliver, and will you tell him that I promise to report back?'

I watch her walk away, gazing longingly at Miguel's book, and a warm feeling engulfs me.

Miranda walks towards me. 'His ex-girlfriend has had a little girl.' Her eyes are red and puffy. 'I need someone to talk to.'

'Why don't I make us both a cup of tea?'

She nods, and I rush out the back. Before long, I'm bringing two mugs of tea back into the bookshop. In my back pocket, I also have two packets of tissues as I sense Miranda is going to dissolve into floods of tears.

She sits behind the counter and wraps her hands around the mug. 'Thank you, Nelly. This is what I need. A cup of soothing tea.'

'Has Frank gone to the hospital?'

'Yes. He left me instructions on what to cook his mother for her tea as he won't be back till late.'

'Oh. Is his mum pleased about the new arrival?'

Miranda shakes her head. 'His mother hates young children as much as I do.'

'I see.'

She takes a sip. 'This is a mess.'

'I'm sorry, Miranda. This must be hard for you.' I watch her put down her mug and dab her eyes. She looks devastated. This is a good reminder for me. Love rarely ends well. I need to remember this image of my broken boss.

Miranda rubs her temples. 'I know this sounds weird, Nelly, but I'm secretly relieved.'

Air gets trapped in my throat. 'Relieved?' I croak.

She sits up and wipes her eyes. 'This situation gives me a way out.'

'A what?' I stare at her.

Something flickers across her face. She sits up straighter. 'If I'm honest, my relationship with Frank has been stale for years. I spend a lot of my time lusting after other men. Frank's new baby has given me a golden opportunity.'

'Look, you're upset—'

She stands and puts her hands on her hips. 'I know what I need to do.'

'Don't make any rash decisions.'

'Nelly, this situation needs rash decisions.' A smile spreads across her face. 'I'm going to leave Frank. This heartbreak is a blessing in disguise.'

Oh, God, the heartbreak has made her delusional. 'Miranda...'

'Nelly, you will need to close the shop. I have things to do.'

Before I can say another word, she's hurried away to the back room.

Even though she claimed it was a blessing in disguise, I believe the shock of Frank's infidelity and the arrival of his child will eventually catch up with her. Tonight, she'll be teetering on the brink of a nervous breakdown while his mother enjoys her favourite meal. There's nothing positive about heartbreak; this is why I've avoided it like the plague for years.

34

'How was your evening?' I ask as Oliver climbs into bed behind the pillow wall.

When I got home from work, I found a note he'd left saying he was going to bathe Alfie and read him a bedtime story. At the bottom, he'd underlined the words, *I will be back for our bed-sharing, so don't fall asleep*. His note had given me a burst of much-needed happiness.

'It was okay,' he says, with an optimistic tone to his voice. 'Rory was home. It was a little awkward, but after, I avoided going into town and went to play Xbox at Jamie's flat.' He laughs. 'I took out all my frustration on the aliens in Jamie's new game.'

'How was Alfie?'

Oliver chuckles. 'He always makes me laugh. It's nice to be back doing baths and bedtime.'

That's odd – why did he use the words 'be back'?

I'm about to question him when he answers for me. 'Molly banned me the other week from seeing Alfie. It was after I'd argued with Rory in a pub and he punched me on the nose.'

'I see. Did Rory start the fight?'

He shakes his head. 'Rory made a comment about how he picks up Alfie from nursery. It made me cross. I tried to punch him, but I missed. He tried to calm me down, so I went in for another punch. Rory blocked it and gave me a whack to the nose.'

'Oh...'

'Molly had every right to ban me from seeing Alfie. Fighting has never been one of my strengths, Nelly.'

'Perhaps you should stick to things you are good at.'

He pauses. 'Then, later in a club, I decided to go home with his sister.'

We both go silent. The thought of Oliver getting intimate with Rory's sister makes me feel uncomfortable. I turn away from the pillow wall and face the opposite side.

'I didn't sleep with her. I stopped myself just in time. It was a stupid revenge tactic.'

His words send my stomach on a nauseating spin. I remind myself that just because Oliver and I share a bed, it doesn't mean he can't still sleep with other women.

'It wouldn't have been right to sleep with her just because I was angry at Rory and Molly for not letting me see Alfie.'

Another silence follows. I think about what he's told me. At least he could see it was wrong and he stopped himself. In a lot of my visions, I rarely see such restraint when it comes to affairs of the heart.

'Nelly? Are you asleep over there?'

'No,' I say in a quiet voice.

'I didn't fancy her. Rory's sister.'

I rearrange my pillow and turn away from the wall.

'I've apologised to her since then,' he says, making me lift my head from my pillow and look over in the direction of the wall. 'She has accepted my apology.'

He's taken responsibility for the pain he's caused. 'That's good, Oliver,' I say softly.

We both go silent for ages. Just as I think he's fallen asleep, he says, 'Nelly, I've been thinking again about all the people who once lived in this house.'

'I am warning you. It's addictive.'

I hear him pat his pillow. 'I am imagining a romance between a footman and a maid years ago.'

'Are you switching genres?'

He chuckles. 'This is an exclusive. Don't tell my agent.'

'Do you have names for your footman and maid characters?'

He pauses for a few moments. 'John and Mary. John's new to the house. He carries coal up three flights of stairs to see Mary, the maid who has caught his eye.'

I smile. 'Naturally.'

'This footman is not supposed to talk to her, so he invents reasons – polishing the same banister twice, lingering by the scullery door.' His voice softens. 'She's quiet. She acts like she's invisible, but he sees her.'

I can't lie – he knows how to put together a good romance story. A silence descends on both of us. My heart is beating so loud, I'm surprised he can't hear it.

'And him?' My voice is almost a whisper.

'John's been through a lot in his life. He's always kept his distance from women and is focused on his work, but Mary is different.'

'Why is she different?'

He pauses before saying, 'Mary has a smile like the dawn breaking over a grey and tired world. It doesn't just brighten his day. Her smile lifts the weight off his shoulders. Even the endless chores seem bearable after he's witnessed it.'

I reach out and run my hand over the pillow wall. This man is doing things to me. He's making my body light up like a row of twinkly lights.

'One night, there's a storm and a leaking roof. The great house becomes chaotic. She slips on the stairs, and he catches her.'

A warm, excited feeling is engulfing my body.

He continues. 'Mary has soot on her cheek, which he tenderly wipes with his thumb. She always looks frightened in front of the other staff, but on the stairs with him, she stares with such intensity it's as though she's looking inside him. In a moment of madness, he asks her to meet him at midnight in the garden.'

I gasp. 'Does she meet him?'

'You'll have to wait until tomorrow.' He laughs, and I fling one of my pillows over the wall at him.

'That's not fair, Oliver.'

'I thought you didn't like romance stories, Nelly?'

I stare at the pillow wall as words jostle on the tip of my tongue.

He starts to clap. 'I'm going to convert you to romantic fiction, Nelly.'

'Careful,' I say, which makes him laugh.

35

When I wake up, I know Oliver is in the bathroom as I can hear the shower running.

The sound of him singing in the shower drifts through the wall, causing my heart to have an early morning flutter. I go to the kitchen to make myself a coffee. I have my back to the doorway when I hear his voice. 'Good morning, Nelly.'

It makes me jolt and spill the coffee I've just poured. When I turn round, he's in his dressing gown. His hair is dripping wet, and he's beaming at me.

'Do you fancy going for a picnic tonight?' he asks.

I blink. 'A picnic?'

He shrugs. 'It's going to be nice weather tonight. What do you think?'

My anxiety climbs into the driving seat. 'I'm not sure what I'm doing.'

He grins. 'Nelly, you've not been out since I moved in. Come on. I need to get you out.'

A picnic. That doesn't sound too bad. I nibble on my thumb, a habit that soothes me.

'Don't worry, it's not a date,' he says. 'We're two flatmates having a picnic.'

I am glad he's clarified that.

He flicks his wet hair out of his face, and in doing so, he lets his robe slip. It reveals his tanned, muscular shoulder, and my heart goes berserk.

'What about Alfie?'

'He's at his gran's tonight, so I'm not needed. How about it?'

'Yes, okay.'

I should never have agreed to this. My body is a traitor. I see one flash of some tanned and well-defined shoulder, and I agree to all sorts.

Oliver's suggestion is making my heart go wild. I am blaming that slip of a robe for everything. On the way to work, I pop in my earbuds and search for a suitable song to soothe my flustered state. To my frustration, I can't find any songs written about two flatmates, who share a bed because of a plumbing leak, and decide to have a completely innocent picnic together.

* * *

My day at the bookshop is quiet. Miranda has decided to take the day off. She rang me as I walked to work. I was expecting her to sound like she'd hit rock bottom, but she sounded almost gleeful. 'I have some things I need to sort out,' she gushed. 'It's exciting. Have a great day, Nelly.'

The ending of a fifteen-year relationship and heartbreak is not meant to sound like this. My curse has always shown me suffering and upset. Maybe the extent of Frank's betrayal has not hit her fully yet.

I've tried to touch as many people as possible, and my list

has reached over three pages. Oliver is still the only person my curse doesn't work on.

Eva pops in at lunchtime, and I talk to her about the picnic.

'What are you thinking of wearing?' she asks, leaning over the counter and fiddling with a glittery pen.

'He said we don't have to dress smart.'

She scrunches up her face. 'Please don't tell me you're wearing grey jeans and a black T-shirt. You need to do something with your hair, too. I'm thinking loose curls.' She smiles and surveys my clothes. 'A pretty dress would be ideal for a picnic. Maybe topped off with some white sandals.'

'It's just a picnic, Eva.'

She raises her eyebrows and grins. '*Is* it just a picnic, Nelly?'

My heart performs a series of flips, which I quickly suppress. Once again, she has not warned me about him. 'You've changed your tune. When you came to my flat you kept telling me to stay away from him.'

After a flick of her blonde hair, she smiles. 'I did warn you but then I thought about this situation. It's time you started experiencing what the rest of us endure. We don't get free dating spoilers. We just put our faith in someone and cling to a scrap of hope that they're not an arsehole.'

I let out a groan.

She smiles. 'Whatever happens between you and Oliver will be an experience and I think you need it. For too long, you've feared getting your heart broken. You need to face your fears.'

'I'm not getting into anything with Oliver,' I say, while secretly praying I do get into something with him while he's wearing that fitted white shirt with the undone buttons.

'Enjoy your picnic. I'll be on WhatsApp waiting for an update,' she says with a wink.

Late in the afternoon, I'm picking up the box of glittery pens that a small child knocked onto the floor when the man who bought the book on dogs approaches the desk. I look up to see him carrying a small puppy. I recall that his ex-wife had taken his much-loved Labrador to Scotland and he bought the book as a comforter. He recognises me and smiles. 'I thought I would come and introduce you. I saw this puppy in the rehoming centre, and I couldn't resist.'

The puppy is a small golden Labrador, and it licks my hand.

'I can't replace Sandy,' he says, 'but this little one is going to help fill in the gaps.'

'Do they have a name?'

He beams. 'She's called Hope.'

'That's lovely.'

'I've also made a new friend with one of the ladies at the rehoming centre.'

As he turns to leave, I make sure my hand brushes his bare arm. I see him as an elderly man sitting by a bed with an elderly lady in it. He's holding her hand and saying, 'I'm so glad Hope brought us together all those years ago.'

The world becomes muffled and I think about how he's giving love a chance and it will pay off – he and his new love interest will grow old together. I smile at him as he places a kiss on his puppy's head.

* * *

Oliver and I are standing in my hallway. He's wearing a fitted navy shirt, sleeves rolled up to reveal his strong, tanned forearms. His hair is messy and tousled. I have an urge to run my fingers through it. In his hand is a wicker picnic basket he borrowed from Jamie, and he claims there are a lot of nice things to eat inside.

'You look great, Nelly,' he says as his eyes wander over my face, my hair – which is not in its usual messy bun but is spread over my shoulders with the ends containing some soft curls – and my pink and white gingham dress.

Earlier, as I climbed the stairs to the flat, I reassured myself that my old grey jeans and black T-shirt would suffice.

I can't read too much into this. We are simply two adults eating outdoors. It won't lead to anything. Oliver and I will be bonding over sandwiches.

Oliver was ready when I got in, and the sight of him in the hallway robbed me of breath. I don't think handsome is good enough for how he looks. There was a stirring in my lower belly, and a warm sensation spread up my legs.

Seconds later, I raced to my wardrobe and opened the section I had locked away while Eva was here. Eva used to comment on my attire. She encouraged me to overhaul my wardrobe and try different hairstyles. She refused to come with me to a cocktail bar if I was going to be dressed in my usual comfort-zone outfit. As a result, I refreshed my wardrobe. When we fell out, I put all the new clothes she had made me buy into a separate part of my wardrobe and vowed never to wear them again. After selecting my gingham dress, I curled my hair and even applied some make-up. When I stepped out of my bedroom, he was standing in the hallway. His eyes widened dramatically and he took a step back. Clearly not expecting such a transformation.

'Where are we going?' I ask.

His dark eyes have been embedded with a glint of excitement. 'It's a secret.'

I let out a silent groan and pray we're not going to a busy park.

As we step out of the flat, he takes a key from his pocket and heads towards the private communal garden. 'Gary gave me a key.' I take a deep breath. The garden is not somewhere I usually go, as I have always preferred to lock myself away.

'Nelly, come on,' encourages Oliver. 'Do something new.'

I think back to how I swam in the sea when I was at Aunt Polly's. That was new for me. It turned out better than I expected. Maybe I should give the garden a chance?

As we enter, I let my eyes sweep over the patch of grass, the scattering of trees and the pretty shrubs. My breath catches in my throat. It's idyllic. Why have I never come in here?

Oliver smiles and strides ahead carrying his picnic basket. I watch as he lays out a beautiful red and white blanket which is more than big enough for both of us. He then takes out an array of fabulous things to eat: little pork pies, cheeses, cold meats, pickles, salad and a bag of crisps. 'Tuck in.' He beams, handing me a paper plate and a napkin.

'This is wonderful,' I say, before biting into a pork pie.

'I have been meaning to ask you, have you seen Juliet at all?'

I smile. 'She came in the other day, and I gave her Miguel's book.'

'Wow, that's great. I bet she was pleased. Did you tell her about my request?'

I nod. 'She's going to keep you updated. Apparently, she's been learning Spanish and has now booked a trip out to Spain.'

'Juliet is giving love a chance,' says Oliver, holding my gaze. 'This is good therapy for you and me.'

'How was your day?'

'I thought a lot about the footman and the scullery maid.' His hair falls softly across his forehead, and his eyes are sparkling with mischief. He looks so handsome sitting in the dappled sunlight.

'Do they meet at midnight?'

'Let's finish the picnic, and I will fill you in.' His voice is warm and low, reminding me of our lovely late-night chats over the pillow wall. I am captivated by his deep brown eyes and his boyish smile.

We make a serious dent into his picnic food and then clear everything away. Our hands brush several times, and my curse is still silent.

Once the blanket is clear, he lies on his side, propping himself up on an elbow. I sit on the far edge of the blanket, hugging my knees but secretly longing to lie down beside him.

'Our maid, Mary, gets caught attempting to sneak out by the lady of the house,' Oliver says, holding my gaze. 'She's sent to help clean up. The leak causes chaos. Everyone in the house goes into a frenzy.'

'Oh no. Does that mean...'

Oliver sits up and nods. 'Our footman, John, is left alone in the garden. He thinks she doesn't love him.' He hangs his head, and I feel an ache in my chest.

'Has he been hurt before?' I make circles with my finger on the picnic blanket.

His finger starts to follow mine. 'Yes, he has, but he can't stop thinking about the maid, her beautiful smile, her sapphire-blue eyes and the way she makes him laugh on the stairs.' He pauses. 'Our footman can also feel the heaviness of lonely nights in her heart while the streets below echo with laughter.'

I don't know how this happened, but we have both inched towards each other. This story he's made up about the lonely footman and maid has made me throw all common sense over the park's railings behind us.

'I want to get to know you, Nelly.'

'Me?' My heart starts to thud. There's not much to tell apart from a lot of books, a leaky ceiling, a cat who should be renamed Houdini... oh, and a curse.

He smiles. 'Don't look so scared. This is me. Let's start with something easy. When was your last holiday?'

'Umm... I can't remember the last time I went away.' I would love to go on holiday and explore distant places, but the thought of enduring a long-haul flight and witnessing a stream of sad, tragic scenes from fellow passengers has put me off.

'Okay. What's the last music concert you went to?'

I squirm and fidget on the blanket. 'I've never been to a music concert.'

He stares at me. 'Really?'

I nod. My face is reddening, and it feels hot. My curse has kept me away from the pain and suffering that love can bring; however, the price it demands is that I relinquish aspects of life like music concerts, theatres and holidays.

'Ah,' he says, 'I bet you're an avid theatre goer.'

This is too much. 'I'm not feeling too well.'

'Oh, I am sorry,' he says, looking crestfallen. 'You have gone very pale.'

'The picnic was lovely,' I say, getting to my feet. 'I need to go back inside.'

He nods and casts me a worrying look as I act like I'm a secret vampire who's been out in the sun too long and needs to return to darkness.

36

It's still light when we climb into bed in our pyjamas.

'Hello,' Oliver says from behind the pillows. The sound of his voice makes my heart beat faster. I think he's facing our makeshift wall. It gives me a rush of tingling sensations.

'Hello.' I am pressed close to the pillow wall.

'Have I said anything wrong?' he asks.

'No.'

'Nelly, you're like a medieval castle with a moat and a huge drawbridge. Most of the time, I feel as though your drawbridge is up, and you've filled your moat with man-eating crocodiles.'

His analogy makes me smile.

'I sense you're keeping something from me.'

I flinch and turn my head away. My defences rise. I don't want to ruin a good evening by talking about my curse. That would kill the mood. It would also mean the end of us, as he'd see me as a freak or a witch.

'Can we not talk about this?' I need to focus on something else.

'Sure.' His voice sounds upbeat. 'Ask me anything?'

I think about the photo of the little boy. 'Is that Alfie in the photo over there?'

'Yes, that's him with his favourite teddy.' I notice the lightness in his voice when he speaks about Alfie.

'I see there's a photo of you and Jamie.'

He chuckles. 'Younger and fresh-faced versions of me and Jamie.'

'How did you meet?'

'We went to school together – Jamie, Rory and me.'

'Oh.'

'We all go back a long way. That's why it hurts so much with Rory. He was my best mate. We've been through so much together. He knew what I went through with Molly. When Molly and I broke up, he made a move on her.'

He goes quiet for a while. I don't say anything.

'When I see him with Alfie, it makes me so cross.' His voice has a firm edge to it.

'That must be hard.'

He rearranges his pillows. 'I can't believe I've been betrayed by the two people who once meant a lot to me.' I hear him let out a heavy sigh. 'I worry about Alfie picking up on the atmosphere when I go over there.'

'How's Rory towards you?'

'He keeps trying to take me aside and talk things through. I have nothing to say to him, and he can stop advising me on my son.'

I'm sensing that Rory is trying to make peace with Oliver.

'Maybe you should talk to him?'

Oliver scoffs. 'It would end up with me punching him.'

'Alfie would want everyone to be happy.' My words don't land well as he goes silent for what feels like an eternity.

'Let's talk about our footman and maid,' he says after such a long pause I assumed he'd fallen asleep. 'John doesn't see Mary the following day. His heart is aching.'

I place my hand gently on the pillow wall. 'Why is his heart aching?'

'He doesn't understand why she didn't show up.' Oliver pauses before saying, 'He senses she's got secrets, but he doesn't care about them.'

'What are they?' I pray Mary is cursed.

'She's carrying an emotional burden, and it's getting heavier by the day.'

Definitely a curse. My heart skips a beat. 'Some secrets need to stay hidden.'

Oliver continues. 'Later that evening, he catches her in the servants' stairwell. The house is silent. A candle flickers in the draught. "You shouldn't be here," she whispers.'

My breath catches in my throat.

'The footman steps closer to her. He says, "If I listened to them, I would never see you. Why didn't you meet me last night?" They both can hear footsteps and laughter from the kitchen downstairs.' He leans closer.

Oliver's voice is silky smooth, making me want to unravel.

'She says, "The lady of the house caught me." There are more voices, and the candle flickers. "Someone could catch us," she whispers as he lifts a hand and touches a lock of her red hair. He bends down and presses his lips...'

'But what about her secrets?' I gasp.

'He wants her to let him carry the weight of whatever she's hiding.'

This is excruciating. He's got such a sexy voice, and I am so involved in this romantic tale about a handsome footman and a shy maid. My body is becoming engulfed in a warm sensation. I want to knock down the pillow wall and kiss him. That would lead to sex. I might be a virgin, but I'm not a complete novice. I know how things work. Sam and I accomplished a few things, but we never had the chance to see it through.

I am still a virgin, though. Not only that, but I am a virgin with a curse.

My heart sinks. I'm like the unicorn of the modern dating world – a rare, mythical creature that no one believes exists.

Oh, God, he's not going to find me attractive.

What am I doing?

He's a romance author. Intimacy will be his speciality. Romance authors enjoy crafting spicy scenes. He's probably used to experienced women in bed. Damn my stupid curse.

I can't do this.

'Are you tired, Nelly?'

'Yes.'

'Goodnight then.'

'Goodnight.'

37

It's early morning. He is still asleep, so I have decided to take a shower. As I dunk my head under cooling jets of water, I recall our lovely picnic and how my overthinking got the better of me.

Having strong feelings for Oliver and not knowing how it will end between us is frustrating. I have nothing concrete to rely on. I now have a newfound appreciation for ordinary people who enter relationships, flings, situationships, and affairs without spoiler alerts. They must navigate dating blindly, hoping that their time, effort, emotions and sanity are not wasted when it ends.

Once I have washed my hair, applied an excessive amount of Tropical Burst Shower Foam to my body and rinsed it off, I step out of the shower and dry myself.

After wrapping my hair in a towel, I put on my dressing gown and notice that the cord is missing. Blast – it's probably escaped. I pull my robe around me and open the bathroom door. The sight of him standing in the hallway makes me gasp. He's removed his pyjama top, leaving him bare-chested, wearing only his striped pyjama bottoms, and his towel is tucked under his arm. My eyes dart to his beautiful broad chest. It's a rich caramel colour and nearly hairless. I want to reach out and run my fingers over his pecs. His dark hair is messy and sexy, and those pyjama bottoms of his are riding low on his hips.

He's staring at me with a newfound intensity. Ripples of warmth are spreading over my body. His eyes shift from my face and glide down my body. I observe them widen in surprise, and then he swiftly covers his eyes with his hand.

My heart grinds to a halt, and I gasp.

My arms are by my sides and… my dressing gown is gaping open like a curtain call at the worst possible theatre.

Oh, God, what have I done?

My face is on fire. This is so embarrassing. I have been a stranger to hair removal cream for some time. I dread to think what images are going through his head right now; a thick, dense forest perhaps?

'I didn't see anything,' he says, still with his hands over his eyes.

With a yelp, I race past him, get dressed in record time and leave the flat.

On my way to work, I pop in my earbuds and frantically search for a song to soothe my shocked state. I need something dramatic about showing far too much of yourself in front of a handsome flatmate. Sadly, music doesn't come to my rescue in my hour of need.

Miranda hurries over to me when I enter the bookshop.

Today, she's wearing a short metallic silver skirt and a red-and-white pinstriped shirt.

'I've joined a dating app. Things are going to heat up.'

'What?' I stare at her in shock. Where's the suffering? The pain that takes months to alleviate? Where's the anger that causes her to cut up all his clothes? 'Miranda – are you okay?'

She nods. 'Never been better. My relationship with Frank went past its sell-by date years ago. It's time for me to move on. He has done me a favour. I'm going to enjoy myself.' With a cackle of laughter, she walks off to the romance section and picks up one of the new spicy romance books that has arrived in stock.

Henry enters the shop mid-morning, carrying a bunch of flowers. It looks like he's tamed his mass of black curls. He's wearing a fitted blue shirt and beige jeans. 'These are for you,' he says. 'I felt like I said something wrong the other day and I don't want to lose your friendship again.'

I take the flowers – pink and yellow tulips. 'Thank you, Henry. You didn't say anything wrong.'

'Nelly, you have an admirer,' squeals Miranda. I groan as I see that she's approaching the counter. Henry casts her a nervous smile.

I introduce them, and Miranda coos over the flowers. 'They are pretty flowers.' She turns to Henry. 'I am going to have to keep an eye on Nelly. She's already proving to be a big hit with a certain bestselling author, and now it seems you are also a fan, Henry.'

My cheeks redden at Miranda's cringy comment. I notice his smile has faded. 'Oh, I see,' he mumbles. 'I didn't realise...'

Miranda giggles and interrupts him. 'Lovely to meet you, Henry. I must dash as I have joined a dating app, and I already have a few admirers myself. Life in this bookshop is certainly hotting up for Nelly and me.'

She hurries away. Henry and I exchange awkward smiles. 'I'd better get back to work,' he says, gesturing towards the door.

'Sorry about my boss,' I mumble. 'She's—'

'Just like you described her,' he says, interrupting me. 'Interesting.'

'Thanks again for the flowers.'

'Let's do coffee again – what about next week, Nelly?'

'That would be nice.'

I watch him leave the shop, and thoughts about Mum race to the front of my mind. My heart aches. If she did have it – why didn't she tell me? Why didn't she warn me?

Eva meets me for lunch. We sit on the bench outside the bookshop. Her blonde hair is full of waves, and she has a hint of sparkly lip gloss on her lips. It feels like the old days. She holds up her hand. 'I want to hug you, Nelly. I know we've been avoiding it, but I want to say something first...'

The word 'hug' makes me flinch. Eva and I have been here before.

'I've been seeing this guy from Tinder. He's sweet, he's the drummer in a band and I think he's a keeper so whatever your curse says, I will ignore.'

'Our hot rocker manifestation board worked then?'

'It only took a few years.' She laughs before pulling me into a hug. 'I've missed you so much, Nelly.'

There's a flash of white light, and when it clears, I can see a tear-stained Eva and a guy with big hair, in a white vest, skintight jeans and carrying two drumsticks. She's showing him her phone screen. 'You have three secret dating app profiles. Let me read what this bio says.' He shakes his head and screws up his face as if she's going to show him something gory. She continues. '"Must be up for something kinky while I'm on tour." You forgot to add, must be okay with being cheated on.'

Why does my curse have to show me this? After everything I've been through with Eva.

The world has gone quiet. She's staring at me intently.

I blink several times as the sound of two women talking

about their morning at work and a child laughing in a buggy greets my ears.

'What have you seen, Nelly?'

I try to look away, but she is insistent. 'Tell me. I'll be okay with whatever it is. Rex and I will work it out.'

I hang my head and let out a silent groan. I'm not meant to have female friendships. Who wants me as a friend when all I do is tell them how the love of their life will break their heart?

'Nelly, talk to me.'

I cling to her assurance that she and Rex can work through his desires to cheat while he's on tour. 'Secret dating app profiles.'

Eva goes quiet for what feels like an eternity. Just when I think my curse has ruined our friendship a second time, she smiles and says, 'He's in a rock band, and they go on tour a lot. I think I was being delusional expecting him to stay single. Friendship is more important to me.'

'Eva, I've just told you—'

She smiles and pulls out a little gift from her bag. 'It's okay, Nelly. Honestly. It's your birthday tomorrow, so I bought you this.'

My birthday. With everything that's happened recently, I'd forgotten about my birthday. 'You remembered?'

'Nelly, I always think of you on your birthday. I will deal with Rex. Are you doing anything nice?'

I shake my head. 'I'm going to see Aunt Polly. She's struggling with the chemo. I was also planning to go swimming again.'

'What?' She looks shocked. 'Are you swimming? You used to say it reminded—'

'It did remind me of Mum, but I have done a lot of thinking, and I read a brilliant book about how the water heals. Mum would have wanted me to keep swimming.'

'That's amazing,' gushes Eva. 'Nelly, I am so proud of you. That can't have been easy.'

She hands me the gift. 'Well, maybe you can take this with you and open it.'

'Thank you, Eva.' I look at the little blue gift wrapped up with a gold ribbon.

She remembered my birthday.

I watch as she takes out her phone and brings up a photo of Rex, the drummer.

'Will you dump him?' I ask.

To my amazement, she shrugs. 'I might just use him for sex and fun.'

'But I saw—'

She turns to me. 'He's cute, he makes me laugh and we are going to some cool gigs. At least I know where things are heading. I might hang around for the good parts.'

My eyebrows arch. 'Good parts?'

'Nelly, love isn't all about how it ends.'

'But that's all I have ever seen.'

She smiles. 'One day you will see that love is about the glorious starts and the lovely middle bits.'

'But what about the pain and heartbreak?'

She shrugs. 'We all get through it, Nelly. Yes, there are days when you're going through that, and all you want to do is lie on the sofa, eat cereal and binge-watch sad films, but it's survivable. It also teaches you things like if you have suspicions about your boyfriend fancying your sister, it's probably best to do something about them as opposed to ignoring the smell of her perfume on his clothes and pretending he didn't murmur her name when he was asleep.'

An awkward feeling passes over me. 'Really?'

'Nelly, I blamed you when I had been ignoring the signs for ages. I got through the break-up. It was hard, but I did it, and I am still here smiling – aren't I?'

'You are, Eva.'

'Sometimes, heartbreak is nothing more than a few days wandering around the house feeling sad and eating cereal. Sometimes you don't feel right for a few months, like an annoying dose of the flu. Sometimes it is like standing in the eye of a hurricane as, once the winds stop, your old world has been destroyed.' She looks at me. 'But you will get through it. How was the picnic? You never updated me.'

'There was nothing to tell. He does know how to put a good picnic spread together, though.'

She giggles. 'I love it.'

'I'm sorry about my curse, Eva.'

'I don't care about your curse, Nelly. You are more important than Rex's secret dating profiles.'

We both laugh and I am flooded with a lovely warm feeling. Eva is back in my life and she's not afraid or angry about my curse.

As I head back to the bookshop, I find myself reflecting on what she said about heartbreak. She says it's survivable and love isn't about the endings. Maybe there is hope for me?

38

'Happy birthday, Nelly,' gushes Aunt Polly as she opens the door. She goes to hug me but sees my wet hair. 'I see you've been for an early morning swim.'

'It was my birthday, so I thought – why not? The water was lovely, and I swam for ages. I could do with a shower, though.'

She laughs. 'Come inside, go get freshened up and we will go to The Sailing Boat café for a birthday treat.'

'Are you sure?'

She nods. 'The fresh sea air will do me good.'

Once I have showered and washed my hair I come downstairs.

I watch as my aunt surveys my outfit. 'Nelly, you look great.'

This morning, after I woke up, I put on my swimming costume under my clothes, and I also decided to pack a different outfit for once I'd showered after my swim. I remembered the other evening, of the picnic, standing in front of my mirror and feeling good. I also recall the look Oliver gave me when he saw me step out of my bedroom. I return to the part of my wardrobe I had once closed off after Eva left. My fingers flicked through the hangers. I pulled out a white shirt and some blue jeans, folded them neatly and put them in my bag.

I do feel different standing in my aunt's hallway, wearing my white shirt and smart blue jeans. I have also let my hair down and not put it into a bun.

It's a slow walk to the café, but it's nice as Aunt Polly and I walk arm in arm along the promenade. We make frequent stops to watch the salty waves break on the shore, while excited children race across the golden sand. I recall floating in the sea earlier, watching the sunshine dance on the surface like golden glitter being poured onto blue paint. I remember feeling a sense of relief as I let the sea hold me. I'd seen an upsetting vision on the train, and it had been on my mind as I entered the water; a woman finding her husband in bed with her boss. The water seemed to carry away my sad thoughts. When I got out, I felt lighter and excited about my birthday.

On the last stop, Aunt Polly turns to me with watery eyes. 'I tried to bake you a birthday cake, but I felt so terrible this morning and...'

'What is it?'

She puts her hands over her face. 'I had a disaster. The kitchen is a mess,' she says through her fingers.

'You don't need to bake me a cake, and I'll clear everything away.'

She takes her hands away and shakes her head. 'You're not tidying up the kitchen on your birthday, Nelly.'

I smile at her. 'I am, and you're too weak to fight me.'

She laughs and we carry on walking.

We have a lovely time at the café, and Aunt Polly treats me to a cake.

When we return to her bungalow, she groans as I survey the baking disaster zone. The work surfaces are strewn with flour, bits of dough, dirty bowls, utensils, and sat in a tin is a sad-looking cake with a saggy centre.

'Wow – you have been busy,' I say, jokingly.

She laughs. 'Can we never mention this again?'

'Go and sit down. I will sort this.'

She doesn't put up much of a fight. I watch her head for the sofa. While she sits and watches TV, I clear away the mess, put the cake in the bin and wash up. As I am putting the clean baking equipment back in her bottom drawer I spot a pile of letters. That's weird. Why would she keep letters in her baking drawer? I am about to have a closer look when my aunt calls me. 'Nelly, come in here, I have something to show you.'

Aunt Polly looks up at me as I enter the living room.

I sit down in her armchair and notice a cardboard box. 'What's in there, Aunt Polly?'

'That's the box of stuff I found at the back of my wardrobe. Remember that photo album I showed you? The one where we both got sad and had to put it away?'

'What else is in the box?' I peer into it.

Aunt Polly reaches down to underneath her coffee table and pulls out a little wrapped gift. 'This was at the bottom of the box. I've been saving it for your birthday.'

'What is it?' I ask.

She passes me the gift and rolls her eyes. 'Nelly, it's a present, and I'm not going to tell you before you open it.'

I take it from her and smile at the rose-patterned paper and pink ribbon.

She watches me as I carefully unwrap it. Once I remove the paper, I'm left with an old notebook.

'It was your mother's,' says Aunt Polly. 'She would have wanted you to have it. I didn't realise I still had it.'

'What's inside?'

She shrugs. 'I haven't read it. That's your job.'

I run my fingers over the soft blue cover. Holding it up, I fan the handwritten pages. The sight of her swirly letters makes the air catch in my throat. I think about what Henry told me. Aunt Polly can sense something is wrong. 'Nelly, talk to me. What's on your mind?'

I explain about meeting Henry, our coffee and what he told me. 'Do you think Mum had my curse?' I blink away tears. 'Why didn't she tell me?'

'You were nine years old, Nelly. If she did have it then maybe she was planning to wait until you were a bit older. It's quite a big thing for a child to understand. Also, can you stop calling it a curse? It's a gift.'

I hold up her notebook. 'Maybe this will explain things?'

Aunt Polly smiles. 'If it does give you answers, great, but if it doesn't, don't be upset with your mum. She was doing her best.'

'I'll save it for later,' I croak.

On the train home, I decide to read Mum's notebook when I am alone. It feels too special to read on a busy train, crowded with a constant stream of visions. Even though the visions I see are heartbreaking, I notice they don't make me feel heavy or sad. I acknowledge each one and remember what Eva said about heartbreak. I also recall being in the water and that light feeling I had when I got out.

Tiredness washes over me as I climb the stairs to my flat. I'm worried that tonight I won't be able to keep my eyes open, and I want to because I really enjoy my chats in bed with Oliver. He doesn't even know it's my birthday – I left before he woke up and haven't mentioned it.

I stagger along the hallway and as I put my key in the lock, the door opens. He's standing behind the door. 'Come in, birthday girl.'

'Wait – how do you know?'

He grins. 'Miranda texted me.'

'She told you?'

Miranda never fails to shock me, but then again, she was behind me and Oliver flat sharing. She's desperate for us to work because it will benefit her business.

He nods. 'Now come in as I have a surprise.'

I walk in, and he leads the way into the living room. The sight that greets me makes me gasp. He has decorated my chair with coloured bunting and tied two balloons on strings to each arm. The coffee table has been transformed. It contains little plates of sausage rolls, sandwiches cut into triangles, crisps, baked pizza slices and sticks of carrot and celery. 'Welcome to your birthday party, Nelly.'

I look at him. 'You've done all this for me?'

He grins. 'Sit down. Let's eat. Lenny is around here somewhere. I had to guard the sausage rolls as he had his eye on them.'

We have the most delightful party meal. When we've finished, he clears everything away and brings out a little cake with candles on it.

It's a wonderful evening and one of the best I've had in a very long time. I open Eva's gift and gasp. It's a tiny silver necklace with an 'N'-shaped charm.

'That's lovely,' says Oliver. 'Who's it from?'

'My friend Eva.' I hold it up and watch the light bounce off the little charm.

Lenny comes for a stroke, which is nice.

'What have you two been up to?' I ask.

Oliver smiles. 'Lenny has been asleep on my writing desk for most of the day. And I managed to get some words down.'

'Oh, wow. That's great.'

He gives me a sheepish smile. 'I'm trying my best. I went back on social media stuff earlier and it was nice. Getting back into it.'

'This is progress.'

I check the time on my phone and suppress a yawn. 'It's nearly nine. Do you fancy an early night?'

He smiles. 'Another instalment of the footman and the maid?'

I start to giggle, and we both laugh.

He looks like a different Oliver to the one I saw in my kitchen a few weeks ago. There's a brightness to his eyes, his brow is not as furrowed and his shoulders are relaxed.

We get up from our seats. I'm so busy thinking about how handsome he looks and how fabulous his birthday surprise has been that I don't spot Lenny weaving himself through my legs. I try to move away from my chair, but trip over the cat and crash into Oliver.

I look up and find myself in his arms.

39

'Can I kiss you, Nelly?' His voice is soft and smooth. 'Lenny is fine... before you ask.'

Without hesitation, I nod, and our lips touch. There is no vision, but I am too wrapped up in him to care. It's a slow and tender kiss. As he pulls me closer and our kiss intensifies, I can't help but compare his style to Sam's. If I am honest, Sam's kiss was more like a fast spin on my washing machine, whereas Oliver takes his time to kiss me properly.

We both come up for air and exchange shocked looks.

'Wow, Nelly,' he gushes, 'that was some kiss.'

I cast him a nervous smile. 'You're not so bad yourself.'

'Happy birthday.' He beams and strokes my hand.

What happens now? Anxiety is coursing through my veins.

'Don't worry,' he says, sensing my worry. 'I'll stay behind my pillow wall tonight.'

'Really?'

He nods. 'I sense you've been badly hurt in the past and I'm not going to rush you.'

Relief floods through me.

We change into our pyjamas in separate rooms. Once finished we get into our respective parts of the bed either side of the pillow wall. 'Have you seen Alfie today?'

'I saw my little boy earlier,' he gushes. I can hear the excitement in his voice. 'Rory was at work.'

'How was he?'

I hear him chuckle. 'Kept showing me his new truck. We played with his toys for ages.'

Hearing this makes my heart swell. 'That's nice.'

'It is different when Rory isn't there. I can relax and focus on Alfie.'

I position my pillow next to the wall. 'Alfie is your priority.'

'I never feel like I am a good father to him.'

'You've moved here to be close to him. You do bedtimes, bath times and you play trucks. You talk about wanting to share your life with Alfie. That's the important stuff.'

I can feel him edging closer to the pillow wall. 'Yes, you're right.'

'You could have stayed in London.'

'I know. I need to stop getting triggered by Rory.'

I pause and wonder whether I should say what's on my mind. Taking a deep breath, I decide to go for it. 'Think about Alfie. He doesn't need arguing adults around him. Kids pick up on that sort of thing.'

He goes silent for ages, and I nibble on my thumb. Have I said the wrong thing? I'm about to open my mouth when he says, 'You're right. I should think of Alfie.'

I smile at the pillow wall. Oliver might be starting to listen to me.

'Shall we talk about—'

I interrupt him. 'John and Mary.'

He chuckles. 'Okay. John and Mary have been meeting in

the private communal garden to kiss after dark. John is falling hopelessly in love with Mary.'

'Really?'

'As I've said before, she's different. One night, under the light of a silvery moon, he begs her to tell him her secret. At first, she remains guarded and tight-lipped.'

'That's how she's survived,' I whisper into the darkness.

Oliver pauses and then continues. His voice softens. 'She says to John, "There's something I need to tell you. I've lied to everyone here."'

I gasp.

'"They think my wages are for my mother,"' Oliver says in Mary's voice. '"But it's for my boy. If I'm lucky, I see him once a year. He's growing and I miss him. I can't go back as I have nothing to offer him."'

'How does John react?'

'He cups her cheek with his hand and says, "You've carried that alone?"'

My heart is beating so loud in my chest.

'Mary tries to pull away as she thinks she's unlovable. John takes her in his arms and says, "You've shown more courage than anyone in this house. How could I not admire that?"'

I wipe away a stray tear. Would Oliver admire me for carrying my secret?

* * *

He's standing outside the bathroom when I emerge after my morning shower. Luckily, I have found the cord for my robe, and there's no danger of it coming apart this time.

His hair is tousled, his dark eyes are shining and he's ditched his pyjama top, which means his muscular, tanned chest is back on show. I can feel myself being drawn to his sexy smile. He's like a powerful magnet, and I am a helpless little paper clip.

'Good morning,' he says, taking my hand. It makes me hold my breath in case a vision appears, but there is nothing. We gaze at each other, and the chemistry between us sizzles up my arm. He pulls me towards him and tilts my chin up to meet his coffee-coloured eyes. They dazzle with affection as he kisses me. The kiss is sensuous and ignites a fire within me. We both start to giggle and he kisses me on the forehead before going into the bathroom.

After getting changed we sit at the kitchen table and have coffee. He holds my hand, which still feels odd. 'Did you have a nice birthday?'

'One of the best,' I murmur before he leans over for a kiss.

When we come up for air he asks about Aunt Polly. I explain she's struggling with the effects of the chemo. He strokes my hand. 'Did you find out about what happened between your aunt and Hilary?'

'I've been so wrapped with helping her and going swimming.'

His face lights up. 'Swimming? Really?'

I nod. 'Margo Lane's book worked. I love being back in the water.'

He kisses me again and I must tear myself away from him or I will never get to work.

* * *

Today, Miranda is wearing a denim mini dress and strappy brown sandals. After I have complimented her outfit, she reaches down behind the counter and, to my amazement, pulls out a book-shaped wrapped gift. 'Happy birthday, Nelly.'

I open it and let out a silent groan.

Miranda giggles. 'It's time you read your new boyfriend's novel… I mean, flatmate.'

'Thank you, I appreciate this.' Perhaps Miranda is becoming a nicer person?

She points over to the romance section. 'You need to use your feminine charms on him as I could do with him hosting a regular book signing event here. Now that I am a single woman, I need all the financial help I can get.'

I feel a prickle of irritation. I thought she was being thoughtful for my birthday, but she has not changed.

Alice appears at the counter. Her cheery smile helps calm me down.

'I've been doing some thinking,' she says, fiddling with one of the glittery pens on the counter. 'About the message in the balloon. You were right to warn me about his kids, but…' She pauses. 'I like the sound of Amber's dad, and I have been getting weird signs.'

'Signs?'

She sighs. 'You'll probably think I am mad, but I keep seeing adverts for Monopoly and last night I watched a film about a man who found a message in a balloon. He didn't know who it was from, but it turned out it was from the new love of his life. The universe is telling me something and I need to give—'

Oliver's words fly out of my mouth. 'Give love a chance?'

Alice's eyes grow bigger in surprise. 'Weird – that's what I was going to say. That's another sign.'

I smile at her. 'Good idea. I can help you.'

She casts me a puzzled expression. 'Last week, you were not so sure.'

I recall the way she and Ben looked at each other that day. There was a definite spark of attraction. Kate's face flashes up inside my mind. She loved a good romance book when she was part of Miranda's book club, especially plots where the characters were brought together in the most unlikely of situations. The idea of a woman responding to a message hidden inside a balloon and wanting to contact the sad, widowed father sounds like something out of a romance book. If Kate is looking down on us, she would love this.

I take a deep breath. 'I think you and Ben will make a great couple. His kids are lovely.'

She frowns. 'I thought you said they were a handful.'

I can't mess this up. 'When you saw me, I was having a bad day. I am sorry.'

Her face softens. 'No worries. What shall we do?'

'Leave it to me. Are you around today?'

'I am.' She takes out her phone. 'This is my number. Do you think I will like him? Is he good-looking?'

I don't want to give the game away. I know she will be more than impressed. 'He's okay.'

I make a note of her number. 'Right, let me get to work.'

She's about to go when she turns back. 'Did you know Kate, the mum?'

'Yes, I did. She came to the book club here. Kate was lovely. She loved a good romance novel. She would have raved about that film you saw.'

Alice smiles. 'That's another sign.'

I watch her leave the bookshop and glance at the romance section. A woman who has the same red hair that Kate had is flicking through a pink novel. I smile to myself and tidy up the box of glittery pens on the counter.

An hour later, I'm serving a customer when Amber walks in,

chewing her gum, AirPods slotted into her ears and inspecting her silvery nails. Once I've finished with my customer, I go to find her in the young adult section.

'Amber,' I say as she flicks through one of the books on the display table. 'I have news.'

She whirls around to me.

'A woman brought in your balloon, and she wants to meet your dad.'

Amber's face falls, which is not what I was expecting to see. 'Oh no.'

My heart grinds to halt. 'What's happened?'

She shakes her head. 'Dad met someone a few days ago, and he's been talking non-stop about her ever since. I don't think he'll go out with anyone unless it's this mystery woman. He even turned down Sue, the neighbour.'

'Sue – the neighbour? The one he was confiding in about his loneliness?'

Amber nods. 'It was a ploy on Sue's part. She wanted a date with him. Anyway, he turned her down and told her he only had eyes for someone else. Sue was gutted. We won't be getting an invite to her dreadful summer barbeques, though, which is a bonus.'

'Who is this mystery woman?'

She shrugs. 'I don't know her.'

I think back to when Ben was in here a few days ago and how he couldn't keep his eyes off Alice. Is there a chance he could be referring to Alice?

Amber sighs. 'I spoke to him last night. He said he would only consider dating someone else if it was this stranger.'

'Did you get any details?'

'Brown hair.' Amber rolls her eyes. 'He's useless at noticing things. Oh... I think he said her name was... Alice.'

I gasp and clap my hands. This is perfect. Ben and Alice are in for quite a shock. 'Oh, wow, Amber.'

She looks at me with teenage suspicion. 'Are you okay, Nelly?'

'I know who Alice is,' I say, feeling giddy with excitement. 'She's the one who wants to meet your dad. They met in here the other day.'

Amber's eyes grow wide and she starts to dance on the spot. 'OMG, Nelly. Was she the one who found the balloon and read my message?'

'Yes,' I gush, as my body is engulfed with excitement. In a moment of madness, I mirror her dance moves. She raises her eyebrows. 'Nelly, you need to stick to selling books. Your dancing is cringe.'

I ignore her comment. 'We need to get them to meet.' I can't believe how excited I feel at the prospect of bringing two people together. What has happened to me? 'Amber, Alice lives next door,' I squeal.

Amber starts to dance again but this time I remain still. 'Is she nice? Does she give you evil stepmother vibes?'

'What?'

Amber ignores me and taps her long nails on the spine of the book. 'There's only one way to find out. Dad is up a big tree today. I'll have to persuade him to come down from it.'

'Can you do that?'

'He doesn't like to be disturbed.'

'Amber, I will leave that with you. Let me know when he can pop in, and I'll tell Alice to turn up at the same time.'

Amber is looking troubled. 'I don't know how to get him to get down from that tree and come here.'

'Use your imagination.'

I restack a few shelves, tidy up the children's section, answer several queries on books about insects and rearrange some of the history books when I hear Miranda gasp.

'Nelly,' she shouts, 'Ben's here, saying Amber has called him to say she's been taken hostage in this book shop.'

I let out a groan. Why the hell did I tell a fifteen-year-old to use her imagination?

'I'll go find her,' I shout.

I head for the young adult section to find Amber hiding behind the armchair. 'Is my dad here?'

'You told him you'd been held hostage,' I hiss.

She nods. 'I had to get him down from that tree. My father doesn't respond to most of my texts.'

I roll my eyes and take out my phone to message Alice. I quickly tap out:

Come now. He's in the bookshop.

'Let's go see him,' I say to Amber. 'You can tell him what you've been up to.'

She groans. 'I can't do that.'

'Amber – you have to explain.'

We walk over to the counter, and Ben glares at Amber. 'What is going on? I thought you'd been taken hostage?'

Amber grins. 'I had to get you here quick.'

He runs a hand through his brown hair and casts her a bewildered look.

'Amber, you better explain,' I say, seeing Alice enter the bookshop out of the corner of my eye.

'Dad, I did something bad.'

Ben lets out a loud groan. 'Oh, God, Amber, what have you done now?'

'I put a message in Mum's balloon.'

'A message? What sort of message?'

She's about to answer when Alice interrupts. 'It was one of the nicest messages I have ever read. I am Alice by the way.'

Ben stares in amazement at Alice. She looks amazing. Her brown, glossy hair hangs in loose curls, and she's wearing a yellow dress and sandals.

Amber grins. 'I said that my dad needs a girlfriend.'

He looks at Amber. 'You wrote that?'

She nods. 'I told whoever found the balloon to contact me. Don't worry, I told them you were miserable a lot of the time, but also that you like Monopoly, coffee and you have three kids.'

His face softens, and he turns to Alice. 'Did you find this message?'

She smiles. 'I did. Are you Ben?'

He nods. 'Yes, I am, Alice.'

I watch Alice's smile get even bigger. 'Well, Ben, I would love to beat you at Monopoly.'

'Is this a challenge?' he asks with a wry smile.

Amber grins at me and gives me the thumbs up. The same warm feeling I experienced after seeing Mr Ellis reading Barbara Plum's cookery book and Juliet walking out hugging Miguel's book rushes back to me.

40

Oliver wanted to go out for dinner when I got home. He resorted to sneaky tricks to get me to agree. It's worrying how he knows I have a traitorous body. We had one passionate kiss on the sofa and the words 'Okay, let's go out to eat' flew out of my mouth.

I can't believe I am here. The restaurant he's chosen is dimly lit and filled with flickering candles and purple velvet booths. It's the sort of place I used to see in my nightmares where couples feed each other garlic mussels and lock eyes over goat's cheese tarts.

We're sitting close together in a velvet booth. While we waited for our table and struggled to keep our hands off each other, he asked me whether playing footsie under the table and sexy back rubs would be permitted. Before I had a chance to answer he kissed me and I came up for air gasping the word 'yes'.

'You look great, Nelly,' he says as his eyes wander over my face, my hair, which is not in its usual messy bun but is spread over my shoulders with the ends containing some soft curls, and my pearl-coloured satin shirt.

'How was your day at the bookshop?' he asks after we have given our food order to the waiter.

I tell him about Amber, Ben and Alice. His face lights up when I explain how I brought Ben and Alice together. 'Nelly, this is brilliant. I am proud of you. Soon you will be filling up your bookshelves with my romance books.'

'Careful,' I say as he leans in for a kiss.

Our starters arrive, and the waiter's hand brushes mine. Once the light clears, I can see him listening to a woman letting him down gently in a bar. She's talking about how there is someone else, a waiter who works in a nearby restaurant. I watch as she stresses that nothing has happened yet, apart from some flirting over garlic bread, but she can't stop thinking about him.

The world becomes muffled. Oliver is speaking to me, but I can't hear him. What I have noticed is that my visions don't have the same effect on me recently. I don't feel sad about what is going to happen to this waiter. There is no ache in my chest.

The sounds of cutlery, clinking of glasses and someone exclaiming at the size of their steak rush towards my ears.

'Nelly, I'd love to know what's going on inside that head of yours.' Oliver has placed his hand on my arm.

With my fork, I attack my goat's cheese tart. 'Trust me, Oliver, you don't want to know.'

'But that's where you are wrong.'

'What do you mean?'

He takes a sip from his wine and looks at me with his warm brown eyes. 'I care about you, Nelly.'

His words ignite what feels like a firework display inside me.

I shift in my seat as bursts of energy shoot across my chest like rockets, and my heart spins like a Catherine wheel.

'Really?'

He laughs. 'You say that in a shocked way.'

I smile. 'It's nice to hear.'

He kisses my cheek, and I sigh with contentment.

We finish our starters and kiss a lot before our main course arrives. I must say his footsie skills underneath the table are impressive.

'How long have you been single?' he asks as we surface for air.

His words make me think of Sam. 'About a year.'

'What happened? If you don't want to say, I understand.'

'I caught him kissing his ex-girlfriend in the back room of the bookshop.'

Oliver's eyebrows travel up his forehead at speed. 'Really?' I nod, and he takes my hand. 'That's horrible.'

I notice there is still no sad ache when I think of Sam.

'Are you willing to give me and love a chance, Nelly?'

With a smile I press my lips against his. 'Yes, I am.'

When we get home, it's a struggle not to knock down the pillow wall. Our goodnight kiss is intense. Ripples of pleasure pass through my body as his hands brush over my hips. I'm desperate to see his chest, so I start unbuttoning his pyjama shirt. At this point, my brain awakens. What on earth am I doing? The old me would not recognise this wild new version of me who goes to restaurants, plays footsie under the table, and starts undressing a man.

I stop myself. He smiles as my face turns the colour of beetroot. 'I'm happy to take it slow, Nelly.'

41

I am on the train and on my way to take Aunt Polly to chemo.

My head is pressed against the window, and I'm thinking about the dreamy kiss I shared with Oliver at the door before I left. It was punctuated with brief pauses that heightened my anticipation. When I finally pulled away, he grinned and said, 'I miss your lips already.'

Even though we have kept the pillow wall in place, our kisses in the evening and in the morning are becoming more passionate. At some point, I am going to have to think about taking things to the next level.

Yesterday's embarrassing moment in the bookshop rushes back and makes me shudder. While Miranda was discussing outfits for a first date with her online stylist in the back room, I managed to sneak a book behind the till. It was titled *Losing Your Virginity – An Adult's Guide.* This is one of the many advantages of working in a bookshop. Information on any topic is never far away. I was three chapters deep when a customer asked me to help him find a book on medieval myths. After locating the book, I gulped and returned to the counter.

Miranda was casually flicking through the book. My cheeks have never felt so hot.

'Nelly, if there's anything personal you want to talk to me about, I am here for you,' she whispered as I approached. I wanted the ground to open and for me to fall through the hole. 'It's for a customer,' I said, thinking on my feet. She gave me an odd look which I ignored.

Apart from that little incident, the last few days with Oliver have been idyllic. He has cooked us incredible meals, cuddled me in every part of the flat, kissed me goodnight, and made me belly laugh with his funny tales over the pillow wall.

'Excuse me, is anyone sitting here?' I am yanked out of my thoughts by a young woman who wants to sit on the seat next to me. The train jolts, and as I am thrown forward, our hands brush. Once the light fades, I see her crying as she watches a young man pack a suitcase. On the coffee table in front of her is a magazine cover featuring her man. The headline reads: *The Export – How a new British actor became Hollywood's most wanted.*

He is telling her not to cry and that she will one day meet someone new.

The train carriage becomes muffled, and an uncomfortable feeling passes over me. Oliver is already a bestselling author and one day he could achieve bigger fame and fortune. How would I cope if, like the man in the vision, Oliver decides I am not part of his glitzy world and that he wants to move to Hollywood alone?

I get off the train feeling anxious. Since an early-morning swim is now part of my routine, I leave my clothes behind a rock and enter the water. Today, the sea is a brilliant royal-blue colour and shimmers in the early morning light. The waves are small and playful. Once fully submerged, I let the water hold me, and I think about the vision I saw on the train. I can't control Oliver's career, and if that happened, it would be sad, but as Eva said, it would be survivable. There would be a period of eating cereal, binge-watching sad films, and... this – swimming. I would somehow get through it. There would be tears, but I would survive. A little wave splashes over me which makes me smile. The water will always be here for me. I do need to think about what I will do in the winter when I can't swim in the sea. I make a mental note to check the times of the local swimming pool near my flat. Once again, the sea carries away my worries, and I start to feel lighter again.

I smile up at the blue sky. 'Mum, if you're watching me from heaven,' I whisper, 'I have finally returned to swimming.'

* * *

It's the middle of the afternoon. Aunt Polly went for a lie-down when we got home from chemo. It went smoothly, but there was a new lady having chemo, and I thought she looked like Hilary, with a sleek, bobbed brown hairstyle and enviable cheekbones. I don't think I was the only one who recognised the similarity, as my aunt kept glancing at her. Mentioning Hilary's name only makes my aunt agitated so I kept my thoughts to myself.

I have Mum's notebook on my lap. I am about to dive in, but the corner of Aunt Polly's photo album is jutting out underneath the coffee table and has caught my eye. I put the notebook to one side and pick up the album. The lady from the hospital is still on my mind and so too is the way my aunt kept looking at her. I recall Oliver encouraging me to find out what happened between my aunt and her best friend Hilary. I turn to the back page. The sight of Aunt Polly and Hilary both getting ready for their epic road trip makes me smile. I feel behind the photo. The envelope is there. Taking a deep breath, I slide it out.

My heart is pounding. I shouldn't be snooping into Aunt Polly's private life, but as Oliver said they could have fallen out over something silly, and that would be a waste of a friendship. He is right about Aunt Polly being special to me. I will do what I can to help her through this difficult time. And there is only one person in the world who can make everything better – Hilary.

This envelope could hold the answer to the mystery of what happened between them.

With a trembling hand, I open the envelope and pull out a letter written on posh cream paper. I instantly recognise Hilary's swirly handwriting.

It has a postmark from ten years ago. That was when they fell out.

I take a deep breath and read...

Dear Polly,

Please don't throw this away.

I never wanted us to fall out like this.

You won't answer my calls, reply to my emails or write back.

This is all my fault, and I'm sorry for the hurt I've caused you.

Our road trip was special, and I will never forget what happened between us. I don't regret what happened. I don't regret kissing you, and I don't regret the nights we spent together in bed. Those memories will stay with me forever.

If things had been different, I would have leapt at the chance to start a life with you. But I have my girls to think about, and I have Mike, who wants a second chance. You know how my girls have dreamed of Mike and I getting back together. I want to make them happy.

You will always have a special place in my heart.

I love you, Polly. Always have and always will.

Hilary x

I stare in disbelief at what I've just read. I reread it. After pinching myself to check that I wasn't dreaming, I read the letter for a third time.

Aunt Polly and Hilary – really?

I wasn't expecting that. They were more than best friends. I knew they were close, but I never thought it was anything more.

The words in her note sink in.

Hilary broke Aunt Polly's heart by giving her husband a second chance. She'd put her family first.

I've been staring into space for ages. Is this why Aunt Polly has been telling me for years that she doesn't believe in love any more?

This must have hurt Aunt Polly.

My heart is hammering away inside my chest. I am in shock.

I put the letter back in the envelope and stick it back behind the photo.

Knowing that Hilary hurt my aunt makes me feel sad. I sink into the sofa. What happened between them happened a long time ago, and I need to remember that. My aunt has rebuilt her life and forgotten about Hilary. However, I think back to my aunt in the hospital. The way she kept glancing at the woman who looked like Hilary makes me question whether she is over her.

My mind wanders. I wonder if Hilary and her husband Mike got their second chance. Did Hilary send more letters to my aunt? My breath catches in my throat. The memory of the letters in the baking drawer comes back to me.

There's no sound from upstairs. She must still be asleep. I open the drawer and reach inside for the pile of letters. They all have an Exeter postmark. My heart starts to thud. I recognise Hilary's swirly writing.

I take the most recent envelope which is dated a month ago. It's been opened. I pull out the letter inside. I take a deep breath and read.

Dear Polly,

I have rewritten this letter five or six times. You always teased me about my perfectionism.

The truth is, I think about you a lot.

Mike and I split up again years ago. He moved out. The girls were upset, but I think they have realised I got back with him for the wrong reasons.

Polly, I love you, and I don't think I have ever stopped loving you.

I have a horrid feeling you will read this letter and throw it away.

I heard through a contact on Facebook that you've not been well, and it breaks my heart to think about you being so poorly.

I LOVE YOU, POLLY. ALWAYS HAVE. NEVER STOPPED.

Hilary x

As I read the letter for a second time, I recall what Oliver said about Juliet and love lingering and waiting for years.

I put the letters back in the drawer and decide to talk to Oliver later.

Before I leave for the train, Aunt Polly hands me the car keys for Nigella. 'Why are you giving me these?' I ask.

'I've been doing some thinking. That car sits outside my house day in day out. I only use it for the hospital, and you drive it all the time. Also, I think it would be quicker and less hassle for you to drive here on the days you come to visit. What I am saying is, Nelly, take Nigella and put her to good use.'

This is a generous offer, but Nigella is problematic at the best of times, and I think she will cause more hassle than the train. 'It's okay, you keep her here.'

My aunt shakes her head. 'Please, Nelly, it would make me happy.'

I silently let out a groan. 'Are you sure?'

'Nigella will be excited at the prospect of spending more time with you.'

42

Nigella is on her best behaviour as I drive her home. There's no seatbelt strangulation or stalling. She also doesn't spit out the CD I listened to.

My legs ache as I climb the stairs to my flat. All the swimming I have been doing is good for my mind but it's hell for my muscles.

Oliver isn't home when I get in. After making myself some beans on toast, I sit with Lenny on my chair and think about my aunt and Hilary. I want to sit down and talk to my aunt about what I've found and ask her why she's not replied to Hilary. She has probably been trying to forget about her, but from what I saw earlier, Hilary is still on her mind. The vision I see whenever I touch Aunt Polly is bugging me as well. For years I have assumed the silver bracelet with the padlock belonged to Sandra; now I am wondering whether it's Hilary's. The problem I have is that my aunt gets defensive whenever I talk about Hilary and right now, she's going through a tough time, and I don't want to cause her any more pain. Perhaps when she's in remission I could take her for a long walk on the beach and talk to her.

I still haven't read Mum's notebook. With everything that has happened with my aunt and Hilary I feel emotionally and physically spent. It will keep.

Oliver is not home by the time I go to bed. I try to stay awake, but exhaustion takes hold of me.

CRASH. I sit up in bed with a thudding heart. What was that?

The flat door slams. I can hear someone staggering up the hallway. The bedroom door bangs open and Oliver bursts through and falls onto the bed, knocking over the pillow wall. I can smell beer.

Anger floods my body. 'Oliver,' I yelp. 'You said you wouldn't wake me up in the middle of the night.'

'Fucking Rory,' he slurs, rolling onto his back. 'I hate him.'

'Oliver, I need to go to sleep.' The clock is telling me that it's half past one in the morning.

'I hate Rory.'

He's so drunk. I can't sleep here. I snatch a pillow and get out of bed.

'Where are you going?' Oliver groans.

'I'm not sleeping here.' I stride across the bedroom. 'You're drunk and you've ruined the pillow wall.'

'Nelly, I'm not that drunk. I had two pints.'

'Oliver, we both know drinking is not one of your strengths.'

He rolls over onto his back. 'Rory made me angry.'

'This is not healthy, Oliver.'

'Tell Rory that.'

I turn to him. 'Oliver, you need to sort out your issues with Rory because this is not right.'

'What's not right?'

'This…' I point to him. 'You should be focused on Alfie, not Rory.'

He sits up and rubs his face. 'Rory is playing happy families with my son. I want to…' He falls back on the bed and shuts his eyes. His words fade and are replaced by loud snores.

I can't sleep. I'm so angry at him for doing this. I stupidly assumed he was dealing with his issues. I hug my knees and sit in my chair.

My anger subsides after a while.

* * *

'Nelly, wake up,' says Oliver. 'Your alarm is going off.'

I wake up in a fright. I must have fallen asleep here in my chair.

He's standing opposite me, and he's dressed. He's even tamed his hair. What's going on?

I watch him scratch his stubble-coated chin. 'Nelly, I let you down last night and I'm sorry. I woke up an hour ago.'

I rub my eyes. 'You're dressed.'

He nods. 'I've decided to go back to London. Living here hasn't worked out.'

My heart grinds to a halt. The words hit like a slap. 'What?'

'Last night I got in a fight with Rory.'

I gasp. 'A fight?'

'Yes. I was drunk. He had put this video of Alfie on Facebook…'

'What was the video?'

He bows his head. 'Alfie was calling him Daddy.'

A lengthy silence descends upon the both of us. I know that must have caused Oliver pain.

'All I've done since I moved in is hurt you, Nelly, and annoy Rory. It's time for me to return to London.'

I stare at him. 'What about Alfie?'

He shakes his head. 'I will see him when I can.' I watch as he bows his head. 'Thank you for everything, Nelly. It was…' His voice cracks.

Tears rush to my eyes. 'You're leaving?'

'I'm sorry for everything,' he says with watery eyes.

I watch him head for the door and pick up a bag. 'I have sent you money for two months' rent via my bank account. I have also you texted you my address in Acton. My flat hasn't sold, which is a sign. I need to go back.'

'But what about us?'

He looks back at me. 'I can't hurt you any more, Nelly.'

After he leaves the flat, tears stream down my face. This must be what heartache feels like. The urge to go to get a bowl of cereal, return to my bed, switch on daytime TV and stay there for the rest of the day is strong. However, I have a job.

The bookshop is busy, which is a blessing as it keeps me from stewing over Oliver leaving. I see a few sad customer visions, but I am already feeling low, so I don't pay much attention to them. Seeing Oliver's books on the display table makes my chest ache and I quickly blink away my tears. At lunchtime, after a little cry in the back room, I google the opening hours of the local swimming pool and decide to pay a visit after work. What I have learnt over the past few weeks is that water can help me.

The day goes by quickly and soon there is only fifteen minutes left till closing time. I am looking forward to going home, grabbing my swimming costume, driving to the sports centre and entering the water.

'Hello, Nelly,' says a familiar voice. I look up to Henry. He's smiling, and for a few fleeting moments, I forget about my heartache. 'I was wondering whether you fancied meeting up one lunchtime this week. We could try the new coffee house which has opened on the high street.'

I want to hide away and feel sad about Oliver leaving. 'Thanks, Henry, but I'm—'

He interrupts me. 'Please let me take you for a coffee. I want to make it up to you after I told you about our mothers arguing.'

His eyes have a sorrowful look about them. He's an old friend and if it wasn't for him asking me to keep hold of Margo's book I would never have gone back to swimming. Perhaps he could cheer me up – or at the very least provide some respite from my thoughts about Oliver.

'I will come,' I say. 'When?'

He takes out his phone. 'Tomorrow – Friday?'

'Sounds good.'

With a smile he nods. 'I'll come in about midday, and we can go from there.'

I watch him leave the shop and then I inform Miranda I'm leaving a few minutes early. The water is calling me.

43

It's Friday, and I have thought about Oliver non-stop. The bookshop is quiet, and I have a throbbing headache. Last night after work I swam until I felt exhausted. I think I overdid it. At one point I did stop to float and let the water cradle me. When I got out later, I felt a little lighter, but the second I arrived home and saw Lenny camped out by the door, waiting for Oliver, the heavy sad feeling returned.

It's mid-morning and I feel like cancelling my plans with Henry. I am not in the mood to make friendly small talk. Miranda comes up to the counter and studies my face. 'You look unwell, Nelly.'

I rub my forehead. 'Just a headache.'

She frowns. 'Why don't you go home after your date with Henry?'

'It's not a date,' I snap.

'Well, go home and take the rest of the day as sick leave. You look deathly pale.'

I eye her with suspicion. What is she up to? I can't recall her ever sending me home sick. 'Are you okay, Miranda?'

She giggles. 'I have been on a date with a new man and he's coming into the shop this afternoon.'

Ah, I knew there was a reason.

'I can't have him seeing you looking like you've been dug up. Whatever will he think?' She smiles. 'Get some rest, Nelly.'

I watch her hurry away. The thought of going back to my flat after Henry's coffee and wallowing in my sadness is appealing. I can buy some new cereal on the way home too. Last night I messaged Eva and she recommended that sugary cereal and chocolate work best on a broken heart. She also offered to come over but I was too tired.

'Can I buy this please?' a man says, presenting me with the book he wants to buy. It's on the history of the motorbike. After he makes a payment, I slide his book into a bag and hand it to him. Our fingers brush and when the light clears, I see him as an elderly man sitting by the bedside of another elderly man. He's holding the man's hand and telling him he loves him. His love will last a lifetime. I gulp back a wave of emotion as Oliver's face appears in my mind.

The man puts his card back in his wallet as sound comes back to my ears. He looks around the shop. 'My partner was supposed to be meeting me in here. I don't know where he's got to.'

'Is he busy shopping?'

The man smiles. 'Probably. I am not moaning. He can shop for as long as he wants. I am just glad he's back in my life.'

I nod and fight back tears. How I wish Oliver was back in my life. 'That's nice,' I croak.

Oblivious to my emotional state, the man starts to talk. 'We split up a few months ago. He moved to the other end of the country. Newcastle, which is a long way away. I was sad for ages and then one day I decided I wanted him back in my life.'

My curiosity has piqued. 'What did you do?'

He smiles. 'I got on my bike and I drove to Newcastle. Just kept driving. Once I got there, I convinced him to give us another try.' With a chuckle he says, 'He'd been missing me and wishing he'd not moved away.'

'That's lovely.'

His phone starts to vibrate. 'That's him now. Goodbye.'

I watch him leave the shop and I serve a customer who is buying a book about Egyptian history.

Henry bursts into the shop at midday and the first thing I notice is the sweat on his brow. His jaw is clenched and his arm is trembling. 'Are you okay, Henry?'

I am secretly hoping he wants to cancel our coffee trip.

'I'm fine,' he says, taking out a tissue to dab his forehead. 'Shall we go?'

Miranda takes over from me at the till and winks as I leave.

The coffee shop, Bean & Cup, sits at the end of the high street. On the outside, it is painted a soft sage-green, and inside, the air is filled with the scents of espresso and cinnamon. After ordering we sit at a table nestled amongst some tall pot plants. Henry keeps checking his phone as we wait for our coffees. 'Everything alright?' I ask.

He sighs. 'My nan had a fall in the night. Mum is in A & E with her.'

'Sorry, you should have cancelled.'

'I couldn't do that, Nelly.' He lifts his gaze to mine and takes a deep breath. 'I wanted to bring you here today to apologise for what I said the last time we met and—'

I don't give him chance to finish. 'It was okay, I'm not upset.'

He runs a hand through his hair, and his curls look like they're quivering with excitement. 'Nelly, I also brought you here to tell you how I...'

The waiter brings us our coffees, and Henry pauses. I sense he has something on his mind as he looks like he's willing the waiter to leave.

As the waiter smiles and hurries away, I look at Henry. He takes a deep breath and his phone starts buzzing. With a groan, he looks at it and answers. I watch as he leaves the table to talk in private. My coffee tastes delicious and I make a mental note to bring Eva here. A tall man enters with brown wavy hair and I think of Oliver. My heart lets out a series of aches. Last night I rebuilt the pillow wall and lay in my half. I sobbed in the darkness. 'Oliver, I wasn't done with loving you,' I croaked, running my hand over the pillow wall.

Henry returns to the table. 'I'm going to have to leave, Nelly. I need to get to London. My nan's not great and my mum needs me to come home.' He checks his phone. 'There's a train in half an hour.'

An idea illuminates the inside of my mind like Christmas lights switching on. I could drive Henry to London and go see Oliver. I could convince him to give us another go. I recall how my bookshop customer drove to Newcastle when he and his partner broke up. Oliver texted me his address in Chiswick West London, near where Henry lives.

Excitement ripples through me. 'Henry, I have a better idea.'

* * *

Henry doesn't think much of Nigella. When I first showed her to him, his first words were, 'We're driving in that? Please tell me you're joking?'

I ignored him and opened Nigella.

We're on the motorway. Henry is talking about his nan and how he just wants to hold her hand and tell her everything is going to be okay. I am silently praying Nigella is in a good mood and gets us to London so Henry can see his nan, and I can persuade Oliver to give us another go. I can't believe I am doing this. I have become one of those delusional people I used to moan about who will go to extreme lengths for love.

'Thanks for this, Nelly,' he says, putting his bag by his feet. 'I wanted to tell you something in the coffee shop, but we kept being interrupted.'

'What is it?'

He takes a deep breath and glances out of the passenger window. 'I've been thinking about you and...'

BUMP. Nigella suddenly lurches to one side. 'Oh, God,' I cry out.

'A tyre has gone,' shouts Henry, 'pull over onto the hard shoulder.'

Luckily, we are near the hard shoulder and it's not far for Nigella to crawl to. We jump out and I groan at the sight of her saggy front tyre. 'Damn it,' I snap.

Henry takes out his phone. 'I've never changed a tyre. Are you with a breakdown firm?'

I climb inside the passenger side and pull down the compartment. Once I have found Aunt Polly's insurance details, I see that she's part of the AA. While Henry calls his mum, I call the AA.

Dark clouds are scurrying across the sky, and the sun has gone into hiding. It's cold being on the side of the motorway and it's not long before I am shivering. To make matters worse I can feel spots of rain.

Henry looks in the boot and finds an old travel blanket plus the black cap I bought Aunt Polly which she didn't like. He hands them to me. 'Put the blanket around your shoulders and stick the cap on.'

We stand by Nigella as cars and lorries thunder past.

'My nan's better,' he says, reading a text from his mum. 'She's having a cup of tea and flirting with doctor.'

Relief floods through me.

'Who were you going to see in London?' he asks. 'You said something about seeing a friend.'

'Oh... Oliver. He was my flatmate, but he's moved back to London.' I gaze into the distance at the winding stretch of motorway.

'Was he the bestselling author?'

'Yes,' I murmur. Instinctively I take a few steps and turning away from Henry. Nigella having a flat tyre is a sign, I tell myself. I was not meant to go see Oliver. We're over. A wave of emotion crashes over me.

44

Henry and I parted ways once the breakdown van towed Nigella home and back to a garage. He said he was going to go catch a later train. I sense something had changed between us as he looked sad and crestfallen. We said goodbye and he said we would catch up again soon.

Nigella's tyre has been fixed and she's back to her usual difficult self. Every time I go swimming, she stalls and the other day she tried to strangle me with the seatbelt outside the supermarket.

I miss Oliver terribly, but I know life must go on. Swimming every day has been a godsend, and it's now over a week since he left. Miranda has been on cloud nine, as her new younger boyfriend (forty-two) thinks she's amazing at fifty-five. I am halfway through Mum's journal, which is full of funny diary entries about Dad and me. There's been no mention of my curse, and I am starting to doubt whether she even had it.

Eva has been a godsend. She's been over several times, clutching a plastic bag containing two bottles of wine, a box of tissues and a massive box of chocolates. We've had a few lengthy emotional evenings and talking to her about Oliver has helped me a lot. She's also agreed to move back in to help with the rent. According to her, we're going to have some fun again, and I am looking forward to it. She is proud of me for starting something with Oliver. According to her, it was an act of bravery.

I have admitted that there are benefits of giving love a chance. With Oliver, there were lots of little pieces of joy. For the first time in my life, I also didn't feel like the world was hostile.

It's Sunday. I am pulling up outside Aunt Polly's house in Tide-Leigh. Last night, she sounded sad on the phone, and I have had a sleepless night worrying about her. She opens the door, and I can see her eyes are pink and puffy. Her woollen hat is pulled down over her bald head, and she's wearing a dark top and baggy trousers. She looks like a shadow of her former self.

I wrap my arms around her and ignore my vision. The world goes quiet as my vision shows me the tiny padlock on the bracelet. I can feel her sobbing into my chest. My eyes dart across the other photos on the wall of her hallway. A picture on the wall catches my attention. The image shows Hilary and my aunt standing, laughing into the camera. Their eyes sparkle, and Aunt Polly's smile is stretched wide from ear to ear. It dawns on me that her extra-wide smile is something I haven't seen on her face for quite some time. Half of me wants to ignore it, but the other half yearns to look closely. I look at the other photos while she sobs, and I see the same wide smile is reserved for Hilary. The biggest clue to Aunt Polly and Hilary's rift has been here on her hallway wall all along. This was why she's never taken these photos down. Love has been lingering inside these photos.

I guide her to the sofa and sit her down. 'Nelly, I used to think I was fine without love – that I could survive being single.

But I see now how much it really matters to me. Not just to survive – but to live.'

I look into her eyes, and I can see that she's still holding on to something. 'It's Hilary, isn't it?'

She's blinking at me in surprise. 'I still love her, Nelly. How did you know?'

I explain about the photo album, the letters in the baking drawer and the hallway photos. 'Why haven't you contacted her?'

'I'm scared of what she will think of me in this state.'

I fight back a wave of tears. 'She loves you though.'

My aunt smiles. 'I know, but I am now a slightly mad and bald little woman.'

'You're still you,' I say softly, recalling what Amber said about Ben and his choice of photo for Kate's balloon. He saw past her bald head and her ill state and just saw Kate, who he loved.

An idea unfolds in my mind, and inwardly I groan. I know what I must do. I need to give their love a chance. In my head I can see the faces of Ben, Alice, Juliet, and Mr Ellis. I helped them to give a love a chance and now I must do the same for my aunt.

'How are you feeling physically today?'

She shrugs. 'Just a bit tired and sad. Why do you ask?'

'Get your bag, a blanket and some pillows. Also, any medication you need.'

'Why?'

'We're going out for the day.'

If I tell her we're going on a road trip, she won't come. Once I'm on the motorway, she won't be able to complain.

While she's getting her bag, I go to the kitchen, pull open

the drawer, and find Hilary's address from one of the letters. I take a picture on my phone.

I fill up some water bottles in her kitchen and grab some biscuits.

At a garage on the outskirts of town, I check Nigella's tyres, water, and fill her up.

'Where are we going, Nelly?' Aunt Polly asks from the back seat. She's got a pillow and a blanket for if she's cold.

'Somewhere nice,' I say, and pray Hilary is home, as this is a risky trip. If things get too much for Aunt Polly, I will have to turn back. If Hilary isn't home, I might cry.

Once we're on the motorway, Aunt Polly falls asleep, and it's just me, my thoughts, the satnav app on my phone, and Nigella, the car.

I have no idea how this will turn out. I just hope my aunt can handle a long drive and the same again later tonight.

My mind brings up Oliver's face. I wonder what he's doing back in London. I hope he's happier there and less troubled.

Before we left, I sent Eva a text message to ask if she can feed Lenny. She has a key to the flat and was going over today to say hello to Gary, who I am sure will be elated.

I need some music. I turn on the car radio and find a decent station playing eighties hits. Aunt Polly often sleeps through my music when I take her back from chemo, so I know she won't mind. I'm halfway through enjoying a Duran Duran song when Nigella decides she's heard enough and switches off the radio. I try to turn it back on, and a few seconds later Nigella switches it off again. Muttering under my breath, I reach into the glove compartment and pull out an eighties CD. After shoving it in and pressing play, the sound of A-Ha fills the car and soothe my anxious mind.

She's just spat out the CD and now I cannot get the radio or the CD player to work. 'You are a nasty piece of work, Nigella,' I mutter under my breath as I'm forced to drive the rest of the journey in silence.

Aunt Polly wakes up as Nigella stalls for the third time at a roundabout. I'm close to losing my rag with this car. We're on the outskirts of Exeter, and Nigella has misbehaved non-stop for the past ten miles. The air in the car is blue.

'Talk nicely to her, Nelly,' my aunt advises from the back of the car. 'Nigella is a delicate soul.'

'She's a car,' I groan as I feel my seatbelt starting to tighten. This is Nigella's payback.

Aunt Polly looks out of the window and sees a sign for Exeter. 'Nelly… where are you taking me?'

'It's a surprise,' I say, getting Nigella to start and trying to make it across the roundabout.

She gasps. 'Please tell me you're not—'

I interrupt her. 'Taking matters into my own hands. Yes, I am doing that.'

'No,' she says. 'Hilary can't see me at my worst. I want to wait until I'm in remission, and I have hair.'

'You're not at your worst.'

'I don't have any hair.'

I shake my head. 'Love can't wait for your hair to grow back.'

'This is madness, Nelly.'

I look at her shocked face in the rearview mirror. 'You're right about that. I'm becoming a supporter of love and romance.'

As we pull into Hilary's street, I send a load of silent prayers to God.

Please let Hilary be home. Please let Hilary be home.

I park Nigella opposite number 43 and look up at the little

terraced house. My heart has started to pound away inside my chest, and all the saliva in my mouth has evaporated.

For a few seconds, I grip the steering wheel and close my eyes. 'Believe, Nelly,' I whisper. 'Believe.'

I flick my eyes open and clamber out. I help Aunt Polly out of the back seat. She casts me a look of terror. 'I can't do this.'

I stroke her face, and as she's trembling, I put my arms around her. There is a flash of light and when it clears, I see the hand with the silver padlock bracelet. The world goes quiet as my vision passes and Aunt Polly looks up at Hilary's house. When the sound of the wind rustling the trees and a distant police siren returns, I look at my aunt. 'When I touch you, I see a hand holding yours. The owner of the hand is wearing a silver bracelet with a padlock charm.'

She smiles at me. 'I bought it for Hilary many years ago. I have the same one but from mine hangs a tiny key.' To my surprise she pulls up her jumper sleeve and there it is.

'Wow.'

'It's not a curse that you have, Nelly. It's a wonderful gift.'

As we walk up the path, someone clears their throat in the garden opposite. I turn to see an older man pruning his roses. 'Hilary's out. She left early this morning.'

My stomach takes a nosedive. Driving all this way without checking to see whether Hilary was home was a stupid idea.

I feel Aunt Polly's hand on my shoulder. 'Let's go home. She could be anywhere.'

We walk back to the car. 'I think we should wait for a bit.'

'It wasn't meant to be.'

I glance at her bracelet, which is still on show. I remember Alice talking about signs. 'We should wait. Your bracelet is a sign.'

I climb into Nigella and watch my aunt through the

rearview mirror. She's staring up at Hilary's house, and her cheeks are damp. The sight makes my heart ache. Silently I urge her to be patient.

'Let's go back to Tide-Leigh,' she says. 'Maybe I'll contact her when I'm better.'

Oliver's face flashes up inside my mind. 'We need to give love a chance.'

45

His voice echoes inside my head. *Give love a chance.*

I glance in the rearview mirror at my aunt. She's dabbing her eyes. I need to believe. Hilary – where are you? We need you. I need you and my dear Aunt Polly needs you.

A screech of wheels makes me look up. A white Golf races into the street and pulls up in the space opposite me. I stare at the driver taking off their dark shades.

'Hilary.'

My aunt lets out a shocked yelp.

Hilary is staring at me through her windscreen.

Relief floods through me. I open the car door as she clambers out. 'Nelly?'

Hilary still has her signature brown bobbed hair, and even though there are a few more laughter lines on her face, she looks the same as she did ten years ago.

I turn to the back of the car. 'I have someone who wants to see you.'

Hilary lets out a gasp as Aunt Polly gets out. They both rush past me and towards each other. The sight of both hugging and crying on the pavement makes me emotional. The images of them both go blurry.

I wipe away tears as I can hear my aunt sobbing and Hilary saying how sorry she is for walking away and that she loves her so much.

To see their happy, emotional faces makes that wonderful warm feeling reappear and engulf my body.

Once we have calmed down, Hilary takes Aunt Polly's hand and leads us inside.

Hilary's hallway is adorned with photos of her and my aunt. For a few moments, I stare at the pictures from their holidays, their shopping trips to London, and their road trip. It's as if I am back in Tide-Leigh, standing in my aunt's hallway. Hilary smiles and points at the wall. 'I couldn't forget about you, Polly.'

My aunt rests her head on Hilary's arm. 'Nelly always asked me why your photos were up on my walls. I couldn't forget about you either.'

We're sitting in Hilary's living room. I'm in an armchair while my aunt and Hilary are on the sofa, holding hands and gazing at each other. I hadn't factored feeling like a third wheel into my plan.

When we first came in, Hilary made us all a cup of tea and some sandwiches, which mainly I polished off as I was starving. There were a lot of hushed whispers in the kitchen as Aunt Polly went to see if Hilary wanted any help. It took a while for my cup of tea to arrive, but I didn't mind. I sensed they had a lot of catching up to do.

'Thank you, Nelly,' says Hilary. 'I know I've said this a hundred times since you arrived, but I was starting to lose hope.'

Aunt Polly leans her head against Hilary's shoulder. 'I was going to wait until my hair grew back.'

Hilary laughs. 'Polly, the rate your hair grows at, I would have been in my nursing home and getting ready to see the pearly gates by the time you would have called.'

Aunt Polly chuckles. 'Nelly got bossy with me.'

Hilary smiles. 'I'm glad she did, Polly.'

I survey the sitting room, the cream fabric sofa and chairs, the photos of all Hilary's girls, and the ornaments on her pine dresser. On the wall beside me is a constellation of pictures of my aunt and Hilary. Like my aunt's photo collection, Hilary has visually documented their holidays together, shopping trips, and there are even a few from when they were teenagers. When we came in earlier, Hilary pointed out the photos and said, 'That's my Polly wall.' It made my aunt get tearful.

'This is a nice house, Hilary.' I admire the French windows at the far end of the room which lead out onto a patio garden filled with pots of colourful shrubs.

She nods. 'It's rented.'

'Do you like it down here?'

She shrugs. 'The girls all live up north now with their respective partners. Lilly is in Manchester, Sarah is in Burnley, and Ailsa has just moved to Newcastle. It's a trek to visit them. I'm not sure I want to be down here any more.'

'Where's Mike?' I ask.

She rolls her eyes. 'He moved away.'

'Nelly, how are you?' Hilary asks.

'I'm okay. I never grew out of those visions.'

Hilary gives me a sympathetic nod. 'That must be tough.'

'She's going to take over the TV psychic medium world – aren't you, Nelly?' Aunt Polly says. 'So she can make lots of money and pay for me to go on luxurious holidays.'

'Can I come with you?' Hilary giggles.

I roll my eyes. 'I'm not doing that.'

Hilary gestures to my aunt. 'Did you ever see anything about us two?'

I nod. 'I saw your bracelet with the silver padlock on it.' She lifts up her wrist and there it is.

'Your aunt has always had the key to my heart, Nelly.'

They both hold up their hands and cast each other goofy smiles.

We talk about the days when Hilary and my aunt were friends, and I was growing up. Hearing them laugh and talk about the times Hilary would show up to fix a life problem brings back that wonderful, warm feeling inside me.

'You were my fourth emergency service,' says my aunt to Hilary. 'I have missed being able to call you and—'

I interrupt her. 'And six minutes later, hear a screech of tyres, the slam of a car door, and Hilary's heels on the path.'

Hilary laughs. 'I did time myself door to door and it was six minutes.'

Aunt Polly nods. 'The sight of you coming into the kitchen would be enough to put me at ease. You solved a wide range of problems back then.'

Hilary nods and squeezes my aunt's hand. 'I'll always be your fourth emergency service, Polly.'

They look at each other with such tenderness and adoration that I can feel emotion rising inside of me. Hilary leans closer to my aunt and gently kisses her on the lips.

It hits me. I made this moment happen. I brought them together.

Once we've finished our tea, I think about heading home.

'Nelly,' says Aunt Polly, 'I'm going to stay here for a few days. Hilary is going to drive me back on Tuesday.'

Hilary beams at my aunt. 'We have a lot of catching up to do.'

'Are you sure you'll be okay?'

'Trust me, she'll be more than fine,' says Hilary. 'Your aunt has agreed to let me nurse her.'

'God help me,' says my aunt, jokingly. 'Nelly, take Nigella back to your place and drive over on Wednesday.'

'Are you sure?'

She smiles. 'Have some fun with her.'

I stare at my aunt. 'I'm not sure I'd ever call driving Nigella fun.'

What I have noticed since being at Hilary's is that my aunt doesn't look so pale, and when I leave, her smile is a little wider.

46

Aunt Polly texted me while I was on my way to work. She apologised for missing my message last night and was glad Nigella had got me home safely. I left out the part where I screamed and hit the steering wheel every time Nigella spat out a CD, turned off her radio, or stalled whenever she felt like it. Aunt Polly didn't need to know that. She and Hilary had a lovely time together after I left, although she had to go to bed at eight because she was exhausted. She told me she's had the best Monday morning in ages as Hilary made her breakfast in bed. That brought a smile to my face.

'Are you missing him?' Miranda is meant to be opening the bookshop doors but is lingering near the till where I am standing. 'I hear he's returned to London. It didn't work out.'

I lie and shake my head. She doesn't need to know that he has never left my mind for more than ten minutes.

'He has a few issues,' says Miranda. 'Let's hope being back in London will help.'

I feel a prickle of irritation and recall how little she told me about him. 'You didn't say anything about all that scandal he went through a few years ago.'

She lets out a nervous laugh. 'Didn't I? Sorry about that.'

She gestures to her outfit. A floaty floral dress and sandals. 'My stylist's advice for this week is for me to look like a romcom goddess who's just been frolicking in a meadow.'

'That's lovely,' I say, forcing out a smile.

In my lunch break, I sit in the back room and read Mum's notebook.

I get to the last few pages and then her entries change.

1st July 2001

I watched a couple on the bus today. She was laughing at something he whispered. Her face was open and unguarded. Everything changed when I got off the bus and touched her arm.

I blink and stare at Mum's words.

After rubbing my eyes, I reread the last sentence. My heart is hammering inside my chest. All saliva in my throat has evaporated. The word 'touched' is triggering for me. It makes me think of my curse.

The question that is on my mind is whether Mum was cursed too. I assumed it had started in me because of the car crash, but recently, since Henry mentioned the argument between our mothers, I've been considering that Mum had it too.

With a trembling hand, I turn over the page.

2nd July 2001

Some people believe love is like a form of light. It burns so brightly until it flickers out. But for people like Penelope and me, it isn't light we see, it's endings. Quiet, inevitable endings of love. Some gentle. Some brutal. Some that never have the chance to have a proper beginning.

My jaw is hanging open, and my eyes are so wide with shock they are almost popping out of their sockets. Mum and I share a curse.

I thought it made me cold towards others and isolated. I thought I was unlovable. But it wasn't me. It was the knowing. I know how things fall apart. When you possess this ability, it's hard not to become wary of people and terrified of forming connections. You learn to look and not touch.

Mum's handwriting has become blurry. Tears have rushed to my eyes. They start to pour down my cheeks. I try to wipe them, but more keep coming.

I reach out and run my finger over the pages. 'Oh, Mum, you don't know what this means to me. Knowing you suffered with this curse means that I am not alone.'

There is no date.

I didn't understand the gift at first. I thought I was cursed. I have spent years pretending I didn't feel the weight of it, but I know now that pretending doesn't make it go away. I can't take back all the moments I held myself back from love. But I can write this now for you, Penelope.

It doesn't have to make you afraid. One day, someone will hold out their hand, and you'll want to take it. You'll want to try – even if you don't know how the story ends.

Maybe you'll be lucky to touch someone and see nothing at all.

I'm sorry I force you to wear those awful white gloves. You don't have a skin condition. I was protecting you. I knew you had the gift from a young age, and I didn't want you to suffer like I have done. When you're older, we will talk about it.

I never saw anything when I touched your father. It was the most terrifying thing of my life, but he showed me that it's not the ending that matters. It's everything in between. It's about deciding to begin.

Much love, Mum.

P.S. Swimming helps with the gift. It helps our minds find peace, and in the water we don't have to worry so much about touching anyone.

47

Miranda is tidying up the non-fiction section while I'm rearranging the crime display table. I keep thinking about what I read in Mum's notebook earlier. I felt so connected to her when I read it. Knowing that she and I shared the same... gift... was life-changing for me.

I've been saying the word 'gift' in my head repeatedly. It does sound better than the word 'curse'.

The part about Dad and Mum made me think about Oliver. I never saw anything with Oliver, but he's gone now.

'Hello, Nelly,' says a familiar voice.

I turn around to see Mr Ellis. He looks transformed from when I last saw him. His skin is full of colour, his nose is no longer bright red, and his eyes have added twinkles. 'Mr Ellis, what a wonderful surprise!'

He smiles. 'As you can see, the casserole worked wonders. I started feeling better after the first mouthful.'

'That is brilliant.'

'You and Oliver were amazing that evening.'

'Mr Ellis, it was worth it.'

He gestures for me to follow him over to the empty armchair in the crime section. Once he's settled, he clears his throat and says, 'I would like to invite you to a thank you dinner, tomorrow evening.'

'Mr Ellis, you don't need to do anything. It was a pleasure to—'

He waves his hands to stop me. 'Nelly, I would like you to come over and have dinner with me.'

'What are you cooking?'

I giggle as he touches his nose and winks. 'That's a secret. But it will be something from Barbara's book.'

'I'm visiting my aunt tomorrow. I won't be back until about six.'

He nods. 'That's fine with me. I will wait.'

'Mr Ellis, Oliver has moved back to London.'

Something flickers across his face, and I detect a glint of mischief in his twinkly eyes. What is he up to?

'We don't need him, Nelly.' He laughs. 'Do you remember where I live?'

The thought of him slaving over a hot stove worries me. 'Yes, I do. Please don't go to a lot of trouble. I would be happy with a sandwich.'

'I want to say thank you. I'll see you at six.'

I watch him heave himself out of the chair and lean on his stick.

'See you tomorrow, Mr Ellis.'

Before he hobbles away, he winks at me. 'Looking forward to it.'

* * *

It's early evening. I am in my happy place, the swimming pool.

I have spent the last hour or so travelling up and down the pool. It's quiet tonight as people are outside enjoying the summer evening. I am now resting in the shallow end and thinking about my aunt and Hilary. Their story goes against everything my gift has taught me. They have shown me that love isn't about first chances. Sometimes it's about the second ones. The kind that proved the first heartbreak wasn't the end, just the beginning of something more profound. Love can come back as something softer, wiser and more substantial.

Perhaps some endings are not endings. Maybe love has seasons. Some break-ups are like a plant shedding its leaves in the autumn and going back into the soil. When spring arrives, the conditions change, and love grows again.

Mum's face flashes up inside my mind. Reading her notebook was transformational. I now know why she made me wear those awful gloves. Knowing she also had this gift has made me feel closer to her.

A man has entered the pool. He has the same black curly hair as Henry. My mind drifts back to the last time we saw each other on that dreadful day when Nigella's tyre burst. I recall standing on the hard shoulder and him passing me the blanket and cap. I gasp as I remember the vision I saw when I touched Henry. His love for someone ended when he was on the side of the motorway watching a figure standing in front of him. My heart falters. That was me. He was looking at me.

Oh, God. The memory of him in the coffee shop and in the car trying to tell me something.

Was he going to ask me out on a date? I gulp.

Was Henry in love with me? This is new territory for me. I have seen myself in a vision.

He must have watched me stare into the distance and yearn for Oliver. Henry hasn't been in contact since. I feel a twang of guilt. There was never an attraction on my part. He was a good friend to me, and I will always be grateful for him showing me Margo Lane's book.

As I kick off from the side and start to swim, I think of Oliver and I hope he's happy. It will take time for me to forget about him, but I am no longer alone. I have Lenny, Eva, Aunt Polly, Hilary, Mr Ellis and my newfound love of swimming. The water will always be my friend.

My gift is still with me, and I have accepted it will never go. With everyone's help I am going to find a way of living with it and not let it stop me when I eventually meet Mr Right.

48

Mr Ellis answers the door. The huge smile on his face at seeing me makes me giggle. 'Nelly,' he cries. 'Come inside.'

As I step inside, I notice something I missed when Oliver and I were here before. Mr Ellis's hallway is narrow and softly lit. The pale wallpaper is slightly faded with age. A quiet gallery of memories unfolds along the length of the wall. There are framed photographs of Joan, some in black and white, others in muted colours. In one, she's young, laughing in the sun with a book on her lap. In another, she stands in a kitchen wearing her pink apron. There are wedding photos, travel pictures, and candid moments. Joan is still here, and so is his love for her. It's embedded in these photos, and it is between the pages of Barbara Plum's recipe book. Love doesn't die. It lives on.

As I head for the living room, a delicious cooking smell greets my nostrils. Mr Ellis has been busy.

I walk into the living room, and I spot the dining table is laid for... three.

Mr Ellis is standing by his mantlepiece, and someone is coming out of his kitchen.

I gasp. It's Oliver.

'Hello, Nelly,' Oliver says as my heart goes berserk. 'I hope you don't mind me joining you and Mr Ellis tonight.'

'No... umm...' I'm struggling to get my words out. He looks different. His stubble has gone, his brown hair has been styled, and he's wearing a crisp blue shirt with beige jeans.

'Nelly, I'm not letting you or Alfie go.'

His words rob me of my breath. 'What?'

He nods and I notice his hands are twitching by his sides. It's as if he doesn't know what to do with them. 'I've been doing a lot of thinking about what's important – or who, I should say – is important to me. I've also signed up for some counselling, which is something I should have done years ago, and I found a buyer for my flat.'

I can't believe what I'm hearing.

He walks towards me. 'I'm going to fight for you and Alfie. I have been behaving like a child.'

His dark eyes lock on to mine with a newfound intensity. 'I won't let you go. I fell in love with you over our pillow wall and I don't want us to end.'

Tears rush to my eyes as he takes me in his arms. My heart falters. There still is no flash of light or vision.

'Say something, Nelly.'

'Oliver,' I whisper.

He presses his lips against mine and his kiss is electrifying.

His words are still echoing inside my head. My heart is a gooey mess. Oliver fell in love with me over the pillow wall and he's returned. He breaks for air and smiles. 'I've missed you so much.'

I gaze into his eyes. He has come back because he loves me. This is something my curse has never shown me. It is quick to show me endings, but not what happens after two people have walked away and then realise they still love each other.

Mr Ellis starts to clap and cheer, which makes us both laugh. 'Can we eat now?'

I bury my head in Oliver's shoulder, and he presses his face in my hair.

We all sit down at Mr Ellis's table and Oliver puts a plate of casserole in front of us. I look up at Mr Ellis. 'I can't believe you have gone to so much trouble to make this, Mr Ellis.'

He laughs. 'Firstly, call me Roger, and secondly, it wasn't me who cooked this.'

Oliver comes to sit next to me and squeezes my hand under the table. I turn to him. 'Did you cook this?'

'Nelly,' he says, softly, 'I had a lot of making up to do. I needed to pull together my best team. The other day I came to see Roger and we hatched a plan. Jamie brought over the ingredients last night and today I cooked the casserole.'

Roger laughs. 'I love keeping a secret. Was I convincing in the bookshop?'

'I didn't suspect a thing.'

Oliver beams at Roger. 'How is the casserole?'

'It's not as good as Joan's,' says Roger, with a wink, which makes us chuckle.

After we've had a cup of tea, washed up and tidied away, Oliver and I say goodbye to Roger. 'Do you promise to visit soon?' he asks.

Oliver nods. 'Let's make this a weekly visit. What do you think, Nelly?'

'I would love that.'

'Promise me you'll bring your little son next time too, Oliver.'

'I will and your tidy living room will not be the same again,' Oliver says, jokingly.

Roger laughs. 'I can't wait. I'm so pleased you both have found each other again.' He nudges me. 'I did ask Oliver what we were going to do if you stormed out. I told him that whatever happens, I will eat the casserole.'

Oliver extends his hand to mine. 'I'm a lucky man, Roger. We will see you next week.'

'I look forward to it.'

49

We walk back towards my flat. When we pass the entrance to the private communal garden, Oliver pulls us to a stop. 'I never gave Gary the key back.' He gestures to the garden. 'Shall we have a moment to talk?'

We hold hands as we enter and sit down on the patch of grass.

He turns to me and takes a deep breath. 'I'm asking for a chance to show you that I'm here to fight for us, to fight for you and Alfie. Because you both are all I've thought about since I left.'

'Have you spoken to Molly and Rory?'

He leans over his legs, placing his elbows on his thighs. 'It was the hardest thing I had to do. Jamie went with me yesterday. I apologised to both, and I've committed to focusing on co-parenting Alfie and moving on from the past.'

'That must have been tough.'

He nods. 'Rory said he could understand why I got angry about the video.'

'He did?'

'Yes, which I thought was a start. Hearing my child call another man Daddy is hard, but when that man used to be your best friend and is now with your ex-girlfriend, that's when the red filter slipped over my eyes.'

I place a hand on his shoulder. 'I understand.'

He sits up and runs a hand through his hair. 'You were right. Alfie doesn't need all the adults around him squabbling and fighting. When Molly and I both lived in London, it was simpler. Every time I went to her flat, Rory wasn't there. I would put Alfie in his buggy, and we would go out, or I would play with him on his activity mat. When she moved here and told me Rory was moving in with her, everything changed. It was like his betrayal actually magnified *her* betrayal, and I felt a hundred times worse.' I watch him gaze out across the park. 'The last few years, all this resentment and anger have been bubbling away inside of me. When I stopped writing, I came undone.'

We both go silent and listen to the evening breeze rustling the leaves on the trees behind us.

He places his hand over mine. 'I'm sorry for the trouble I caused you and the late nights.'

I smile. 'It's okay. I have missed you, Oliver.'

He leans in and presses his soft, warm lips against mine. His kiss is slow and sensual. Once we pull apart, he strokes my cheek. 'I've missed you too.'

'A lot has happened since you left.'

'Tell me.'

'Eva, my friend, is going to be my new flatmate,' I explain, feeling a prickle of worry. Perhaps Oliver thinks he's going to move back in?

With a smile, he puts his arm across my shoulders. 'That's good. I can date you properly now.'

'Really?'

He nods. 'I'm living at Jamie's for the time being until I can buy somewhere. It will be nice to be able to take you...' His words fade away, and something flickers across his face. He remembers my anxiety. 'Are you going to be honest with me? I've had a feeling you've been hiding something. In my story, you were like Mary, burdened by some terrible secret.'

I take a breath. 'I related to her.'

Taking my hand, he looks into my eyes. 'Whatever it is, I will still be by your side.'

I take a deep breath.

This is it. The crucial moment. I look into his dark eyes and he strokes my cheek. 'Nelly, you mean the world to me. I am not going anywhere.'

'OK...' I take a deep breath, 'When I touch people, I see visions in my head. They're about things that happen in the future.'

He casts me a puzzled look.

'I've always regarded it as a curse.'

He's giving me a look of surprise. 'A curse? What, like someone has put a spell on you?'

'I see how love ends. Mostly I see break-ups, cheating and sudden deaths.'

'That sounds intense.' I watch him thinking about what I've said. 'That's why you don't go out – isn't it?'

'Yes. It's draining when all you see inside your head is a constant stream of dating spoilers.'

'Why do you think you've been cursed? It sounds more like a special ability to me.'

'My aunt says I have a gift, but I have always viewed it as a curse. I see so many visions. They always come true. When I touch someone, I get a flash of white light and then I see how their love ends. The visions always come true. There's no time limit on them.'

I look at him and try to catch the words precariously balancing on the tip of my tongue. They tumble out of my lips. 'I don't see anything with you.'

His eyebrows arch with surprise. 'Nothing at all?'

I shake my head.

A grin spreads across his face. 'I always knew I was special.'

We both start to laugh.

'What does it mean?' he asks after we've both stopped laughing. 'Wow – so with me, you have no spoiler alerts?'

'No.'

He smiles. 'You haven't had your gift guiding you.'

'That's right.'

I think of Mum's notebook and what she said about her gift and Dad. 'My mum never saw anything with my dad.'

He lets out a mock groan. 'Oh, I thought I was special there for a few moments. Like immune to magic curses.'

We both giggle, and he pulls me into a hug. 'How do you manage this... gift?'

'You've helped me a lot by encouraging me to give love a chance.'

He puts his arm around me and pulls me close.

'That must be hard if all you see is how things end. I bet it put you off dating.'

Resting my head against his shoulder, I think about how tough it's been. 'The only way to survive was to lock myself away and avoid physical contact.'

I can feel him turning to face me. 'Will you be my girlfriend, Nelly?'

'Yes, I will, Oliver.'

Cupping my face with his warm hands, he kisses me. 'You're also the best kisser.'

As we kiss, my mind reminds me of my virginity. I decide to tell him everything when we break for air. 'I will be your girlfriend, but there's something else.'

'What is it?'

'You will have your work cut out with me, Oliver.'

He nods. 'I am ready.'

'I am not only cursed, but I am also a cursed virgin.'

He blinks for a few seconds, smiles, then kisses me on the lips. 'You're not cursed, and we can wait...'

I let out a wail of frustration. 'We're not waiting, Oliver. The sooner I say goodbye to my virginity, the better.' The shocked look on his face makes me giggle, and then we both start to laugh.

When we leave the bench, he extends his hand to me. 'Shall I walk you back to your flat?'

'Yes, Papa Tiger,' I say with a cheeky smile.

'Careful,' he says with a mock-deadpan expression, before we both start to laugh.

Once we've hugged and kissed some more, I take his hand and remember Mum's words. This is about deciding to begin.

50

THREE MONTHS LATER

The chairs in the romance section are arranged in neat rows. The bookshop is busy, with people standing behind the chairs, some squeezed between bookcases, and a group of young women sitting cross-legged on the rug. This is the busiest author event I have seen in a long time. Not only is there pink bunting hanging up, but all the fairy lights in the shop are on. Oliver's books are everywhere, and it looks like a secret romantic fiction cult gathering.

Miranda has chosen to wear a little black dress for the occasion. She's no longer using her stylist. Her latest love interest is a portrait artist called Graham, who loves painting her. She spends more time at his studio than she does at the bookshop nowadays, which is a bonus for me.

I survey the familiar faces gathered to listen to his talk. In the corner are Ben and Alice, who look more loved-up than ever. His arm circles her waist, and she's gazing up at him adoringly. Alice loves playing Monopoly and climbing trees, and it's rumoured that they have been spotted kissing high up in trees around the town. She's also been a big hit with Ben's kids, including Amber, who we hardly see in here now.

Roger Ellis is sitting by me. We have kept our promise, and every week we all have dinner together. Alfie and Roger have become the best of friends.

Eva and her boyfriend, Rex, are here somewhere but keep sneaking off to the quieter book sections.

Aunt Polly and Hilary are standing behind me. They have been like two lovestruck teenagers ever since I reunited them, and there's talk of a wedding once my aunt is in remission. They've come over specially to see Oliver's author talk. Hilary drove, and according to my aunt, she never left the fast lane.

I feel a tug on my hand. Alfie looks up at me with his huge brown eyes and outstretches his little arm. With a smile, I pull him up into my arms. Getting to know Alfie has been great for me. Oliver and Molly have agreed a co-parenting rota and Oliver now has Alfie for two full days. Alfie has helped me to stop paying attention to other people's love stories and he's shown me a different type of love.

Oliver walks out to a warm burst of applause, looking like a fashion model who accidentally wandered into a bookshop. His white fitted shirt is rolled up to his sleeves, his hair is wavy, and he's beaming from ear to ear.

He waves and sits down. Miranda rushes over with a mic. He takes it from her. 'Hello, I'm Oliver James and I write love stories.'

Everyone claps, and a few of the girls on the rugs give him a whistle.

'Thank you for coming to this event. It means a lot to me. Writing about love is one of my passions in life because love is everywhere. It's in the stolen glances, shared coffees and the holding of someone's hand.'

He goes on to talk about his journey as an author and how he achieved publication. Miranda has placed a stack of his pink books by the chair, and he explains the story behind each one. He comes across as comfortable and at ease. The audience loves him, and they laugh at all his jokes and the funny story about the time he met his agent and accidentally knocked coffee all over her. Once he concludes his talk, he asks for questions.

Hands shoot up across the bookshop. He picks a woman from the second row of chairs. Miranda races over with a mic.

She smooths down her frizzy brown hair and takes a breath. 'In a recent interview, you said you'd stopped writing. Are you back to writing now, and what made you return to it?'

He glances over at me, standing by the display table. 'For a long time, I stopped writing. I had stopped believing in the very thing I was writing about. Love had started to feel like fiction. And then a special person entered my life. She became a voice in the darkness that made me want to listen more, so I returned to the page.' He holds my gaze. 'To the woman who made me believe again and reignited my heart. I know how difficult it has been for you to take a chance on me, and I love you so much, Nelly.'

My heart swells as Alfie whispers, 'Daddy.'

Oliver will never know how different my life was before he entered it. He made me break free from the shackles of my gift and believe in love. My gift will always be a part of me, but Oliver has shown me it's not about the ending of love that matters, but everything in between. It's about deciding to give love a chance and choosing to start. I have also learnt that heartbreak hurts, but it is survivable. I know now that if he had not come back into my life, I would have been okay. My gift will continue to show me the dangers of heartbreak, but it will never again have as much power over me. I, Nelly Blake, am a believer in love.

* * *

MORE FROM LUCY MITCHELL

ACKNOWLEDGEMENTS

Thank you to everyone who made this book possible.

Boldwood Books for giving me this wonderful opportunity.

Emily Yau – my fabulous editor who has helped me transform Nelly and Oliver's story into something wonderful.

My agent, Anna Klerfalk, for believing in me and creating such a supportive environment at Intersaga Literary Agency.

My amazing husband, Huw, for his support, love, delicious cooking, and the antique, Gothic writing bureau.

My daughters, Seren and Felicity, for the stress-busting trips to Newport Retail Park and the coffees in Café Nero.

To Mum and Vez for the love, support and the trips back home to Leeds (walking Vez's dog).

To Jeff – the boy from Abertillery, 'he done good!'

To Kathy – for the love and support.

Sue and Catherine, for their friendship, encouragement, and the occasional 'Get a grip!' on WhatsApp when needed.

Rachel, for the much-needed cocktail nights at the Celtic.

Bettina, for the funny voice notes and our creative FaceTimes.

The RNA Cariad Chapter, who listened to the idea I had for this book during one of our catchups and gave me so much encouragement.

To the Key family at The Nags Head, Usk, for their love and support.

To my dad, Michael, and my mother-in-law, Kris, who are no longer with us but would love to see this book published.

Finally, thanks to my dog, Apollo, and Harry the cat, for reminding me that my writing is of secondary importance to their needs.

ABOUT THE AUTHOR

Lucy Mitchell started out writing contemporary romance, but these days she can't resist adding a magical twist. Her stories celebrate hope, connection, and the magic of finding love. She's based in Wales with her husband, her two daughters, three unruly cats and one excitable Labrador. When she's not writing, she can be found curled up with a stack of books, sipping coffee, daydreaming about "what ifs," or walking her dog.

Download your exclusive bonus content from Lucy Mitchell here:

Visit Lucy's website: www.lucymitchellauthor.blog

Follow Lucy on social media here:

facebook.com/lucymitchellauthor
x.com/LucyMitchAuth
instagram.com/lucy_mitchell_author

Printed in Dunstable, United Kingdom

83067975R00188